More praise for
Photographing Fairies

"Delightfully whimsical . . . This sweet little tale turns darker by degrees as little acts of viciousness multiply and the whimsy becomes almost terrifying. It's a delicately constructed maze at turns funny and frightening, and leaves readers perplexed and entertained."

The Milwaukee Journal

"Szilagyi has written a sprightly first novel full of gentle humor, weird sex and unlikely happenings. Szilagyi writes with a sort of careless half-smile that keeps the reader reading. *Photographing Fairies* is a small, deft enchantment."

Kansas City Star

"Extraordinary . . . While Szilagyi walks the line separating the magical from the mundane, he also weaves together fragments of fiction and history."

The London Free Press

"An adeptly controlled cross between a mystery, a fantasy and a historical novel."

The Cleveland Plain Dealer

"An enjoyable mystery-fantasy."

The San Diego Union-Tribune

"Brilliant."

Buffalo News

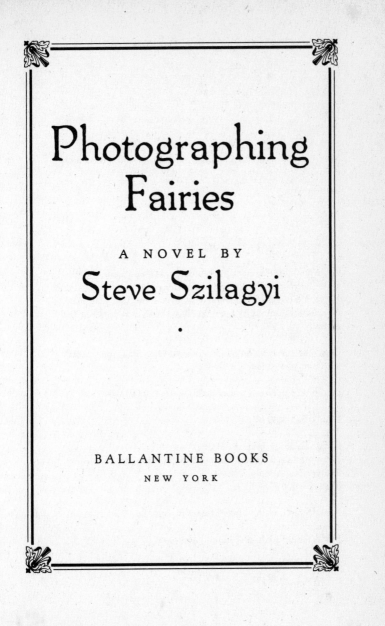

Photographing Fairies

A NOVEL BY

Steve Szilagyi

•

BALLANTINE BOOKS
NEW YORK

 Published in the United States by Ballantine Books, a division of Random House, Inc., New York, and simultaneously in Canada by Random House of Canada Limited, Toronto.

Originally published in hardcover in 1992 by Ballantine Books, a division of Random House, Inc.

Library of Congress Catalog Card Number: 92-97320

ISBN 0-345-38323-0

Cover design by James R. Harris
Art by Edward Robert Hughes, "Midsummer Eve"/Fine Art Photographic Library Limited
Text design by Debby Jay

Manufactured in the United States of America

First Trade Paperback Edition: May 1993

10 9 8 7 6 5 4 3

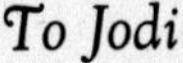

To Jodi

Chapters

Book One

Book Two

Photographing Fairies

THERE IS SOME QUESTION HERE. It rages in the council of my solitary consciousness. One party of thought says "Yea." The other says "Nay." A vexing dispute. But one, you would think, it would be easy to bring to final resolution. After all, I could come forth and testify as my own expert eyewitness. But while so much remains incised with perfect clarity in my memory, this one detail resists the still camera of my brain. And so the embattled query shall echo forever; its answer guessed at, but unknown. That is the question: Do the fairies have wings?

How much easier to ask: Do they have eyes?

The answer: Yes.

Do they have lips?

Yes.

Do they have arms, legs, pert bottoms, and tiny feet? Do they have knees, chins, bare pudenda, flowing hair, and bright nipples, red as rubies?

Yes, yes, yes, yes, yes, yes, and decidedly yes.

But do the fairies have wings?

Silence.

I shut my eyes and visualize the place where wings

might be expected to sprout. On the upper back, just below the cervical vertebrae, where the scapulae and trapezius glide silkily past one another. And what do I see there? Nothing. Not even the expected anatomical landmarks. Just a blur.

Now, this blur could be evidence of wings that move so quickly, they are invisible to the naked eye—like an airplane propeller, or the wings of a hummingbird. Or it could indicate something else. A point of contact, a kind of spiritual umbilicus connecting the fairies with another plane. It could be the vibrating nexus between two worlds, the natural and the ecstatic. If so, the link would be logically located. Do not our deepest aesthetic experiences signal themselves with a thrill up the spine? Does not beauty lodge like a cool, tense bubble between the shoulder blades?

I think it does; though I could not prove it. And so this whole wings business refuses to come into focus. I cannot resolve the issue. But it does lay to rest one of the world's best-known saws. How does it go? That wise old chuckle that says, "Being hanged on the morrow concentrates a man's mind wonderfully"?

Well, let us see . . .

Book One

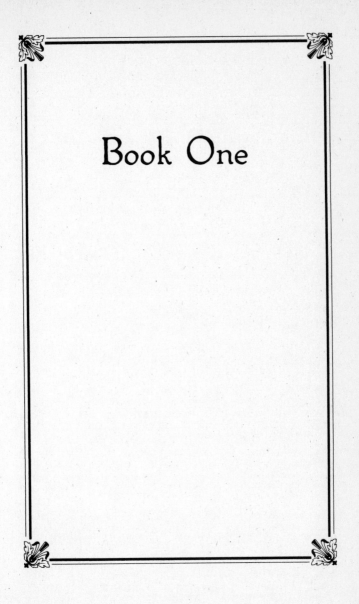

CHAPTER ONE

How I Met the Policeman

YES, TOMORROW I AM SCHEDULED to die. But as I contemplate this incipient event, I am troubled by the thought that I leave nothing behind. Oh, of course, there are hundreds of undistinguished photographs and some sketches and studies that might have amounted to something if I had worked them up; but for the most part, after thirty-two years of life, I leave a barren legacy. No children to mourn me. No widow in weeds. And, as the only child of now-deceased parents, no family or relations to shame by the manner of my death.

I have been sentenced to hang for the crime of murder. I crouch now in a small, dark cell, with a metal cot, and a smelly little hole in the corner. High above me, to my right, a tiny, barred window admits a trace of dim starlight. To my left is an iron door, with thick, dollopy bolts and a sliding peephole. Behind my cot, the wall is scratched with names and curses, a Psalm, and a home-made calendar. A previous tenant has even charcoal-sketched the familiar stick figure from the game "Hangman," which another has smeared to near obliteration with what appears to be spittle. Beyond the walls of my cell, I know (though I cannot see them) are the grim guard towers, the dusty exercise yard, and the prison garden, its meager blossoms lovingly tended by some of the older inmates. If I close my eyes, it is easy for me to imagine that I am not here— That it is four months ago, and I am in another small, dark room. . . .

It is London. In this nervous, third decade of the twentieth century. These giddy years after the Great War. I was up to my bare elbows in chemicals, developing group photos of the Kennel Hill Cricket Club. The pictures were routine: a score of white-garbed goops standing in ranks, staring out over each other's shoulders; crossed bats; one wag waving a whiskey bottle . . . But wait. Here is a bit of advice for young photographers: Never miss the chance to do this type of mass photograph. Team pictures can be a short road to big business for the commercial photographer. Each head in those serried rows will someday get married or have children, or know someone who intends to do one or the other, and that wedding, christening, and anniversary business can be yours if you are willing to hustle for it. All you have to do is bring a generous supply of your business cards and scatter them among the assembled multitude, making sure that no member of the team, squadron, or enlightened society leaves without your name stuck in his pocket, breeches, or waistcoat.

I, for my part, had forgotten to bring a single one of my expensively embossed business cards to the Kennel Hill shoot, and I was cursing my own stupid forgetfulness as I lifted one of the crowded negatives from its chemical bath.

Suddenly, I was startled by a report and ricochet from without. It was the door to my studio slamming open and hitting the wall.

I couldn't leave the darkroom to see what was going on. So I shouted, "Hello?"

There was no answer. The floor of the studio trembled as footsteps crashed over the boards. Out of the confused noises, two voices rose in loud argument. I recognized the officious tenor of my assistant, Roy. The other was a voice I had not heard before. It was deep, thick, and rough. Its accent was rural, and as redolent of England's farms and fields as Roy's chirp was of its centrifugal capital.

The thick, rough voice was demanding to see me. Roy informed its owner that I could not be disturbed.

"And why bloody not?" demanded the stranger.

"Because Mr. Castle is in the darkroom," said Roy.

"Where is the dark room?"

"Right over there."

I heard footsteps crossing the floor. They stopped right outside.

"Behind this wall?"

"Yes."

I was startled by a scraping sound not far from my head. It was the stranger's hand, probing the wall. I felt strange, vulnerable, removed from it all, floating blindly in a lightless pool.

"What's he doing in there?" the stranger asked.

"He's developing pictures."

"In a dark room?"

"That's right," said Roy.

There was a moment of silence as the stranger seemed to meditate. Finally, he observed, "Well, maybe Mr. Castle could use some light—"

Car-pock! The darkroom wall seemed to explode. A shaft of daylight shot past me. Along with it came a cloud of plaster dust, bits of lathing, shreds of wallpaper, and a large fist. The fist wriggled free, leaving behind a ragged hole, gushing brightness.

My first thought was for the negatives. There was a demure ping from the egg timer, a sigh of relief from me. The period of sensitivity was over: The light would not damage. Wiping my hands, I reached for the door and threw it open.

Daylight dazzled. Restless clouds paced across the bright blue in the skylight; a silvery airplane cut a trim diagonal across the glassy grid. Beneath it, Roy stood in the rolling shadows assuming a boxer's stance before a stranger wearing a loud brown-and-mustard-checked jacket.

Roy was much smaller than his adversary; the battle was over as quickly as it began. With surprising gentleness, the stranger parried Roy's fistic attack and flipped him to the ground. Once Roy was subdued, the stranger sat on his head. From this low perch, he scowled up at me.

"I'm looking for Mr. Charles P. Castle," he said.

"I am he," I said.

"The photography expert?"

"I suppose I'm some sort of expert, yes."

Roy was struggling beneath the stranger's posterior.

"Can he breathe?" I asked.

"What?" the stranger said, as if he'd forgotten all about where he sat. "Oh," he said, looking down, and lifted his rear end enough to allow Roy to slip out.

Roy gasped and rolled across the floor. "I'm calling a policeman," he said, getting to his feet.

"That won't be necessary," said the stranger, dusting his own behind.

"And why not?" asked Roy.

"I'm a policeman," said the stranger.

He was a tall man, sun-browned, with bushy brows and a thick, rubbery scowl. Aside from his checked jacket, he wore a tight bowler hat, ill-fitting green trousers, and bullnose shoes. Noticing that I was studying him, he removed his hat, revealing a low forehead creased with a pink line from the sweatband.

"If you are a policeman," Roy challenged him, "where is your uniform?"

"I don't wear it on holiday," he said.

"Is this some kind of official business?" I asked.

"No, sir," he said. "It's personal."

"Then you have no right to come in here smashing through our walls," said Roy. "It's outrageous. This isn't Russia. What's your name?"

"Please, please, please, Roy," I said. "Let me handle this."

I turned to the stranger.

"I don't believe we are acquainted," I said, trying to put the exchange on some kind of civil basis.

The visitor smirked in Roy's direction. "Walsmear," he said. "Constable Michael Walsmear."

He put his hat up under his arm and offered me his hand. The trip through the wall had made the knuckles look as if they had been passed over a cheese grater.

After I shook the proffered appendage, Roy tried to give me his handkerchief. I waved it away.

"What can I do for you?" I asked our visitor.

"I want to know what you think about some pictures," he said.

"What pictures?"

"Some pictures I have here in my pocket."

"What would you like to know about them?"

Constable Walsmear looked over at Roy. Then he looked at me. "It's private," he said.

I could see that he was worried about Roy.

"Roy is perfectly trustworthy," I assured him. "He's my Dr. Watson. Anything you say to me, you can say to him."

"Doesn't look like a doctor to me."

"I didn't say he was a doctor. I meant he was like a doctor—Watson, that is."

"Get him out of here."

Roy laughed and straightened his tie. "I hardly think," huffed he, "that Mr. Castle would take the chance of being left alone with you—whatever you claim you are."

I looked from Roy to the visitor and mused inwardly. Roy was correct inasmuch as I was in no hurry to tête-a-tête with this large, violent individual. On the other hand, Walsmear was refreshingly different from my usual clients; and his mysterious "private" mission seemed like the beginning of an adventure—something I fancied, in my exquisite insanity, I wanted just then.

Recklessly, perhaps, I told Roy not to judge too hastily. "I think I'd like to see what the constable has to show me," I said.

"Do you mean you want me to step outside?" Roy said.

"Not step outside. Nothing like that. I have it. You can go to lunch. It is almost noon. I'll talk to Constable Walsmear here, and when you come back, it will be all over."

Roy stared in disbelief. "He could kill you," he said.

I told him that I doubted that would happen. And after giving the loyal and able Roy a great many assurances that I would take every care for my safety, I was able to get him to agree to leave me alone with our visitor.

"I'll be back," he said, plucking his hat from the rack and giving Walsmear a warning look. "I may just come popping back a bit early, too."

"Yes, yes, yes," I said, patting his head. "I appreciate your concern, Roy."

He stepped out the door, then pushed his way back in for a moment. "Don't forget," he said. "You have an appointment at one-thirty. Mrs. Skorking."

"I'll remember," I said. "Now go off and enjoy your lunch. And don't worry about me."

Roy started down the five flights from my studio to the street. The stranger did not move until the sound of Roy's footsteps had narrowed to a point and disappeared.

Then he visibly relaxed, and smiled.

CHAPTER TWO

How I Was Shaken by Some Photographs

THE STUDIO WAS SET UP from my session of the day before, when my clients had been a violin duo. Let me note here that the ambitious young photographer would do well to cultivate his contacts among the theatrical and musical professions and among those who aspire to them. Actors and musicians are in constant need of photos and prints to promote their shows and concerts; and many a professional photographer has built an entire career entirely on this trade. In this case, the musicians had wanted a "salon" look for the background of their picture. To please them, I had dug a couple of overstuffed chairs out of my prop room. Behind the chairs, I crossed a pair of ostrich-feather fans over an oriental vase big enough to hide a body in. Then I dusted off a bouquet of fabric roses and scattered the false blossoms around the set to look as if they had been hurled there by an ecstatic audience.

The fiddlers thought it was just the thing.

Now I motioned for Walsmear to take a seat in one of the overstuffed chairs. He tested both chairs with his fingers. Then, throwing up the short tails of his coat, he spun around and dropped heavily into the softest one. Reaching down, he picked up one of the fabric roses still on the floor. He sniffed.

"A fake," he pronounced.

I nodded, asked if he was comfortable; and, with heavy sarcasm, regretted that I couldn't offer him a cigar.

Walsmear said he had a cigar of his own.

This, half-smoked and crushed like a tent peg, he removed from his breast pocket. Lighting it, he puffed expansively. A yellow cloud enveloped the chair. From within the billows, I heard him smacking his lips.

"Comfortable?" I asked.

"Quite."

"Good."

After a few minutes of silent puffing, Walsmear asked, "You're not English, are you?"

"No."

"Australian?"

"No."

"Canada?"

"American. From Boston. Though I've lived here in London for eight years."

"I met some Americans in France. Didn't think much of them. That was in the war. Were you in the war?"

"Too young," I said.

The smoke was making my head ache. I walked over and opened a window. Fresh air rushed in along with the noise of the street.

"Didn't think much of them at all," Walsmear reiterated.

"Yes, well . . ." My voice must have sounded testy.

"But I appreciate you," Walsmear said, flicking ash into the oriental vase. "You're civil. For a Londoner."

"Thank you."

"I've been in London for two days now. And you may be the first civil bloke I've met."

"You may bear some of the blame for that," I said. "I mean, you've got a distinctive way of entering a room. Do you punch holes in walls everywhere you go?"

"I'd apologize for that. Only I make it my business never to apologize. Let me just say I was angry. At your friend."

"My friend? Oh, you mean Roy. Roy's not a friend. We're friendly, of course, but he's mostly my assistant—"

"Not the runt. I'm talking about Doyle."

"Doyle? Who's that?"

"Your friend."

I ransacked my brain. I didn't have any friend named Doyle. Unless he meant Jimmy Doyle, back in school. I shook my head at Walsmear. "I don't—"

"Sir Arthur Conan Doyle," he said exasperatedly. "The writer bloke. The bloody spiritualist. The Knight of the bloody Garter, or whatever."

"Oh, him."

"What do you call him? 'Arthur'? 'Artie'?"

"I think I called him Sir Arthur when I took his picture. But that was months ago. And I hardly know him personally."

"He knows you."

"Why do you say that?"

"He had your card in his desk. He told me to see you. He said you could tell me what you thought about—my photographs."

"Photographs, eh?" I said knowingly. "A local blackmail case?"

The policeman eyed me narrowly. "What makes you think it's blackmail?"

"Not difficult," I chuckled. "Or should I say 'elementary.' Ha, ha. I simply deduced it, as Sherlock Holmes might have."

"Who's Sherlock Holmes?"

"Sherlock Holmes," I repeated.

"Who's that?"

"You went to see Arthur Conan Doyle and you don't know who Sherlock Holmes is?"

The policeman looked at me blankly.

"Don't you read?" I asked.

"I'm a simple man," he said, jaw tightening.

"Why, may I ask, did you go to see Sir Arthur?"

"To show him," he said, "these."

Setting his bowler on his knee, he reached in his pocket and pulled out a dirty brown envelope tied with string.

"And what are those?"

"The photographs," he whispered.

Once more I tried to guess his business. What kind of crime involving photographs would bring a rural policeman ignorant of Sherlock Holmes to consult with Arthur Conan Doyle?

"Dirty pictures?" I asked.

Walsmear's head took on the color of a red bell pepper. His eyes popped and he leaped to his feet.

"What?" he thundered.

"I meant—"

"Who do you take me for?"

"Really, I—"

"You think I've come down here to London with a packet of dirty pictures to sell? Is that what you think?"

"Not at all—"

"Is that how I look to you? Well, you're no better than the rest of them."

"That's not so," I said.

"It is, too."

"It is not. But please let's get back to your business. If it's not blackmail and it's not dirty pictures, what in the name of heaven is it?"

"Never mind."

"What is it?"

"No, no, that's all right. Never mind. I'll go someplace else."

"Please tell me."

"You've had your chance."

This new outburst from the common, seemingly mad policeman made a strong contrast with my recollection of Sir Arthur Conan Doyle, a dignified man, despite his sometimes outlandish views. I wondered at the connection between the policeman and the writer. Why had the writer recommended me? I recalled my brief era of acquaintance with Sir Arthur. I had photographed the eminent author for the frontispiece of his collected works, to be published in Italy. Afterward, there had been some problem with the bill. Who was to pay? Sir Arthur's English publishers? Or the Italian publishers? Or Sir Arthur himself? My invoice went back and forth between the angry parties, until someone mediated a solution that saw the Italians paying, and Sir Arthur and his English publishers saving face for the Italians by blaming the whole thing on my somehow inept billing practices. It was even noised abroad that I had tried to bilk them in some unnamed way.

Was Sir Arthur still abiding by this absurd fiction?

Was he taking revenge by sending lunatics to harass me?

"May I ask a question?" I said.

Walsmear sniffed an affirmative.

"What else did Sir Arthur say to you? I mean, besides giving you my card. . . ."

"He said I was wasting his precious time. Then he had me thrown out."

"Why did he do that?"

"He didn't like the photographs."

"What's wrong with them?"

"Said they were poppycock."

"Well, let's have a look."

"After what you said?"

"Oh, come on."

"All right. I'll show them to you. But watch what you say, I don't like to be stepped on."

"You can trust me."

"I may be a fool," he went on. "And if I act like a fool, you can say so. But whatever you say, Mr. Castle, don't you dare—" and here he leveled a long finger at my nose "—don't you dare say a word against those girls."

"What girls?" I asked.

Walsmear's expression grew woeful. "I suppose you ought to see for yourself."

He held the package out toward me. As I reached for it, he suddenly drew it back.

"Doyle said you would know what you were talking about," he said.

The package was coming toward me again. Again I reached for it. Again it was withdrawn.

"If it turns out that I am wrong," he said, "I don't want you gloating. I don't want you humiliating—"

Here I fairly snatched the package from his hand.

He gave a surprised jerk, coughed into his hand, and said, "Yes, of course."

I pulled my chair under the skylight, right over a brilliant, bright square on the Oriental rug. I put the package on my knee and began undoing the dirty string with my fingernails. It was the devil to get off, and I was tempted to use my teeth. Finally, however, the knot was undone; the string floated through the air, and I pulled away a lot of extraneous wrapping material to expose two ordinary postcard-size snapshots.

"These are them?" I asked.

Walsmear nodded.

"The photographs?"

Walsmear nodded again.

I studied the top picture. It showed a pretty little girl, dressed in a modest white pinafore, standing in a garden. There were beds of delphinium to either side of her, and a gnarled tree in the background. The second picture showed another, younger girl, blonder, and similarly dressed. She was standing in almost the same spot, in profile and reaching out to touch the longest petal of a drooping iris.

The pictures were in crisp focus; but the frames were skewed, and both shots were marred by small, bright splotches here and there around the girls' figures.

These splotches immediately struck me as somewhat odd, if not exactly remarkable. There was something familiar about them. After musing about it, I recalled the way sunlight plays off the surface of a running stream and dapples the bottom of an overhanging bough. But how did such dapples get onto these photographs? They were not on any surface, but scattered around the image. I attributed the phenomenon to dust, or some other factor extrinsic to the scene.

"Now, tell me, what am I looking at?" I asked. "What do you see?"

"Two charming little girls. Two poor photographs."

I suddenly remembered what Walsmear had said about being "humiliated."

"What I mean to say," I hurriedly added, "is that the photographs are not bad, in the sense of being 'bad photographs.' I mean, for an amateur. They are just poorly printed. Did you—uh—take them?"

"Not me," he said. "The girls took them. One of the other."

"Oh, well, for being taken by children they're very good. How old are these girls?"

"One is six and one is nine. What else do you see?"

There wasn't much else. But I had to say something. So I bent closer and studied the girls' faces.

"I see," I said, "innocence. I see purity. I see the springtime of life."

The words came out of my mouth, but I couldn't believe I was saying such cornball stuff. I looked up at Walsmear. He was looking back at me as if "innocence, purity, and the springtime of life" were exactly what he expected me to say.

"What I mean is—"

What did I mean?

Get a hold on yourself, Castle, I thought. I looked back down at the photographs. I was reassured. There was nothing special there. The pictures were mundane in the way that only amateur snapshots can be. Of course, the girls were beautiful. That was something. And they were beautiful in their own special way. There was nothing of that insipid, dimple-cheeked sweetness that usually passed for childish beauty. There was a golden, unsullied quality about these two girls. I'd call it "goodness." But what does that mean anymore? Suddenly, I had a horrible thought.

"Are these girls missing?" I asked. "Have they been kidnaped?"

Walsmear shook his head. "They gave me these photographs themselves."

I was enormously relieved. But I was also becoming annoyed with Walsmear's guessing game.

"Listen here," I said. "I can't imagine what this is all about. Why did you bring these photographs to Sir Arthur, and now to me? What am I supposed to be seeing here? You have to give me some help. Or I'll have to start preparing for my next appointment. I don't have time for this nonsense."

Walsmear didn't move. He gave me a look that seemed to say that I was acting just the way he was expecting me to act. But how was I supposed to act?

"That's it," I said, handing him the photographs. "That's all. You'll have to go."

Does that sound harsh? Was I being a little short with the man? I was, but the snapshots of the two girls had a peculiar effect on me. They'd gone down inside me and were stirring my feelings. I felt like I was a great vat of yeasty dough being churned by a giant oar. (I'd actually photographed such a thing for a commercial bakery—like many industrial concerns, a good source of jobs.) I was upset, you see.

How unfortunate that I had sent Roy away. My next client was coming in soon, and Roy would have been invaluable. He attended to many details well, but the most important thing he did was chat up the clients. He was full of those polite obsequiousnesses and commonplace observations that make ordinary people comfortable. I used to have a knack for that sort of thing myself back when I was first starting out and the choice was to chat or starve. Lately, however, a thick tide of mopery and introspection had been rolling in. Now I dreaded meeting this new client; and why? Simply because I would have to think of things to say to her.

The second factor contributing to my uneasy state of mind was Walsmear's having revived some latent bitterness in reminding me of that Arthur Conan Doyle business. It was really a small disaster! I was made the scapegoat there. It was a matter of small print in his contract with his Italian publishers; and while Sir Arthur and the Italians had long since signed a peace treaty, I had been stuck with a reputation for shady billing practices. It was not fair. (But let the young photographer note here that business is not necessarily fair. The prizes go to the quick, the canny, the forceful, and the manipulative.)

Finally, there were those two little girls in the photographs. Damned how they affected me! It is strange the sort of things that breach the walls of criticism, skepticism, and irony we build around our emotions. A good cheap song will do that. Or when Little Eva dies in *Uncle Tom's Cabin*. (Maybe that's just me.) But that's just what the angelic faces of those two little girls did. They seemed to burst right out of those common, uninteresting snapshots and right into my heart.

And the thought occurred to me: Just like Little Eva, those girls were going to die. Not soon, I hoped, or not for many decades; but someday their bright, fresh, freckled faces would wither and disintegrate. Just as those cheap photographs would someday turn brown and curl up at the edges.

I looked down at my hands. I was kneading them.

This was surprising to me. Hand kneading was not in my repertoire of anxious gestures. I stopped and watched as the blood rushed back into my pallid fingers. I couldn't think why I was doing this. Now that I'm reviewing the incident, I think I understand. My hands were working in concert with deep impulses. They were trying to grab something: Time. They were trying to stop it, shape it, and mold its passing beauties into some permanent form. (I find it interesting that my hands instinctively sculpted. They tried to shape time as if it were clay. Does this say something about sculpture as an art form? Is sculpture the most fundamental artistic medium? Is it the medium most directly responsive to the most primitive sectors of our nervous systems? Isn't it a wonder that I can still take an interest in these questions—even though I am scheduled to hang tomorrow morning?)

So much to be done! I felt a strange urgency. A thousand plans and notions swamped my brain. So much beauty in the world. I had to find it, celebrate it, immortalize it. I had places to go, things to do. Tableaux, compositions, still lifes, interiors, portraits, landscapes, catalogues, close renderings, and luminous vistas.

I forgot about the policeman, Roy, my next client, the studio, and the gaping hole in my darkroom wall. Why was I sitting on my duff when so much beauty was out there, waiting to be crystallized into art? It was a crime to let it decay. Hell, it was almost immoral. Right then and there, I almost dug out my old paints and brushes and struck out on the road for—where? Why not—where did those little girls live?

CHAPTER THREE

How I Came to Be a Photographer

PHOTOGRAPHY HAS BEEN MY LIVING. Painting, however, is my metier. Many years ago, back in America, I studied drawing, painting, and printmaking under no less a master than Nolan Price, "The Bouguereau of Bridgeport." It was the noble Price who advised me to quit the U.S. and (since I couldn't speak French) move to London; to follow in the footsteps of his personal hero, John Singleton Copley. From a base in London, he argued, I could take advantage of the Continent's centuries-long tradition of drawing, painting, and sculpture. And if I worked hard enough, if I worshiped nature and paid her patient homage with pencil and brush, I might someday hope to join the fraternity of immortals: Giotto, Raphael, Michelangelo, Rubens, Rembrandt, David, Landseer . . .

By the time I got to London, however, the fraternity of immortals had altered its membership policy. Once there might be said to have been a single branching line of artistic descent from ancient Greece to modern Europe. Now that line was shattered into a thousand "isms." Each artist began history with himself. The past was a thing to be ridiculed, nature a thing to scorn. I myself was not immune to this trend. For a time, I stopped studying nature; I called myself an "oatist," and wore an empty rolled-oats tin on my head for a hat. I smashed up bowls and crockery and stuck the broken pieces to canvases; was briefly successful with women; felt like an idiot.

In time, I came to hate the pretensions of modern art; but I was too young to consider myself a conservative. Quite by accident, I made friends with some young photographers at a Chelsea pub. I discovered that photography was the great alternative. In practicing it, I could be modern without abandoning the pleasure of observing nature, and without having to worry what brush stroke was in fashion that week.

To ground myself thoroughly in photography's most basic processes, I went to work in a commercial darkroom. From the darkroom, I moved on to work as an assistant in the studio of Pierre Marquand, the famous portraitist. Marquand showed me that photography was a business as well as an art. In his company, I began to yearn for professional rewards and the sight of my own name in gold letters on a portrait case. After much planning, I broke the news to Marquand: I was going out on my own; starting my own studio. What an adventure! The high point of my life; and an adventure I hoped only to enjoy once—the studio I established I intended as a life sinecure.

Something about those two girls—I suddenly felt that maybe I'd taken the wrong turn in life. I felt like I'd sold out Art and Beauty for security. And I was still so young! Only thirty-two!

I turned away so I wouldn't have to look at Walsmear and his blasted photographs. My mind was in a turmoil. Where to rest my eyes? I looked across to my right. My eyes fell on a little alcove. That was a bad place to look. That alcove was where my desk stood.

My desk was a sight I usually avoided. Why? Because it was the place from which I conducted the business side of my studio. Its blotter was covered with unanswered letters and unread notices. Due bills spewed from the pigeonholes.

Some artist I turned out to be. My paths of glory had led only to a life of debt and petty calculation; I was no different from any miserable little shopkeeper or pin manufacturer.

It was all too much for me.

"Go," I croaked, turning back to Walsmear. "Go back to wherever you come from. Or go bother somebody else. I don't know who you are. I don't know what you want. And you know what? I don't care. You and Sir Arthur can all—"

Policemen don't like being told off. Walsmear stood up. I could see his fingers reaching instinctively toward the place on his belt where his truncheon ordinarily hung. As he took a step forward, I took a step back and tumbled over a prop Greek column. My back thumped against the floor; breath deserted me.

While I gasped, the policeman continued his minatory advance. I fully expected to share the fate of the cigar he now hurled to the floor and mashed with his foot. I closed my eyes and felt the floorboards tremble beneath his tread. When I opened them, Walsmear had passed. He'd stepped right over me and made for the window. I raised myself and twisted around to see what he would do. What he did was put his foot up on the sill and stare thoughtfully down at the street.

The thoroughfare was giving forth its usual midday

cacophony. If you weren't used to this commotion, it sounded like a combination of a train wreck and the rape of the Sabine women. But if you listened closely, the sounds separated out. You could distinguish street vendors, taxicab horns, gear-grinding omnibuses, and the shrieks of the street arabs. It was all tied together by the hum of motors and the murmur of the million conversations taking place in the heart of the greatest city on earth.

Walsmear spoke without turning from the street. "Mr. Castle," he said. "You may think I'm a funny man. You may get a good laugh from my clothes and my way of talking. You may think my pictures are funny. You and your friend Doyle may think I'm some kind of rustic clown. But you know something, Mr. Castle? I think you lot are pretty funny. You live in a dream world. You think you're so bloody important. But I don't think you're so important."

I was touched. I could tell he was not a man accustomed to making such speeches. His feelings had been hurt by someone, somehow, in some indefinable way and he was—very painfully—admitting it.

"I'm sorry if you feel that way," I said.

He dismissed me with a wave.

"Really," I said. "If there's anything—"

"No, no, no. It's too late."

"Please. Mr. Walsmear." I got to my feet. "What you said. It's very true. The world is a cruel place. I don't see why any of us should ever want to make it more so. And that other thing you said about me—what was that?"

Walsmear looked at me. "About you being a snob?"

"No."

"About you having a face like an ass?"

"Did you say that? No. It was something about a dream world."

"You live in a dream world?"

"That's right. You know, sometimes I do think I'm living some kind of dream. I feel insubstantial. Like I'm not even here."

Walsmear raised his hand to his chin and gave me a dubious look. Perhaps I shouldn't have confided that feeling to him. He was probably too crude to appreciate it.

"But listen," I said. "Let me help you. I'm at your service. Tell me what you want and I'll try to help you."

He now looked me up and down as if measuring my sincerity. "I'm prepared to pay you," he finally said.

"For what?"

"For your services."

"What services?" I was literally begging him now. "What do you want from me?"

"Sir, I want to know about these pictures."

He held the prints between his thumb and index fingers and shook them in my face.

"What do you want to know about them?" I snatched the prints from his hand. "What am I supposed to be looking at?"

"I want to know if they're real."

"What? The girls?"

"Not the girls." He grabbed my hand and held the prints in front of my face. "These," he said, pointing to one of the bright little splotches: the ones that looked like glints of sunlight, reflecting off a river. "And these, and these."

"Yes, I see."

"They're real, don't you see? The girls told me. I

believe it in my heart. But I want solid proof, too. Someone's got to prove that they're true."

"True? Real?" I said. "What are you talking about, for God's sake?"

"Don't you see them?" He beat his fingertip against the little splotches. "There's one there, and there's one there . . ."

"See what?"

He stopped and gave me a furious stare.

I spoke the words slowly. I implored him: "What are they?"

He looked at me like I was the biggest fool on earth. "Why, they're fairies, damnit. Fairies!"

CHAPTER FOUR

How I Struck a Deal with the Policeman

JUST THEN, THE WHOLE BUILDING seemed to shake. Actually, it was just the stairway. (It did that whenever more than one person came up it at a time.) Out of it came the high-pitched screech of a child and a rich, petulant female grumble. A moment later, my next appointment, a Mrs. Skorking and her ten-year-old daughter, came pounding through the door.

"Never again," gasped Mrs. Skorking. She flew straight to the chair where Walsmear had been sitting. There she collapsed. "This is absolutely the last time I go to a photographer who is on the fifth floor. I am absolutely dying and—" She whipped a small mirror out of her reticule. "I look a fright. G-r-r-r-r-ace!"

The little girl did not respond to her name.

"Do not touch the furnishings."

Little Grace, however, had gone behind my favorite backdrop. She was punching holes in it with a pencil.

Fanning herself furiously, Mrs. Skorking lay back and closed her eyes. A huge pile of hatboxes and garment bags entered the room in the arms of a servant girl.

"Heather—is that you?" Mrs. Skorking said, not bothering to look.

"Yes, m'um," answered the servant.

"Come here, Heather."

"Yes, m'um."

"Where are you, Heather?"

"I'm under these boxes, m'um."

"Tell my secretary to find another photographer."

"Yes, m'um."

"I am not a mountain goat."

"No, m'um."

"I want to look pretty and rested when I have my picture taken."

"Yes, m'um."

"Put those boxes down, I can't see you, dear."

The servant did so, curtsied, and withdrew. She was young, and might have been pretty if she didn't look so tired.

Mrs. Skorking opened her eyes and snapped shut her fan.

"You there—you're the photographer, aren't you?"

"Yes, m'um—I mean—" I coughed and tried to sound authoritative. "Yes, yes. I'm your photographer. And how are we today, Mrs. Skorking?"

"I don't see why you're standing there with your

mouth hanging open. I'm the one who's just climbed five flights of stairs."

"Oh yes, that is a problem. But you see, high up . . . natural light . . . best for the complexion. . . ."

A crash and a tinkle came from the darkroom.

"Excuse me." I rushed in to find little Grace standing over a pile of broken glass plates.

"Dear me, Grace. What have you done?"

The girl crunched over the broken glass as she made her escape. As I picked up some of the larger shards, I heard Mrs. Skorking addressing her servant.

"Heather, I don't want to be dark."

"No, m'um."

"You aren't making me too dark, are you?"

"No, m'um."

"Let me see that mirror."

"Yes, m'um."

"Oh, there. You've done it. You've made me too dark."

"Sorry, m'um."

"More powder."

"Yes, m'um."

When I came back out, madame and her servant were sitting knee to knee, a makeup box between them. The servant grabbed a huge, dribbling powder puff from the box and applied it to her mistress's face with vigor. In a moment, the two women were hidden in a billowing cloud of powder. It was like the stage magician's cloud of smoke. I found myself wishing Mrs. Skorking might vanish in it. She didn't, of course; but when the cloud had settled, I noticed that someone else had disappeared: Constable Walsmear.

Shouting his name, I grabbed my hat and made for the door. Behind me I heard another crash. A monitory "G-r-r-r-race!" rumbled from Mrs. Skorking. I couldn't check what else had been broken. I was flying down the stairs, swinging around banister poles, and almost left footprints on Mrs. Skorking's chauffeur who was having a smoke in the vestibule. As I hit the street, I saw Walsmear about to step aboard an omnibus.

"Hi, yo, ho!" I shouted, dodging traffic and crossing over to him. "Please, please, just a minute."

Walsmear raised one foot toward the omnibus steps. I grabbed his lapel and spun him around.

"Please." I caught my breath. "I wanted to help. I wanted—you didn't tell me what it was—what it was I could do for you."

"Yes, I did." Walsmear detached my fingers from his jacket.

"No, you didn't."

The omnibus roared off belching smoke. After waiting for me to complete a coughing episode, Walsmear continued: "I showed you the pictures. And I want you to prove that they're authentic."

"Authentic what?"

"Authentic pictures of fairies."

"What fairies? The girls? Are you saying the girls are fairies?"

"Don't be daft."

"Then what are you talking about?"

Walsmear removed the photos from his jacket pocket. "What do you call this?" He pointed to one of the bright splotches there. "And this?" He pointed to another splotch.

"It's a reflection," I said. "A halation. An irradiation. A dab of nose grease on the lens. Very common sort of thing, spots like these. Those cheap cameras and celluloid film are extremely unstable. And lenses magnify the slightest smirch or mote."

Standing in the middle of the crowded sidewalk, I was battered by women carrying packages, had my toe stepped on by a messenger, was jostled by preoccupied businessmen, and had my ear nipped by a cart horse. Walsmear stood above it all, for some reason unmolested.

"Photography is a delicate process," I went on. "There are a million places where imperfections can creep in."

"But they're just in these pictures," he said. "The ones the girls took in the garden. Not ones they took in the house."

"You can't predict what a speck of dust will do. A bit of grit can slide on and off the lens or piece of film. And it can do all sorts of prismatic things."

"Can you prove that these are only spots of dust?"

"Not necessarily dust. Like I say, they could be anything."

"Then they could be fairies."

"Anything but fairies. I'm sorry. What I mean to say is, what you have there is on the lens or film. It's not out there where the girls are. It's in the camera."

"Can you prove that?"

I thought for a moment.

"Well, you can't see anything very well in these little prints. Do you have the negatives?"

"Yes."

"Good. Now, if I enlarged these spots you'd be able to see better."

"See what better?"

"See the dust or whatever."

Walsmear pulled out his handkerchief and unwrapped the negatives. "Here," he said.

"All right." I slipped them from his fingers. "This should help settle your bet."

"I beg your pardon."

"This should help settle your bet," I said.

"What bet?"

"Whatever bet you've got going."

"I don't have any bet going."

"You mean you haven't bet someone that these splotches are fairies? And they haven't bet you that they aren't?"

"No."

"Oh."

"What makes you think that?"

"I just couldn't think of any other reason. For you to be interested, I mean."

"I have my own reasons."

"I'm sure."

"I'm paying you. So why should it matter?"

"It doesn't."

"Good. Here."

He reached in his pocket and drew out a wad of bills.

"Not here," I said. "I mean, not now. When I'm finished."

"When you're finished proving I'm right."

"Look," I said. "I can't prove anything. But here's what I will do. There are about a dozen of these little spots here. I'll enlarge each one of them to eight inches by ten inches. That should be large enough to settle any question. And I'll just charge you for the paper. Not the labor or anything."

"I'll pay full price, thank you."

"Have it your way."

"And take a deposit."

"It's not necessary."

"Take it."

"Oh, for—"

I took the money from his hand and quickly stuffed it in my pocket. I felt like a costermonger or something, doing business in the street.

"When will you be finished?" he asked, climbing onto the next omnibus.

"The day after tomorrow," I shouted after him. "Morning."

The bus ground gears and moved on.

I stood for a moment in the street. I wondered what I had just got myself into. Suddenly, I remembered Mrs. Skorking. She was still in my studio. Waiting. And probably breathing smoke and fire from every aperture in her face.

"Crikey."

I raced back up the stairs. I was doomed, I thought. Mrs. Skorking will be furious. Nothing can save me now.

But saved I was. The U.S. Cavalry had arrived in the form of Roy. He'd decided to come back early from lunch, and he had the session well in hand.

"Surprised to find you in one piece," he whispered to me.

"He really wasn't dangerous," I said, peering through the big studio camera. Standing up, I held high the red bulb. Mrs. Skorking and daughter suppressed their inner gargoyles for a fraction of a second. I squeezed.

"That will be wonderful," I said.

It was amazing how quickly the scowls settled back on their faces.

"Tough life, eh?" I whispered to the servant girl as they prepared to leave.

"Are you talking to me?" she said, scowling.

"Ah, yes. I was, ah, saying, ah, tough life. Working for that old bat, eh?"

"Mind who you talk about that way," the girl hissed. "Mrs. Skorking could buy you and sell you. She could tear down this building. She could ruin you."

And from this little slip of a servant girl I got the most hateful, malevolent look I've ever received.

The incident wasn't important. Except as I am trying to establish my state of mind here. And that state was: confused.

Why did this girl—a complete stranger—hate me? All I did was make a commiserating pleasantry. For that matter, how did I get stuck with this Constable Walsmear and his fairy pictures? What kind of day was this? Now Roy was standing around clearing his throat and looking at me expectantly. He's going to ask for that raise, I thought.

"Ah, Roy," I said before he could get a word out. "Why don't you go home early today. I have a slight headache. You can see what kind of day it's been. It didn't start badly, you know. When I stepped into the darkroom this morning, all was calm. When I came out there were all sorts of crazed constables and little girls smashing my plates. I don't know why it should be. But there it is . . ."

When Roy had gone, I walked over and pulled the swivel chair away from my desk. I set it directly under the skylight and leaned back in it as far as I could. There was a scattering of fresh weather clouds in the sky. I watched them go pink in the sunset. The street noise lost its harried edge. I tried to think about pleasant things.

That crazy copper Walsmear.

I picked up his "fairy" pictures. I looked at the sweet girlish faces. Surely, I thought, these are all the "fairies" the world needs. Two bright, merry children. An English garden. Isn't there enough enchantment there? Why, I wondered, did this Constable Walsmear insist on complicating the scene with his "fairies"? Of all the shopworn fantasies! You could see fairies everywhere: in advertisements, on the stage, in picture books, on perfume bottles . . .

But the innocent loveliness of those two girls. Now that was rare. It probably only existed in isolated places like whatever burg, village, or market corners had produced the likes of Constable Walsmear.

Leaning closer, I squinted into the "fairy" glints on the pictures. Nothing. Zero. I took out the negatives. The glints were there, too. But my conclusion was the same: The spots were grease, water, jam perhaps, on the lens. I decided to have Roy do the enlarging. I hoped the policeman wouldn't be too disappointed.

I locked up and went downstairs to bed.

Half asleep, I saw the little girls from the photographs in my mind's eye. They were standing in the middle of their garden. As I approached, they took me by the hands. They led me to a secret place where the flowertops were alive with figures. Little men and women. Fairies, sprites, fays, gnomes, elves, and peris sported through the blossoms. I must have been fully asleep by that time. My secret heart was "charmed" in every sense of the word. The scene perished in a point of white light as I awoke.

What a sweet fantasy. I wanted it to be true. But I was way beyond all that now. The only route to fantasy I could imagine would be through the eyes of a child. But my life in London was singularly free from childish influences. And being unmarried, thirty-two, and without a close female companion, I couldn't see any children entering my life soon.

CHAPTER FIVE

How I Was Late for an Appointment

THE NEXT DAY, I felt strangely listless. I started thinking about old girlfriends. That's not good. I thought about Sheila—now in Rangoon with her planter. And Jeanne—whom I saw the other day; still a good dresser, but much, much heavier. Then there was Laura, back in Boston. We were only sixteen. Why hadn't I written her? Now, it could never be. I had a fantasy in the darkroom. I saw myself prostrated on her grave, my face nestled in the winding grasses, inhaling the fresh scent of the earth as I'd once . . .

That was no good at all. I flicked on the darkroom light. There were the faces of Mrs. Skorking and Grace looking up at me through a swirl of chemicals. That sobered me up good.

ROY WAS ALREADY WORKING in the darkroom when I arrived at the studio the following morning. It was another nice day, so I took my chair up to the roof. London stretched around me in daunting detail. Spires. Towers. Chimneys. Windows. Rooftops. Pigeon coops.

Smokestacks. And bricks, upon bricks, upon bricks, enough to drive you mad if you tried to include them all in a painting; revealing to me that there was at least one sure road to riches in this town: brick making.

A shadow fell across my lap. I looked up. It was Roy.

"I've finished those enlargements," he said.

"Which ones?"

"The splotches. For that constable. I enlarged every last little splotch on those negatives."

"Anything, uh, interesting?"

I hadn't told Roy about the "fairies."

"Hardly. Chap's bonkers, right?"

"It's his money," I said, taking the prints.

Roy went back down through the hatchway.

I flipped through the enlargements. Isolated and blown up to eight by ten, the splotches were even less inspiring than before. Their edges were vague. Inside were only a few indistinct shadows.

Not that I had expected anything. Nonetheless, I took it badly. The world seemed a little more barren than it had a few minutes before. Of course, there were no such things as fairies. But still . . .

The hatchway popped open with a thud. Walsmear's bowler-hatted head popped up. The rest of his body, wearing the same loud, checked jacket, followed. He appeared to take no interest in the spectacular view around him. He walked over to where I sat.

"Phaugh," he said.

A cloud of smoke rolled over us from a nearby chimney.

"Where are you?" he called out through the smoke.

"Over here."

I crossed over to another part of the roof, but I

couldn't get away from the smoke. It seemed to follow me.

"Come on over here," I said, going back to where I originally sat. The wind changed, however, and the smoke followed again back to where I had come from.

"Just a minute," said Walsmear. He feinted a few steps toward the other side of the roof. The smoke started blowing that way.

"Ha!" Walsmear turned around and trotted back to me. The smoke stayed where it was.

I showed Walsmear the enlargements.

"As you can see," I said. "There's nothing here. It's just some everyday optical phenomena. Dust, grease, bits of pollen . . ."

I parceled the prints out slowly. I wanted him to sense that he was getting something for his money.

Walsmear studied each dim shadow on each print. I felt bad for him. From the look on his face, I'd just wiped out a big emotional investment.

"I'm sorry," I said. "I really am. You know, you don't have to pay me for these. I'll give you your money back."

"Mr. Castle," he said. "Don't treat me like a child."

"I'm not treating you like a child."

"Yes, you are."

"I am not."

"Ain't I good enough to pay your full fee?"

"Of course you are."

"Well?"

"Well, it's just that—that is—they came to nothing, didn't they?"

"And?"

"And I'm sorry it didn't work out. All right?"

"What do you care?"

"I don't care. But see here, let's not argue. I thought the whole thing was charming. Fairies and all that. Here, let me have another look at those prints."

Walsmear looked glum. He handed them over.

"These enlargements," I went on, "don't prove anything. Not if you don't want them to. You don't have to accept them. Nor do the little girls. I mean in the larger sense. Of course the splotches are some kind of technical error. But who's to say they aren't really fairies?"

"What do you mean?"

"I mean that if you believe that these splotches are fairies, and the girls believe that these splotches are fairies, who's to say that they are not? These or any other photographs. It's all imagination, man. That's how we interpret the world. And God bless it, eh? Do you think I want to crush anyone's belief in fairies? Not a bit. Here, take a look at that cloud over there. By St. Paul's dome."

"What about it?"

"What does that cloud look like to you?"

"A cloud."

"Now, now. You can do better than that. Here's an example. When I look at that cloud I see—ummm—I see a white buffalo."

"You're barmy."

"I am not."

"You are, too."

"If I believe something is so, then it's as good as being so. In a certain sense, I mean. Now, look at this enlargement. There's nothing here. But it isn't exactly empty. Maybe it's just some dust on the lens. But look here. If you turn it this way . . . and you sort of look over at the edge of this shadowy thing here . . . why, that, there—that could be an almost perfect outline of an arm. Right? It's an almost perfect outline of an arm. And if you follow the line down here, that looks just like a shoulder. Oh, look. And here's the chin. Quite remarkable, really. Down here. Look where it swells. That could be a hip. And a knee. I studied anatomy, you know. In art school. Ah, and look right there. That's the other leg. Just in the right place. . . . And what's that you're looking at there. Heavens to Betsy. Those fingers look just like—fingers. . . ."

I chattered away like an idiot. My mind was a little late in catching up with my eyes. Not so the hairs on my neck. They stood up and leaned forward, stiff as ski jumpers.

I was looking at what had previously appeared to be nothing more than a murky pattern of grays. Now I saw that the murk contained a human figure, or what appeared to be a human figure. It was hidden in the shadowy pattern the way objects are hidden in those illustrations for children; the ones that conceal spoons, frogs, and teacups in the hills and foliage of seemingly ordinary landscapes. The figure was there if you looked for it. But could anyone else see it?

I glanced at Walsmear. His eyes were glittering.

Still, I kept on babbling. It was too much to accept. What were we looking at? Just the edges of some vague shadows. Each edge was nothing by itself, but in relation to one another, the proportions were unmistakable. It was a human figure—a female figure.

"It comes out at you," said Walsmear, breathing with difficulty. "Like a deer out of the woods."

He was holding the enlargement by one corner. I was holding the other. Neither of us wanted to let go.

"Now let's just take a second here," I said. "Let's

pause and make room for a little sanity to creep in. I'm going to look away from this thing. Now I'm looking away from it. I'm looking out at the city. It's a beautiful day. It's the 1920s. My name is Charles P. Castle. How do you do? Now. Let's have another look at that enlargement."

I looked. The figure was gone. In its place were the same vague shadows I had seen the first time I looked; the same relationless chaos. What a relief. I exhaled. My mind relaxed. Suddenly, the figure popped back, clear as before; the way an optical illusion will when you stop searching for it.

"I don't believe it," I said.

Walsmear laughed. He guffawed quite loudly. Then he snatched the print from me and held it to his chest.

"Those dear girls," he said, wiping a tear. "Those dear, dear girls."

I'd encouraged all this. Now I felt I should be the cold water bearer.

"Oh, come now," I said, "this proves nothing. You see a shape. It's just a bunch of shadows. I might as well say I see Calvin Coolidge in the moon. You know, the craters and all."

"I don't care what you think," he said.

"You don't really believe—"

"I certainly do."

"Would you look any man in the eyes and say, 'Yes. I believe in fairies'?"

"I would."

"I wouldn't if I were you."

"Why not."

"You're a policeman. You could lose the public's confidence."

"Bah. Tell me, which one of the pictures does this come from?"

"I don't know. Let's go downstairs and have a look."

I led the way down the hatch to the studio, with Walsmear's feet above me, treading my fingers on the rungs of the ladder.

Fortunately, Roy in his excellent way had numbered and cross-referenced the splotches with their enlargements. The splotch in question had come from the photo showing the taller of the two girls. There were flowers all around her, and that trunk of a great, gnarled tree in the background. The splotch which held the figure was at her feet—and judging from the girl's size, the figure was less than ten inches tall!

It was all too absurd. At first I was fancying the figure to amuse myself and—well, to patronize Walsmear. Now I really believed it. How could I not believe it? It was there! I thought to myself: If this is silliness, by God, let's make the most of it.

"Constable Walsmear," I said.

"Yah?"

Walsmear had reverted to his usual tone of voice. Crude. Challenging. I paused. What sort of person was I getting involved with? You can never tell, I decided, and plunged ahead.

"Constable Walsmear, I wonder if I might stand you lunch?"

"Eat?"

"That's right. Yes. I'd like to take you out to eat. And talk. We ought to talk. Not that I think there's anything to these pictures—"

"Yes, you do."

"I'd never tell anyone—"

Just then, Roy appeared at my elbow. He'd slid over from my desk, where he'd been doing some kind of work.

"Excuse me, Mr. Castle." Roy almost had to stand on tiptoe to talk in my ear. His face was its usual self: pink and shining with ambition. "I wonder if I could have an important word with you."

"Can't it wait?"

"I suppose it could."

"Good. Good man, Roy. It shall wait. So it shall. I'm leaving you in charge here while the constable and I go out to lunch. See that everything runs smoothly, would you? I know you will."

"Good man, that," I said to Walsmear as we descended to the street not exactly arm in arm, but in a friendly sort of way.

The next question was where we would have lunch. I had a few places in mind; modest establishments where the policeman would be comfortable—and where no one I knew would see me dining with a man in a loud, checked jacket.

Walsmear, however, had his own ideas. We were barely around the corner when I felt his hand on my shoulder. I was thrust down into a shadowy doorway. A wave of heat slapped my face. I heard a roar of voices. The smell of old grease and stale gravy smacked my nostrils.

"Beg your pardon. Excuse me, excuse me . . ."

I felt myself rolled through a crush of bodies. By the time my eyes got used to the dim light, I was being pushed down into a chair.

It appeared to be some kind of eating establishment. I'd never noticed it before, even though I'd lived around the corner for six years. If I had noticed it, I might have complained to the authorities. Not only the smell, but the din was terrific. The vocal intonations were Covent Gardens, blacksmith, and street tough all talking at the same time. Engineers with greasy arms gobbled meat pies and shouted in each other's faces. Lean cobblers sipped beer, muttered, and eyed the crowd. Everybody knocked against my back as they walked by, shoving their way in and out.

A waiter's belly appeared over our table. Walsmear ordered every heavy, oily dish imaginable. I asked for beer and some bread.

"That's all?" asked Walsmear.

"I'm not really hungry."

"I am. I get hungry when I feel good. And today, I feel good."

He leaned back and stretched his legs expansively into the aisle. Someone tripped. Walsmear ignored the curses. I got a wedge of boiled potato thrown at me.

Our beers arrived. Walsmear downed his in a gulp. I picked through the bread.

"You want to talk?" Walsmear said. "Do it now. I'm off right after we eat."

"Back to wherever you—?"

Walsmear nodded. A shepherd's pie was shoved under his face. He disappeared in the steam.

"It's about this fairy business, of course," I said. "I was thinking I could help you."

"Don't need help."

"You may. This discovery has to be properly handled if you want to make the most of it. Now, I'd suggest we first contact the British Museum. Get the science boys involved. Just to show we're on the level. Then we start parceling out information to the newspapers. Not too much at first—"

"What—are—you—talking—about?" Walsmear uttered each word between forksful of food and sops of gravy.

"I'm talking about the fairies," I said. "Don't you want to tell the world what you've found?"

"No."

"I thought you did."

"I don't."

"Isn't that why you went to Sir Arthur?"

"Bah. They told me he was an expert. That's why I went to see that bloody high-and-mighty bastard. He was no help. Now you were help. I'll grant you that. But I don't need any more help. I'm letting the whole thing drop. I'm satisfied and that's all there is to it."

"That's the end of it?"

"That's all."

"You mean to tell me that you have what appear to be actual photographs of fairies in your possession and you're just going to let the matter drop?"

"Yup."

"And what are you going to do with the photos?"

"That's my business."

"What about the girls?"

"What girls?"

"The girls in the pictures. What about them?"

"What about them?"

"Don't the pictures belong to them?"

"They gave them to me."

"Did they give them to you officially? As a policeman?"

"As a friend, Mr. Castle. As an old friend of the family."

"So you know the family?"

"That's right."

"For long?"

"I've been a friend of their father for most of my life."

"What does he do? Are they wealthy?"

"He has a private income. But they're not wealthy."

"And the mother?"

"She's dead."

"I'm sorry to hear that. How did she die?"

"I killed her."

Walsmear's eyes stared at me coldly; his bushy brows lowered like storm clouds.

The conversation pretty much stopped dead in its tracks.

Several minutes passed in uncomfortable silence. When next Walsmear opened his mouth, it was to release an enormous belch.

"Ah, that felt good," he said. "You know, the Gypsies consider it good manners to belch after a meal."

"Do they now?"

"That's right. Say, what's that behind your ear?"

"What? Where?" I reached back with my fingers.

"There."

"Where?"

"Right here—"

Walsmear suddenly lunged over the table. I ducked in fear. His hand passed behind my ear. It came out with a coin in the fingers. Walsmear grinned and smacked the coin on the table.

"And look, here's another one." He reached and pretended to grab another from behind my ear. He placed it next to the other. "For lunch."

He rose and stuck out his hand.

"You've been kind, Mr. Castle," he said. "But don't press your luck."

Picking up his hat, he turned and walked out the door.

I drank two more glasses of beer before I left. Outside, I felt light-headed. The fresh air contributed. Of course, I couldn't go back to the studio in that state. I had to wait a bit and clear my head. And, anyway, it was a perfect day for a walk.

I strolled hither and yon, down thoroughfares wide and narrow. Passed parks, palaces, and hovels; plunged into the City. Around me, humanity surged like a pitching sea; black-frocked financiers muttered in doorways; peddlers howled; locomotives thundered. I saw a one-legged veteran begging in the Strand. I passed a jeweler's where a turbaned Indian was buying a glittering brooch.

"O London," I apostrophized. "Thou . . ." something or other.

There is certainly no place like London. Especially not New London, Connecticut, where I had an aunt. Or Boston, where I grew up, in the North End, in three rooms over my father's paint store. Or New York, where there is sufficient noise and bustle, but where everything is new.

But London, I stopped to reflect. Now here was history. Right where I stood. Who else might have stood here? Mysterious druids and blue painted savages. Julius Caesar. Arthur and the legendary kings and knights. Spenser. Shakespeare. Johnson. Reynolds. Van Dyke. Turner. Peter the Great. Sir Walter Ralegh. You could go on and on. Not to mention all the great chain of simple, anonymous humanity stretching from before history to this moment. London—England is an ancient place. Something old is built into the people. It's a current. Subterranean. Supernatural. Prehistoric.

Clearing my head with such reveries, I eventually steered my steps back toward the studio. I climbed the five flights that Mrs. Skorking had found so difficult. It *was* rather hard going. My next studio, I decided, would be in a skyscraper. With an elevator. High above it all. In the clear blue empyrean.

Roy was just coming out of the darkroom. He wiped his hands on his apron as I came puffing through the door.

"You missed Brewster," he said. He undid the apron and carefully hung it on a peg on the wall. He removed his jacket from the peg next to that and put it on.

"Brewster?"

"Mr. Lucius Brewster?" he inquired liltingly. "M.P. The political chap? The campaign pictures? He was scheduled for two-thirty."

"Oh, my God." I crumpled my hat in aggravation. "How do I let these things slip my mind? Roy, you handled it, I hope? You've done it before. Good old Roy. Thank you, man, thank you."

"Actually, I didn't do the session."

"No?"

"In fact, I recommended Brewster go elsewhere. To another studio."

"Another studio? Why? And who?"

"The studio of Roy Pecksworth." Roy bowed grandly. "That's what I've been trying to tell you. I'm leaving your employ, Mr. Castle. I'm setting up on my own."

"What? How?"

"I've worked for you for over a year, Mr. Castle. You are a skillful photographer when you want to be. I've learned a lot from you. But my opinion of your business acumen is low. Very low."

Roy walked over to the desk. He picked up a handful of bills and receipts. They dribbled through his fingers. "It's been months since you attended to these things."

"Roy, Roy, Roy," I protested. "Don't you worry about that. That's my responsibility. You've got to relax. Learn how to take a good picture. I mean a really good picture. I've so much yet to teach you. About light, composition, modeling. Why, it's been months since we've taken a field trip to the museum. Let's plan something right now."

Roy held up his palm.

"Mr. Castle, you have to think about more than art. Brewster is the third client this month you've missed. Despite all my reminders. And as far as your business is concerned, I've been doing some rough calculations. In a matter of three months, Mr. Castle, you will be out of business. Bankrupt. Broke."

"Broke?"

"Unless," Roy frowned thoughtfully, "you can come up with, oh, about a thousand pounds before then."

I didn't doubt that what Roy said was absolutely true.

"This is very good, Roy," I said. "I mean, it's very bad. But it's very good that you understand these things, Roy. You can help me. You seem to understand these things very well."

Roy shook his head. "I'm a young man, Mr. Castle. Why should I get sucked under with you? No sir, no debacles for me. I've been saving my money. I rented a studio over on Crofter Street. It's not very large or sumptuous, but it's a start. And I already have my first client."

Stunned, I barely heard the rest of what he had to say. Dutiful to the last, he described his final chores for me. ". . . And I did that extra set of prints you wanted. Those blotch things. For that awful policeman. They're drying now."

"Oh, thank you, Roy," I said sorrowfully, following him to the door. I didn't think I could change his mind, so I wished him the best of luck and assured him that I was always available for consultation—on technical matters.

"We may be competitors in business," I said. "But we'll always be brothers in art."

"Not for long," he laughed, starting down the stairs. "You're going to be out of the game very quickly."

"Now, now, Roy." I clattered after him. "By the way, what did you think of those blotches?"

"The policeman things? I don't know. They were blotches, that's all."

"I mean, what do you think made them?"

"What could have made them? I don't know." He laughed once more as he fitted his hat on his head. "Fairies, I suppose."

He laughed out the front door and all the way down the street.

CHAPTER SIX

How I Vexed a Great Author

THE NEXT DAY, I was walking down Victoria Street with a book in my hand. The book was *Death: the*

Great Illusion, by Walter Barrington. Is death an illusion? Tomorrow morning, I am scheduled to find out. Back then—what seems like a thousand years ago—the question was academic.

I didn't care what the book said anyway. I was more interested in the address inside. It was the address of the place where the book had been purchased: The bookstore operated by the daughter of Sir Arthur Conan Doyle (and financed by the great man himself). This was a bookstore devoted to psychical publications, periodicals, and paraphernalia. Sir Arthur's secretary told me I could find him there that day, signing checks for the daughter.

I found the bookstore located on the first floor of a modest town house. As I was about to put my hand on the door, I felt something seize my elbow.

"So," spoke a harsh, sibilant voice. "Going to see the devil, are you?"

Swinging around, I reclaimed my elbow. It had been taken by a clawlike hand. Stepping back, I saw a tiny, white-haired old woman. She was dressed in black, and wore an old-fashioned "coal scuttle" bonnet.

"What are you?" hissed the crone (a cruel word, but the first that sprang to mind). "Friend? Tradesman? Business associate? Who are you that you come to see the great devil Doyle at this fiendish shop?"

"See here, now," I said. I looked up and down the street, wondering what kind of district this was that it put up with aggressive lunatics accosting honest citizens. Of course, the poor old thing was to be pitied. But still— "Madam," I said, "that is none of your business. Kindly let me pass."

"He's the devil, you know," she said. "Satan. The Anti-christ. Lucifer."

"Please, let me pass."

"All right, all right. Maybe he's not the devil. But he's a very evil man. Lookie here, mister. Look at the number of this store. The street number. It's here in brass numbers. Brazen in every way. Double that number, mister. Do it in your head. Double it and add it to the numerals of the year 1910. Now subtract fifty-nine. That's how old he is."

"I'll do no such thing."

"You don't have to. I already done the ciphering. It adds up to six-six-six. That's right: The evil number. The mark of the beast."

"Oh, please . . ."

"He's in league with the forces of darkness. He conjures spirits. He talks to Ouija boards. He thinks he's talking to the dead, but he's really only talking to demons. Our Savior warned us, mister. Doyle is in league with the strange and ghastly. And it is only through our Lord and Savior Jesus Christ that he can be driven out. Help me, oh brother, that the precious blood of Christ can prevail over—"

Poor mad old thing! I reached into my purse and gave her a coin, patting her withered hand. She was babbling and inspecting the coin as I went into the shop. A little bell tinkled as I walked through the door. I glanced around. The books were separated into categories: Astrology, Automatic Writing, Life After Death, Numerology, Telekinesis, Palmistry—that sort of thing. The building also housed a "Psychic Museum." But a sign said it was closed.

There was only one customer in the shop. He was a pale young man with a wispy beard. When he slunk out with a purchase, I felt like an infestation had been lifted.

"Can I help you?" asked a young lady.

This could only be Doyle's daughter, I thought; she resembled him about the eyes and forehead.

"Ah, how pleased to meet you," I said. "No books now, thank you. I'm here on personal business."

"Personal business?"

"Yes. You may think my business is strange. Well, maybe you won't. I'll bet you hear a lot of strange things in this shop."

The young lady nodded. She gave a knowing smile.

"Why, yes," she said. "We do find ourselves involved in many phenomena that the outside world might consider—unusual."

We laughed together complicitly.

"Actually," I said, "I've come to speak to your father."

She looked startled for a moment. Then she composed herself.

"Of course," she said. "It can be done. I've spoken to him myself, you know."

"I should hope so," I said, laughing.

"Yes," she said, her eyes suddenly gazing into the far distance. "I spoke to him only last week. He said he was very happy. He'd finally found the peace he had been seeking so long."

"That's good to hear—"

"Not in so many words, naturally," she said, flushing slightly. "It was a sort of rapping. One rap for yes. Two for no. But I asked if he was happy and he did rap once."

"There must be some sort of mistake. Isn't your father here? In the shop? I was told he was probably in the back room."

The young lady eyed me with shock; her lip began to quiver. "My father has been dead for four years!" she sobbed.

A man's voice suddenly boomed from behind me. "She communicated with her late father at a séance," said the voice. "I was there. I heard it all."

I turned around to see the tall figure of Sir Arthur Conan Doyle. A beaded curtain shimmied in the doorframe behind him.

"So you're alive," I said.

"I can see there's been some confusion here. This young lady is not my daughter. She is my daughter's employee."

I uttered profuse apologies to the teary-eyed young woman, but Sir Arthur cut them short. He sent the girl on some task behind the counter. Then he peered at my face.

"We're acquainted, aren't we? You are Mr. . . ?"

"Castle," I said. "Charles P. Castle."

The look of standard greeting fell from Sir Arthur's face.

"Oh," he said. "You."

"Did you get my note?"

"You said you had something to show me? Some psychical materials pertaining to . . . ?"

"That's right."

"I'm very busy today. Did you bring them?"

"Yes, I did."

"Would you be good enough to come upstairs?"

The beaded curtain concealed a staircase. We climbed up to a surprisingly sunny second-floor room. There were a desk and chairs, overflowing filing cabinets, and boxes and trunks full of books.

Sir Arthur introduced me to his real daughter, Mary; a tall, stout woman, whose features were a humbler, milder version of her father's.

"Bit of a misunderstanding downstairs, Mary," said Sir Arthur. "Mr. Castle here thought Irene was you.

He asked to speak to her father. It confused her. It was the sort of mix-up that can only happen among people like us—people who actually do communicate with the dead."

"Did Irene think Mr. Castle had come for a séance?"

"Something like that."

"It must have been very funny."

"It was somewhat amusing."

Neither father nor daughter cracked a smile.

"Mr. Castle is a photographer," Sir Arthur went on. "He did my portrait. You remember that problem with the Italian edition, don't you, Mary?"

"So this is him?" Mary looked me up and down. She seemed to be memorizing my appearance for a future textbook on criminal physiognomy.

"Let's leave that in the past," said Sir Arthur. "Mr. Castle sent me a letter this morning. He mentioned a subject very close to my heart right now. Can you guess what that subject is, Mary?"

Mary cocked her head and made a fluttering motion with her fingers, mimicking a flying thing.

Sir Arthur nodded.

"I'm glad to hear you're interested," I said, half-bowing. "I think you'll be excited by what I have to show you."

"I hope so too," said Sir Arthur. He walked behind the desk and sat down. "I'm a publicly avowed spiritualist. The whole world knows my beliefs. I'm interested in spiritualism, the occult, psychic phenomena, and the supernatural. This can be a problem sometimes. I'm besieged by cranks, knaves, and fools of every description. The world of spiritualism is full of such types."

"Charlatans?"

"I take great moral satisfaction in exposing the fakes," said Sir Arthur. "But as an earnest investigator, I cannot afford to overlook anything. I simply hope that you are not going to waste my time."

"I hope not too."

"You know," Doyle began playing with a letter opener, "your name came up a few days ago. Strange thing. It was in my office. An offensive sort of man. Said he was a policeman. He came barging in claiming to have photographs of fairies. Naturally, I was eager to see them. Unfortunately the photographs showed no such thing."

"The man you are speaking about is Constable Walsmear. I know. He came to consult me."

"Well then, I'm sorry about all that, you know. I just wanted to get rid of him. Your card was in my drawer and I just sort of grabbed it and stuck it in his hand. You should have seen this fellow, Mary. There was this air of violence about him. Violence and diffidence—a not unusual combination, really, in both criminals and policemen."

"In Constable Walsmear's defense," I said, "he seemed to be a bit of a fish out of water in London. And he was not really accustomed to meeting with prominent or famous people like yourself."

"Still," said Sir Arthur. "I apologize. I hope you were able to get rid of him."

"Actually, that's what I've come to see you about. Constable Walsmear's photographs."

"Oh?"

"I've studied them. And made a rather curious discovery."

I had taken the liberty of having Roy make copies

of the original photos at the same time he was making the enlargements. I handed one to Sir Arthur.

He waved it away.

"I've seen this," he said. "And those spots. Dust on the lens, wouldn't you say?"

"I thought so myself," I said. "Then I had my assistant make some enlargements."

I pulled the crucial enlargement out of my valise and set it on the desk. The eminent author and his daughter leaned forward to look. After a moment, Sir Arthur asked, "What are we looking at?"

"I don't expect you to see anything at first." I gave a chuckle of undeferable satisfaction. "I didn't see anything at first either. But now, note . . ."

Using a pen as a pointer, I traced the figure in the enlargement. I tapped each anatomical point. I discoursed on the role of proportion in verisimilitude. I pulled out a piece of thin paper, and actually traced the figure off the enlargement. But I could tell early on that I wasn't getting the proper reaction from Sir Arthur and his daughter. They evinced no shiver of recognition. The figure did not pop out at them, as Walsmear put it, "like a deer out of the woods." The enlargement remained inert under their gaze; and my sweat began to give off the sour odor of failure. As I paused for breath, Sir Arthur got up and walked to the window.

"Mr. Castle," he said. "Come over here."

I did as he asked.

"Look up there in the sky, Mr. Castle," he said. "Do you see that cloud? Over behind that chimney there?"

I could see it coming. Sir Arthur was going to dismiss me with the same patronizing demonstration I had used with Constable Walsmear. What goes around comes around, I thought.

"Yes, I see it."

"What does that look like to you?"

"Hmmm. I suppose it looks a bit like an India elephant. Not the African kind. The sort with the small ears."

"Yes, and—"

"And there's some sort of structure on its back. I don't know. It looks like Brighton Pavilion—"

"So you see—"

"And the elephant seems to be holding Henry the Eighth by the ankle, while sliding down a kind of spiral staircase."

Sir Arthur was a patient didact, waiting until I was finished.

"To me," he said, finally, "it looks like a ball of cotton. Not very imaginative. But you see what I mean."

"I think you're trying to tell me that you see nothing in my enlargement."

"I'm afraid not."

"Does Mary?"

Mary slowly shook her head. I think she pitied me.

"Well, then, I'm sorry to have wasted your time."

"Don't think of it that way."

"Oh?"

"I'm impressed by your sincerity."

I bowed with mock humility.

"And I admire your courage."

"Courage?"

"Yes. In championing that policeman. Most people would avoid linking themselves to that type. A snob sort of thing."

"I hope you won't tell anyone." I was abashed.

"No, no, no. And don't feel bad. We're all new to this. We're groping in the dark. We're bound to bark our shins once in a while. You, at least, have an open mind, Mr. Castle."

Sir Arthur exchanged a smile with his daughter.

"And to make up for our differences in the past," he said, "I'm going to show you something. Something that will startle you greatly."

Sir Arthur gestured to Mary.

"Do you think—?" she said hesitantly.

"It will be all right if Mr. Castle knows," he said. "Soon, the whole world will know."

Mary cleared away some boxes. She bent down. I could hear her opening a safe. Hinges creaked. She stood up and handed her father a clean brown envelope.

"Can you guess what's in this envelope?" Sir Arthur grinned with schoolboy pleasure.

"No."

"It contains some photographs," he said.

"Really?"

"Extraordinary photographs. Photographs that will change the world. Photographs that actually show in clear and perfect detail what your policeman's photographs only purport to show."

"What?"

Mary pulled up a chair. "You'd better sit down," she said.

I did.

"Photographs," Sir Arthur said. "Of fairies."

My heart sank. I'd been a dope. Of course Sir Arthur wasn't interested in Walsmear's photographs. He didn't need some vague shadowy stuff. He had the real goods in his safe.

Sir Arthur must have noticed my discomfiture. There was a twinkle in his eye as he undid the envelope.

I must have psychological problems, I thought. That's why I believed that cockeyed constable and his photographs. It's because my business is going under. Roy could see it. Why couldn't I? I resolved to read some Sigmund Freud as soon as possible.

"Are you ready?" Sir Arthur asked.

I nodded.

He placed a pile of prints in my hands.

I picked up the first print. It was an outdoor scene. A lot like Walsmear's photos. There was a young girl, not nearly so pretty or angelic as the girls in Walsmear's photos. (Actually, I thought she looked a little cheap.) She was holding out her index finger. And standing on the index finger was—I couldn't believe my eyes.

I looked up at Sir Arthur. He was beaming. I looked back at the photograph. I looked back up at Sir Arthur. I started to chuckle. Then I laughed.

"What's so dashed funny?" Sir Arthur asked.

"This picture," I said.

"What about it?"

"It's a joke, isn't it?"

"It is not."

"Come on. It's got to be a joke."

"Are you a poor loser, Mr. Castle? Don't you see the fairy?"

"Yes, I see a fairy. But it's just painted on there. Someone's painted a fairy onto the print and rephotographed it. It's not even a good painting. I can see the brush strokes. And look at all these others. They're just the same."

"I misjudged you." Sir Arthur frowned. "You were not the right person to show these to."

"Where did you get those?"

"They came to me from some very reliable people."

"Well, they're fake. It's so obvious. The artist didn't even use human models. It's all out of his imagination. These fairies have popular illustration written all over them. How could you fall for these?"

Sir Arthur was trying to master his anger. "I suppose you think the photograph you have is superior?"

I was full of new admiration for the photographs brought to me by the simple policeman. It was a grand demonstration of how truth makes itself known. It spites our expectations, and thwarts the mighty.

"Yes, it's superior," I said. "It captures an actual phenomenon on film. Even if it's only an optical illusion. Your 'fairies' are flat. They aren't even shaded like the rest of the picture. They're painted on, Sir Arthur. Painted on."

Sir Arthur's gray mustache twitched. His inhalations grew labored. These must have sounded alarms in Mary. She put a hand on her father's elbow.

"Can we talk?" she said. "Outside?"

They went out into the stairwell and held a murmuring conversation. When they came back in, it was Mary who spoke. "Mr. Castle, you do not think our photographs are authentic. Am I correct?"

"Absolutely."

"Is that your professional opinion? Or is it because you have these other photographs?"

"It is my professional and personal opinion that you and your father are the victims of a crude hoax."

"And you say this without having examined them

thoroughly? Without seeing the negatives? Without seeing the camera they were taken with?"

"I don't need to."

"Why not?"

"A child of ten would not be fooled by those photographs. Not even the most benighted, drooling moron would actually believe that those were—"

I stopped myself. Sir Arthur and his daughter believed in the pictures nonetheless. I could see it in their eyes.

Mary coughed into her hand.

"So you believe," she said, "that the policeman's pictures are authentic?"

"I think they show something real. If I look up at a cloud and imagine it's an elephant, at least the cloud is real. It's not painted on the sky."

"And you think our photographs are not real?"

This was getting exasperating.

"No," I said. "Your pictures are crude concoctions pandering to the popular idea of what a fairy is supposed to look like. Look, this fairy here is wearing a gown. Now where did she get that? Are there fairy dress shops? Are there fairy mills where they weave the fabric? And who works in the mills and dress shops? Is there a fairy class system? Are there fairy unions and fairy strikes?"

Sir Arthur burst out, "Oh, so now you're the expert on fairies. You know what they actually look like."

"No, I don't."

"You sound like you do."

"What I do know is that if there are fairies, they don't look like popular illustrations. They'll look how they look. Not how we want them to look."

Mary intervened. "Mr. Castle, do you believe in fairies?"

"That's not a fair question. Not fair at all. You've got to see that, Miss Doyle. It's rather like being called on the line about religion or something. I mean, what is it to 'believe'? A thing doesn't exist just because we 'believe' in it. If a thing exists, it exists. If it doesn't, it doesn't."

Sir Arthur stared me down angrily. "Well, I do believe in fairies," he said.

Mary put a hand on her father's arm.

"The world is changing," she said to me. "A new worldview is opening up thanks to psychic research. Fairies play an important role in that world. We suspect they represent a parallel line of evolution. They may be a kind of intermediate being, straddling the natural and supernatural worlds. From our studies, it appears that they play a beneficent role in the growth of plants and flowers, much like bees and butterflies. We're not quite sure how it works. But somehow, they provide energy that aids the growth of vegetable matter. However it might be, the subject is potentially explosive. And we believe it has the power to change human thought forever."

"You're entitled to your opinion."

"And you're entitled to yours. But you aren't entitled to ruin all our work."

"What work?"

"We own all rights to those photographs you are holding. Very shortly, we will be releasing them to the newspapers. For us, it is the beginning of a campaign, complete with lectures and illuminated slide shows. It will be a campaign to make the world believe in fairies. Our fairies. Not yours."

"This is crazy."

"That is what some part of the public will inevitably say. Fear, disbelief, and ridicule are something that we are accustomed to. That we can survive. But there is something else our movement cannot survive. Can you think what that is, Mr. Castle?"

"It won't survive those phony pictures, I'll tell you that," I said.

Mary pretended not to hear me. "Look at the field of religion," she went on. "Why is it that no single religious idea dominates the world? It is because the first primitive man no sooner put forth his idea of a divinity, than some other primitive man put forward some alternative. And on it went, until today the field of religion is crowded with competing sects, all claiming to be true, and all appearing—to intelligent people at least—to be ridiculous."

"So what is it that you are afraid of, Miss Doyle?"

Father and daughter stood side by side. They stared down at me over folded arms.

"Competition," Mary answered.

So it was that, an hour later, I left the Doyle's psychical bookshop with a most unusual set of contracts under my arm. They were contracts empowering me to act as Sir Arthur Conan Doyle's agent in Burkinwell. My task was to purchase the Burkinwell fairy photographs from Walsmear, the girls, their father, or whoever had the right to sell them. Sir Arthur was willing to pay as much as one thousand pounds. It was in my interest, however, to get the photos for much less; for my pay for acting as go-between would be the difference between one thousand pounds and what the seller of the photographs could actually be persuaded to take for them. In other words, if I purchased the photos for six hundred, I would get four hundred. If I got the pictures for nothing, the whole thousand would be mine.

Of course, I was astounded that Sir Arthur was willing to part with so much to rid the world of rivals to his spectacularly bogus "fairy" photographs. On the other hand, maybe it wasn't so strange, considering his opinions—a few more of which I'd heard before leaving his company.

"We are at a crossroads in history," he'd said. "Mankind has just emerged from a great and terrible war. The current peace is violent and vexing. The next war will be more horrifying than the last. And the war after that—it is difficult to contemplate. Let us just say that to prevent it, we must redirect the path of human evolution. We must point our race toward those regions hinted at by our innate psychic understanding. We must plant our feet firmly in the spiritual. For there is only one route of escape for mankind, Mr. Castle. And that is, in a sense, through the ether . . ."

CHAPTER SEVEN

How I Lost My Valise

I LIKE RAILROAD STATIONS. I like the way they look. I like the way they sound. I like the way they smell—well, I like the way they look and sound. I'm especially fond of railroad stations when I don't have to catch a train. Strolling hands-a-pocket through crowds of harried travelers calms my soul. I seem to be looking down on the masses as if from a great height. Below me the human condition is spread out like a carpet.

What do I mean? Well, each individual bears his burden of miscellaneous parcels and luggage. Each is bent on his own concerns. Above us all is a ceiling of clouded glass. This peculiar ceiling admits light, but conceals what lies beyond. Beneath it the brave and cowardly, fool and wise man, all hurry to their coaches and so to be borne away by the solemn black engine of death, which awaits us patiently, chugging at the end of the platform.

When traveling, however, my concerns are no different from any atom in the churning swarm. I don't contemplate the mystery of crowds and the pattern of intersecting fates. I just want people to get out of my way.

So it was two days after my meeting with Sir Arthur. I was at the railroad station to catch the train to Burkinwell. It was late, and for some reason it seemed that great mobs of louts, laggards, and sluggards of both sexes and all classes had chosen this day to take the air at the station. They discovered the points that would be most inconvenient to me, and there chose to form dense, slow-moving knots.

I was uneasy for other reasons, too. When I'd come out of the psychic bookstore two days earlier, that Bible-crazed crone had been waiting for me. Small, wiry, and dressed in black, she'd leaped out of the hedge. It was like being attacked by an umbrella.

"Ssssssooooo," she'd hissed. "What is it now? Chiromancy? Numerology? Chatting with the dead? Reading cards? Casting spells?"

Recovering from my surprise, I assumed an air of

urbane amusement. "No, granny," I winked. "Nothing sinister. Just fairies. Innocent fays. Gentle sprites."

"Demons," she said, baring long dark teeth.

"No, no, no," I chuckled. "Not at all. Sweet little peris, dancing across the buttercups."

"Call them what you want, sonny," she said. "But I'll tell you—they're demons straight from hell."

It wasn't hard to disentangle myself from this disagreeable person. But it was not so easy to escape her words. Not for the last time I wondered what I was getting involved in. I didn't worry so much for my soul as my mind. I was headed down a garden path. What lay at the end? Madness? Were there actually fairies, or only the demons of self-destructive fantasy?

I was eager to be on my way. I knew that once I was aboard the train and on my way to Burkinwell I would feel better. As I said, however, the crowds at the station did not seem to share my sense of urgency. Worse still were the two porters I had engaged to transport my luggage.

My luggage consisted of a large steamer trunk and two valises. They were piled on a wooden wagon with a long handle, which one of the porters pushed from behind while the other pulled from the front. They were poking along at an exasperating rate, and carrying on an unintelligible conversation.

To wit:

"Your fault, Paolo."

"Your fault, Shorty."

"Not so, comrade."

"Betcher so it wasn't."

"Betcher so it was."

At the time, there was no reason for me to take special note of the way these two looked. Later, however, I had cause to remember their appearance. In fact, their faces and figures were laid into my brain with something like a hot branding iron.

The porter addressed as Paolo was a tall, stalking creature. Middle-aged. His eyes were dead; his skin was dirty and pale; and his cheeks wore deep, lugubrious creases under long side-whiskers.

The one called Shorty was Paolo's opposite number. He was only half his partner's size, and possibly half his age. He had a pink, butcher-shop complexion, and tiny little teeth through which he sieved his breath.

"Your plan," said Shorty.

"It was a good plan," said Paolo.

"It was a stupid plan."

"Was not."

"Was."

"I couldn't plan for everything."

"Guess you were too clever."

"Both too clever."

"By half."

"It'll blow over."

"We'll lay low."

"That's right."

"They'll forget."

"People do."

"But people talk."

"That's right, people talk."

Here both porters stopped. They looked back at me. Was I listening? Not really. I was just walking slowly behind the wagon, head bowed like a mourner. There was a hot little ball of anger in my gut. I ignored it and grinned at the two in a friendly way. They went back to pushing and pulling.

I guess they were satisfied that I wasn't listening in

to their conversation. But I wasn't satisfied. I was late. I coughed in a stern way.

The tall one was at the front of the wagon. At the sound of my cough, he abruptly stopped. Those of us walking behind did not. Shorty fell over the trunk. I fell over Shorty.

Paolo watched us disentangle ourselves. "You in a hurry then?" he asked me.

"Yes," I said. "I am in a hurry."

"He's in a hurry," he said to Shorty. "Imagine that."

"Yeah. Imagine that," said Shorty, straightening his cap.

"You'd think it was our fault," said Paolo.

"Don't blame us," said Shorty.

"No sir, don't blame us," said Paolo. "If you had left earlier, you'd have gotten here sooner, and you wouldn't be late."

"That's true," agreed Shorty. "Some people always wait until the last minute."

"Bad habit that," said Paolo.

"I beg your pardon," I interjected, "but I don't see where it's any of your business when I left. Your job is to get my luggage to the train. And to make it snappy."

"Make it snappy?" echoed Paolo. "He's an American, I think."

"Oh well, fancy that," said Shorty.

"Yeah, well, an American, well. And he thinks it's our fault he's late."

"Our fault," said Shorty.

"Listen," I said. "I left home with plenty of time to spare. But since I arrived at this station, things have been going very slowly."

"And that's supposed to be our fault?" said Paolo.

"It doesn't matter whose fault it is," I said.

"It matters to me," said Paolo. "How about you, Shorty?"

"Matters to me. Yeah."

"So there you have it," said Paolo. "It matters to both of us. Now what I'd like to know is if you are in fact complaining about the way we're performing our jobs. Because if you are, you can't just stand there and complain. You have to file a formal complaint. We're in the union, you know. You can't just say anything you want to us. It's not like the old days."

"No sir, not like the old days," nodded Shorty.

"We're protected. You can't just push us around."

"All right, all right," I said. "I'm sorry if I sounded like I was complaining. Let's forget the whole thing and just get my luggage to the train."

"Oh no you don't," said Paolo. "You don't get out of it that easy. We've still got to get this thing straight."

"Straight, that's right," from Shorty.

"Do you," said Paolo, "or do you not believe we are in error in moving this luggage slowly through the station?"

"I do believe you should move along as quickly as you can," I said. "Not that I'm complaining, mind you."

Paolo chuckled knowingly. "For your information," he said, "we are only following orders. Our supervisor told us that we were to be very careful with this trunk."

"Careful," said Shorty.

"He told us," said Paolo, "that there was glass in the trunk. Fragile, he said it was. Is that or is it not true? Am I mistaken, or am I not?"

"As a matter of fact, your supervisor was right," I said. "That trunk does contain—"

"I mean—" and here Paolo slammed his hand down on top of the trunk, which clinked loudly "—it sounds like glass to me." He slammed his hand down again.

"Please, be careful," I said. "You see—"

"And who do you think would have to pay for it if we broke something inside?" Paolo asked.

"Yeah, who?" asked Shorty.

"I'll tell you who," said Paolo. "We would, that's who. We'd have to pay for your bloody crystal goblets or whatever you lot carry around in your trunks."

"Bloody crystal goblets," spat Shorty.

"My gosh," I said. "It's not crystal goblets. It's darkroom equipment. Jars of chemicals. Cameras. Lenses. Yes, it's fragile. And I appreciate your care. But you can move along a little more quickly. I'm the photographer, and I take full responsibility."

"You taking responsibility?" said Paolo. He straightened up attentively. "Hell, let's go."

He spat on his two hands. Then he spat in my direction. The two resumed their positions at the head and back of the wagon. Now they fairly raced through the station.

"Out of the way," Paolo shouted. "Coming through."

The wagon thundered. Knots of people scattered like billiard balls. I ran behind.

"Hey, Shorty," Paolo shouted over his shoulder. "You hear the one about the photographer?"

"What's that?" said Shorty, somewhat breathlessly.

"What did the photographer say to the lady?"

"I dunno. What did he say?"

"Come into the darkroom, my dear. We'll see what develops."

Shorty briefly extended his tongue in mirth. "That's a funny one," he said. "What's a darkroom?"

The contents of the trunk were clattering and clinking in an alarming way. The two had just taken the wagon around a corner on two wheels. I was about to say something when I saw we were approaching the gate.

"Just pulling out," said the blur of an attendant as we raced past. Out alongside the platform, a shiver ran down the line of carriages. Far ahead, the engine exhaled loudly and began to chuff.

"Damn," I said, slowing to a trot. "We'll never catch it."

"Come on, you," Paolo shouted back at me. "We'll get you on."

Both porters were at the back of the wagon pushing. I ran up between them and the departing train.

"Jump on," Paolo said. "Jump on the train."

I reached out, grabbed a door, and swung into a compartment in the last car. Excusing myself, I climbed over the passengers and ran down the corridor toward the door at the back.

Through the back window, I saw Paolo and Shorty pushing the wagon alongside the moving train. The railcar was a Hastings III, with individual compartments opening out onto the platforms, a corridor running the length of the car, and a iron "porch" and stairway over the coupler. As I watched, they threw the two valises onto the stairway by the back door. Then Paolo, taking a running leap, made it up onto the lowest step. From there he reached down and pulled my trunk onto the train. Once it was in place, he did the same for Shorty.

And it was a near thing. For the last carriage passed the end of the platform the moment after Shorty's foot left it. The abandoned luggage wagon was not so lucky: it kept going of its own momentum and sailed off the end of the platform and crashed into the gravel. A single wheel rolled out of the wreckage.

After fumbling with the latch, I opened the back door. Paolo and Shorty tumbled in at my feet.

Paolo looked up at me from the floor. "Your luggage, sir?"

"My good man—" I helped pull him to his feet. Then I did the same for Shorty.

"I don't know what to say," I said, helping them to brush the dust from their already filthy uniforms. "What you just did there. It was truly above and beyond . . . Really. I don't know how to express my gratitude. You didn't really have to."

That had certainly earned a nice tip.

"Here." I reached into my pocket. "Let me."

Paolo held up his hand.

"First," he said. "Where are you going?"

"Why, I'm going to Burkinwell. It's—"

"No, no," sneered Shorty. "Where do we haul this garbage?"

"Oh. Of course," I said. "I've got to find a compartment. Just a moment."

There was a likely compartment at the other end of the car. It was empty but for two women—an older and a younger. They were sitting opposite each other by the window.

"In here," I said, opening the door and waving to the porters.

In a second, my valises had been whipped onto the seats. The trunk clattered onto the floor between the two women. The older woman gave it a look of distaste.

"So sorry." I raised my hat to the ladies. "And now, gentlemen, this is for you," I said, handing them both banknotes. "And believe me, you earned every penny of it."

Paolo stared down at the note as if it were a bird dropping that had landed on his palm. "What's this?" he asked.

"A little tip," I whispered, giving him a smile and a wink—contemplating, but stopping short of, offering an appreciative pat on the arm.

"A what?"

"Tip," I said less confidently.

"A tip? Is that what you call this?"

"Why, yes."

"For what we did?"

"I don't consider it ungenerous."

"This? Generous? We risked our necks for this?"

"Yeah," said Shorty. "You call this—you know?"

"Bloody disgrace, this is," said Paolo.

"Dis-grace," spat Shorty.

This was very embarrassing for me. Especially in front of the ladies. I smiled and lifted my hat toward the ladies again. I hoped they'd seen the denomination of the notes I'd given the two porters. If so, they would certainly see that the scruffy twosome had done quite well by me.

The porters were looking at me expectantly.

"I'm sorry," I muttered. "I'm not really so very well off . . ."

I had to do something to break the tension.

"Well . . ." I clapped my hands and turned my back on the two. "What say we open this trunk? See if anything got broken."

I unlocked the trunk and swung open the lid. A few

vials were smashed. A smell rose up. It was a homey and familiar scent to me; a nice darkroom smell. Of course, I realize the general public might not see eye to eye—or smell nose to nose—with me on this.

"Pheeeeeew," Shorty said, covering his face with his elbow. "Smells like dirty knickers."

"If you don't mind," I said, "there are ladies present."

"Smells like old piss to me," said Paolo.

"Really." I turned around, arms akimbo. "If you don't like the smell you can go."

"Go where?" asked Paolo.

"Anywhere," I said.

"That's a laugh."

"Can't you go sit down somewhere?"

"Without tickets?"

"Why should you need tickets?"

"To sit down."

"Can't you stand someplace until the next station?"

"Person needs a ticket to stand, too."

"You shouldn't need a ticket at all. You work for the railroad, don't you?"

Paolo and Shorty slowly shook their heads no.

"Do you mean you work for the station?"

They shook their heads no again.

"Who do you work for?" I asked.

"Nobody," said Paolo.

"Aren't you porters?" I asked.

"No," said Shorty.

"You're wearing porters' uniforms," I said.

"That's true, but we're not porters."

"Then what are you?" I asked.

"We're robbers."

Shorty pulled out a knife. It was a long, filthy blade with a rag tied around the hilt.

I looked at his face to see if he was joking, but he wore a triumphant little leer. He was in perfect earnest.

The two women had been observing us. Prior to this, I could tell they were both upset by the unmannerliness of the proceedings. Now that things had passed from unmannerly to rude to practically murderous, they both emitted sharp "Ohs!"

The older of the two women instinctively clutched her bag. This attracted Paolo's attention.

"I'll have that bag, Missy," he said.

Making a grab for the bag, he stretched over the open trunk. The younger woman screamed defensively. It had nice duration and pitch. Paolo was distracted. He clearly felt he had to stifle that scream before going any further. He had one hand on the older woman's purse; with his other, he tried to cover the younger woman's mouth. The effort left him momentarily unbalanced.

The younger woman saw her chance. She reached into the open trunk and pulled out a jar. With a deft twist, she pulled off the cap. Then she hurled the jar's liquid contents into Paolo's face.

The robber shrieked. His sallow face went red. He fell backward, clawing at his eyes.

By this time, the far end of the compartment was a tangle of bodies. The ladies and myself were trying to put as much distance as we could between ourselves and Paolo and Shorty.

With a squeal of rage, Shorty leaped forward. He plunged his knife into the convulsing mass of arms and legs and torsos. The older woman screamed, then fell silent.

I saw the blade pierce the woman's dress at the level of her rib cage. Cursing helplessly, I grabbed a piece of broken bottle out of the trunk. Holding it by the neck, I pushed the jagged end into Shorty's wrist. Then, raising it over my head, I brought it down again and again.

Shorty fell back onto the bench. He grabbed one of my valises and held it up like a shield. I tried to twist it out of his grasp, but he kicked free and fell back into the corridor.

Paolo was already out there, clutching his face, smashing blindly into doors and windows. People leaned out of their compartments to see what was going on.

One old man spotted Shorty. "See here, you," he said.

Shorty punched him in the face. Blood sprayed across the corridor. (It was from Shorty's wounded arm, not the old man's face.)

The corridor was suddenly very crowded.

"Stop them," I shouted, fighting my way through the confusion of bodies. But people did not know whom they were supposed to stop or why.

I stumbled to the end of the car in time to see Shorty push Paolo off the end of the stairway. A moment later Shorty himself jumped. He was still holding my valise to his chest. Fortunately for the robbers, the train was not going very fast. Standing in the doorway, I saw them soon afoot. They made a clean escape, trampling parallel corridors through a field of rye.

Now I fought my way back through the corridor. Two men were pulling my trunk out of the compartment.

"Give her air," someone was shouting inside.

The older woman lay propped limply in the corner of the compartment. A doctor had come forward. He and the younger woman undid the victim's dress down the front. I could see gray undergarments—but no blood.

The doctor probed and prodded. "Not a mark," he announced, cheerfully.

The malign intent of Shorty's blade had been deflected by a sturdy corset.

"It's a miracle," the woman whispered. With trancelike slowness, she gathered her dress about her, signaling the end of her career as a public spectacle. The crowd dispersed.

I turned, but someone grabbed my hand. It was the younger woman from the compartment. She dropped my hand.

I spoke first. "I hope your mother will be all right," I said.

"My mother?" She appeared confused. "Oh no," she said. "Her? In the compartment? She's not my mother. I—we're strangers."

"I'm sorry. I didn't—"

"She seems to be doing fine."

"Yes, she does, doesn't she?"

"So fortunate, so lucky," said the woman. "And yourself?"

"Me?"

"Yes, are you all right?"

"I? Well, I suppose I'm fine. One of them got away with one of my bags, though."

"How unfortunate. Was it the one you stabbed?"

"Yes. The short one. I'm sure he's not hurt badly. But you, how are you?"

She smiled brightly. "As you see me. Unmarked, but for some drops of that whatever-it-was on my dress. I've wiped them off with cold water already."

"I say, that was quick thinking."

"Was it? Well, you've got to catch a stain before it sets."

"No, no. I mean throwing the chemicals in that fellow's face."

"I hope I didn't hurt him."

"I hope you did."

"How cruel."

"I'm sorry if I sound cruel. But those were not nice men."

"I know," she pouted. "I wish the world were more like a fairy tale."

I must have started. "How is that?" I asked.

"Oh, you know. In a fairy tale, the evil villain stubs his toe, and that makes everything all right."

"Does that make everything all right?"

"In a fairy tale."

"Well, those two got their toes well stubbed. And if it makes you feel any better, I'm sure they've already recovered."

"Really? Do you think so?"

"Yes. The last I saw of them, they were tripping through the rye. With my valise."

The doctor and another man pushed past us, excusing themselves. "—thought those corsets had quite gone out of fashion," the doctor was saying to his companion. "The whalebone certainly stopped that harpoon . . ."

The younger woman turned aside to let them past. I took the opportunity to steal a glance at her finger. She wore a wedding ring. As she turned back, I'm sure she noted that I was noting.

The trunk was blocking the corridor. Its top was smashed down over the broken vials and instruments inside. I reached in and began straightening it out. The woman arranged her hat in the window glass. Then she returned to the compartment.

CHAPTER EIGHT

How I Was Given a Ride

THE TWO LADIES AND I were not permitted to continue in peace to our destinations. The attack had become a high police matter. The train dropped the three of us in Devving, a district police headquarters town, where uniformed officers escorted us to the headquarters building.

The exterior of the district police headquarters was squat and ugly, but inside it was quite sunny. This was thanks to some tall, classically proportioned windows. Police personnel sat around with their feet up on chairs and desks. Some smoked. Others looked out the windows. Golden light poured in. Someone was watering the lawn outside, and every so often the spray smacked the glass.

"I'm Detective Cubb," said a young man in civilian clothes.

I didn't like him. For one thing, he was a lot younger than I. That's a problem I have. I don't like all the young policemen, soldiers, and other authority figures you see nowadays.

He also had an annoying know-all attitude. And

very slick, neat hair. And a crisp, white shirt. And he fidgeted impatiently while the two ladies and I told our stories. Before the older lady was even finished, he opened his mind to us.

"Not porters, I'm afraid," he said. "You call these men porters. Do not do so. For porters they are not."

"No?" I said. "You could have fooled me. I mean, they took my bags."

"Taken your bags, they may have," he said, "but they were not porters. The porters' union is on strike. There were no porters inside that station. They are all outside these days. Breaking windows. Rioting. Overturning buses. Whatnot."

"Then who were they?"

"I fancy they were a couple of the riffraff the railway has hired for the duration. Desperate and unsavory types, some of them. Men without scruple. No connections to the community."

I didn't like his smug satisfaction. "Well, I hate to inform you, but the men told me they were in the union."

"Why weren't they out on the picket line? Answer me that."

I couldn't.

Detective Cubb stretched and sniffed. He leaned back in his chair. "Yes, I imagine they signed for work at that station," he said. "Work was not to their taste, they then found. Never is for that type. Probably looking for an opportunity to pull a job. Could be a longstanding crime duo. They often work in pairs. Paolo and Shorty? Never heard the names. But who says those are their real names? They could be some other pair. Maybe they're really Mangraff and Soames. There's a pretty pair. No, no. Couldn't be them. Mangraff's still inside. Another twenty years before he sees daylight. Maybe they're someone else. Cooper and Potts, maybe. No, no, no. Not possible. They went south. They'd never come back. Not after the brewery slashings. Hmmm. How about . . . Tate and Grossman? Tell me, did the younger one have a beard?"

"No."

"Oh."

"Does that matter?"

"Yes, it does."

"He could have shaved it."

"Never." Detective Cubb shook his head. "Grossman was an anarchist. Wouldn't shave on principle."

"So where does that leave us?"

"With nothing to say." Detective Cubb smiled.

"Are you going to try to catch them?"

"Oh yes. Catch them we will. Of fear you need have none."

"How can you be so sure?"

Detective Cubb dangled a pencil between his fingers. "Easy," he said. "Mistakes. They all make them. It's in their wild spirit. It's part of the criminal tendency. They may go for years committing little crimes and getting away with it. But one day that wild spirit takes them over. Like a storm. Then they do something violent and stupid. Agitation of the blood, I take it. Very visible, they make themselves. Start drawing attention. That's when we get them."

"Didn't they just do that?" I asked.

"Yes. And I wouldn't be surprised if they were already under arrest somewhere nearby. Their descriptions are out. Into one of these little villages they'll stumble. Some farm lads'll lock them in a shed."

"What about my valise?"

"The stolen property? Anything valuable inside?"

"Some clothing. Legal papers."

"Cast it aside, they will, in some field or ditch. Farmer'll turn it in."

The older woman was fidgeting. She interrupted the young detective to ask if she might be on her way. She was traveling north to visit her sister, and she needed to make the proper train connections. Knowing everything he needed to about the woman, he let her go. I offered to accompany her to the station, but Detective Cubb detailed some uniformed men to do that. The younger woman and I wished her good-bye. I told her that I hoped to meet her again in court at the trial of our attackers.

With the older woman's departure, our interrogation came to an informal end.

The younger woman—and this is the last time I will refer to her in this impersonal way—requested to make a phone call. She was told to inquire of the sergeant out front.

For my part, I was eager to be on my way.

"Now, about my valise," I said. "How do I get it back if it's returned to you?"

Detective Cubb had begun shuffling papers. He meant to indicate that he was about to get on to the next thing—probably, once we left, more gazing out of the window.

"We'll notify you," he said. "I have your address."

"That's my London address. Suppose I'm not there?"

"Where will you be?"

"In Burkinwell."

"Oh yes. You said that, didn't you?"

"You can contact me there."

"Really? Where will you be staying?"

"At an inn. Let's see." I pulled out the scrap of paper where I had it written. "Here it is," I said. "The Starry Night."

"The Starry Night?" Cubb laughed.

"That's right. Do you know it?"

"Oh, I know it." Cubb laughed again. He craned his neck to see if anyone was listening. Then he gave me a little smirk of male confidentiality. "They call it the Starry Night," he said. "But they should call it the Esmirelda."

"I don't understand."

"She's the main attraction, Miss Esmirelda."

"Main attraction?"

"You'll meet her soon enough. Of course, I don't know if she likes Americans. Ha ha. What am I saying? There's nothing she doesn't like. Ha ha."

"I say, this place isn't some kind of bawdy house?"

"No, no, no." Cubb giggled. "Perfectly respectable. Except for Esmirelda."

"What about her?"

"Just stands out, she does. Not much else going on in Burkinwell. Pretty sleepy place. Hope you're not going for excitement."

"Taking photographs."

"So you said. Land?"

"I beg your pardon?"

"Taking photographs of land? Involved in real estate, you are?"

"Not at all."

"Certain about that?"

"That's not my business."

"Well, you hear things, you know. About speculators. Rumors go around. There's valuable minerals under Burkinwell, they say. Don't know what. Coal. Mercury. Tinned fish. Just rumors, I suppose. People visit the town. Poke around. Americans sometimes. You wouldn't know anything about that, would you?"

"Not a thing. But as far as I know, it's not illegal."

"What's not?"

"Real estate speculation."

"I should say not. But if there's anything going on down there, I'd like to get in on it. Talk about forming a syndicate sometimes, me and the boys. Making some investments."

I thought about my own sorry finances.

"I'm the last person to consult about that sort of thing."

"Too bad."

And here re-entered the woman I'll now introduce by her proper name: Linda Drain. Mrs. Linda Drain. She told us about herself as she made her statement to the detective.

Mrs. Drain was the wife of a minister. She lived in Burkinwell. And she didn't look like a minister's wife was supposed to look. She was fresh, and shapely, and well turned out. In repose, her face had the proper dignity; but when she smiled, her eyes and nose and mouth crinkled into an adorable clown face.

"What were you doing down in London?" Detective Cubb had asked her.

"Seeing some shows, hearing some jazz."

"Hmmm. Minister's wife, you say?"

Mrs. Drain's face crinkled. She laughed from the back of her throat. "Oh, my husband hates jazz. And he fidgets in the theater. So I go to London alone and stay with my sister when I want to have some fun. He's quite grateful not to have to go."

Now she stood in the doorway. She was wearing an ink-blue chemise, with a pattern of small, dark triangles, and a flounce that stopped just below her silk-stockinged knees. A smooth white cap with a little point on the crown clung to her head like an inverted buttercup.

Several times, as we spoke, she lifted her cap and smoothed the crinkly, bobbed hair beneath.

"Can I give you a ride, Mr. Castle?" she asked.

"What? Do you have a car?"

"My husband will. He's coming to pick me up."

"I don't know," I said. "My trunk is rather large. Will you have room?"

We took our leave of Detective Cubb and went outside.

"I don't want to cause you any trouble."

We sat down on a low wall outside the police headquarters.

"Oh, no trouble," she said. "Depending."

"Depending on what?"

"What kind of car."

"Yes?"

"That is to say, what kind of car my husband can borrow."

"He has to borrow a car?"

"He doesn't own one. Doesn't like them."

"How does he get around?"

"He walks or—this may sound strange."

"Go ahead."

"He runs."

"How do you mean?"

"He strips off his shirt and runs. He's a physical culturist."

"You mean exercises and all that?"

"Always. He's always doing exercises."

"And he's a minister? What does his congregation say?"

"They're used to it. Besides, he's got the theology to support it. Written articles about it. The body as a temple of the perfect spirit. Exercise as prayer. I haven't read them myself."

"Sounds like muscular Christianity."

"Very muscular. Lithe. And well-proportioned."

Crinkling irreverently, she took off her hat and dropped it in her lap. Then she began fussing with the pins in her hair. It occurred to me that a longer hairstyle might have been easier to take care of. But maybe constant fussing was the point. I watched the sunlight playing on the wispy golden strands.

"What about you?" I asked. "Are you a physical culturist?"

"Not at all. But I do get exercise. You know how the song goes: 'Dance and Grow Thin'? I dance as often as possible. I just adore jazz."

"Lots of it in London," I observed.

"Gobs," said Linda. "My ears are still ringing."

There was a building boom going on in Devving. No prosperity was visible. Just building. At least a third of the buildings we could see were either under construction or they were being torn down. Not far from where we sat, brick walls were going up around a steel frame. A steam apparatus chugged inside the frame. There was a near-constant hammering sound. Work spilled into the street. Men mixed cement, measured pipe, and cut wood across impromptu sawhorses.

"There's my husband," said Mrs. Drain.

A fortyish man in clerical black strode briskly across the street. He was hatless and cleanly bald on top of his head. As he came up to the building under construction, he paused. Two workers were hauling bags of cement off the back of a truck. The bags were large and unwieldly and the workers were huffing and wheezing. The Rev. Drain hailed them and came up around the back of the truck. He easily hoisted first one bag, then another onto his shoulders; and then, as steady as a Sunday stroller, he followed the two workmen into the building.

A few minutes later he reappeared, dusting his hands and sharing a laugh with the workmen. Before leaving them, he handed them both what appeared to be religious tracts.

Linda hopped down from the wall to greet him.

"Hello, dear," he said, taking her hands. "Had a bit of trouble, then?"

"Nothing, really," Linda said, hitting her husband with the flat of her hand. The Rev. Drain fell back a little. Linda hit him again and again on the chest, arms, and back.

I wondered what was going on. Then I realized that she was beating the dust off his clerical outfit.

"You've got to stay out of those construction sites," she said.

Drain said nothing. He barely flinched under the rain of feminine blows. His head with its attractively tanned dome stood stolidly. His eyes narrowed with amusement. Linda's blows made a good solid thwacking sound. There was a strong torso under that black coat. Drain smiled at me over his wife's shoulder.

"How do you do?" he asked.

CHAPTER NINE

How I First Saw the Garden

REV. DRAIN'S BORROWED MOTORCAR was a capacious old Crollier sedan. The roof was patched, bits of straw clung to the running board, and the bonnet was speckled with what appeared to be chicken droppings.

There was plenty of room for my trunk in back. I hauled it in beside myself, while Linda settled herself in front, and her husband went out to crank the engine.

"Don't make a big thing about the robbers," Linda whispered.

"Pardon?"

"Don't tell my husband what happened. Let me do the talking."

"Why?"

"If he thinks it's dangerous, he won't let me go to London anymore."

I nodded my understanding. A gentle deception. But not wise, I thought. If Paolo and Shorty were caught, her husband would find out the truth.

Did Linda have a boyfriend in London? A young fellow who liked jazz?

Rev. Drain's head bobbed once over the crank. The engine came to life. As he swung into the driver's seat, Linda gave me another look to insure my cooperation. It was insured.

Rev. Drain ground the gears. We were off. He was clearly an inexperienced driver.

On the road to Burkinwell, Linda narrated her version of the day's events. As she told it, Paolo and Shorty were something in the way of overgrown Boy Scouts who'd accidentally walked off with one of my bags. She'd been detained at the police headquarters simply to give a description of the two.

Drain seemed to buy it. "Most unfortunate," he said. "Were there valuables in the valise?"

I had two views of Drain from the backseat. Straight ahead, I could see the back of his head, with its shadowy fringe of shaved bristle under the bald part. To see his eyes, I had to look into the rearview mirror.

He addressed his looks to me through the mirror.

"There were some legal papers in the valise," I said. "If I don't get them back, my business will be delayed."

Drain looked at Linda. "Didn't you say he was a photographer, dear?"

"He is," said Linda. "Aren't you, Mr. Castle?"

"Yes. The legal papers are business things. Photography is my business."

"How did your instruments get broken?" Drain asked.

Linda answered for me. "He was late for the train. And he tripped over the trunk getting on board."

"That's that smell you probably smell," I said. "Lots of chemicals got spilled."

"Some of them must have got on you, dear," said Drain, sniffing in the direction of his wife.

"Possibly. Ha ha. While I was helping Mr. Castle get his trunk off the train."

"Oh," said Drain. "I hope the broken things are replaceable. I know how expensive photographic things are."

"Yes," I said. "They are. Quite."

"We had a camera once," said Drain. "And some darkroom equipment. I bought it for Linda. Do you remember your interest in photography, dear?"

"Yes. That was years ago."

"You took a few good pictures. I mean, where you could tell what you were looking at."

"I wasn't very good at it."

"She wasn't," said Drain to me. "Whatever happened to that camera, dear?"

"Oh, I gave it away."

"You gave away that expensive camera? Perhaps we could have sold it."

"Oh, Tom. You know it wasn't that expensive."

"Perhaps Mr. Castle would have liked to have seen it."

"I'm sure he has much better cameras than that. Don't you, Mr. Castle?"

"Well, I—"

"Who did you give it to?" Drain asked. "I'm just curious."

"Well, there's a dear story to it," Linda said. "I gave the camera to the Templeton girls. Anna and Clara. Do you remember when they were over last year?"

"But they're just children," Drain said.

"I thought they might have fun with it. But I forgot all about it until last Sunday."

"Were they in church last Sunday?"

"Yes. Will you let me go on? I asked the older one, Anna, if they had ever taken any pictures with the camera."

"What did she say?"

"She got all excited. She said, 'Oh yes, Mrs. Drain. We took pictures of the fairies in our garden.' Isn't that sweet?"

I tried to coax the knot out of my throat. "So—" I gulped. "Did you—ahem—see these pictures?"

"What? Oh, it was all their imagination, I'm sure. I used to imagine that sort of thing all the time. When I was a little girl. Didn't you, Tom? When you were young, I mean?"

"What sort of thing?" asked Drain.

"Fairies. And gnomes. And elves. I used to imagine that the world was swarming with little creatures."

"Boys don't imagine that sort of thing," said Drain. "Do they, Castle?"

"No," I agreed. "But did you see the pictures?"

"You don't really think—" Linda laughed.

"Now there's something you might want to photograph," Drain said.

"What? What?" I asked.

"That's right," Linda enthused. "Templeton's garden. It's about the best-looking garden in Burkinwell. Very much worth seeing."

"Is that where," I was gulping ridiculously, "the girls took their—pictures?"

"Yes."

"I say, Castle," said Drain, "I don't usually care for flowers and all that much, but this garden is really quite nice."

"It's strange," I said, "but someone already suggested I might want to photograph there."

"Recommended?" said Linda. "By whom?"

"A friend of mine. From Burkinwell."

"We know everyone in town. Who was it?"

"A policeman. Michael Walsmear."

Husband and wife exchanged a look.

"Do you know him?" I asked. "I mean, he's not a dear friend of mine. More like an acquaintance."

"We know him, of course," said Drain. "Blustery sort of fellow. I suppose he's a good policeman."

"He's an unhappy man, I think," Linda said.

"The accident, of course," said Drain.

"So many years ago," said Linda.

They both glanced at me to see if I knew about "the accident."

I recalled what Walsmear had said during our lunch two days earlier. Just before he had told me not to press my luck.

I took a stab. "The girls' mother?" I said.

"Yes." Linda sighed. "So sad. So terrible. Funny coincidence, all this coming up in the conversation."

We were stopped at a crossroads.

"You know," Drain said. "If I loop over this way, it will take us right past the Templeton cottage. Would you like to see it?"

I tried not to sound too eager. "Hmmm. That might be interesting."

Drain pounded the gas pedal. He turned the wheel hand over hand, and we headed down a rutted, bumpy country lane. Stone walls rose up and petered out. Ruined barns stood atop low hills.

"Mostly farms hereabouts?" I asked.

"There was some industry in the area," said Drain. "Came in about twenty years ago."

"What kind?"

"Some manufactories. Outposts of big factories from up north. There was some kind of notion that there was coal in the area. Or oil, or some other valuable resource. No one seems to remember anymore."

"Doesn't look like coal country," I said. Not that I knew what "coal country" looked like. Unless it were a lot of Pennsylvanians hanging around.

"It isn't," Drain said sharply. "This is no place for industry. This is farm country. And it should be kept that way."

He was studying my reaction in the mirror. I guessed he thought I was an agent for some industrial or mining concern. Or a land speculator. Or some other sinister business figure that neither he nor I could adequately name.

"I suppose you wouldn't care to see that repeated," I ventured, safely.

Drain growled. "I wouldn't. Tearing up the countryside. Young men lured away from healthy pursuits. Stinking smoke."

"Hmm."

"There is nothing valuable under the ground of Burkinwell, I assure you." Drain was emphatic. "No reason to locate a factory here. Why, they've only recently run electrical lines to Burkinwell."

"Hmm," I said again, noncommittally.

It was perfectly all right with me if the minister thought I was something other than what I was. What was I supposed to tell him? I'm not interested in your coal, old fellow. I'm interested in your fairies.

"You'll have to forgive me," Drain sighed. "I do love our English countryside."

"My husband needs the countryside to run over," Linda said.

"It's good for the soul." Drain tucked his chin into his chest.

Up ahead, I saw a large shaggy woods. It was hardly Sherwood Forest, but it was the largest group of trees I had seen yet in the area.

"Not far now," said Drain.

As we got closer to the woods, I saw a long, low building amid the trees. It was the ruin of an old factory. The roof was caved in, the windows all broken. Weeds and saplings sprouted in the interior.

Beyond the factory was a sharp bend in the road. Drain struggled with the wheel. "Right here," he said, stopping the car.

The woods ended. Before us was a splendid garden. It spilled over a low stone wall alongside the road, gloriously amorphous; a mist of pastel colors; waving green stalks; hovering bees; tiny leaves. Beyond the garden was a stone cottage, almost hidden behind clouds of flowering shrubs and the thick, lowering trees. To either side of the cottage two tall cypress trees rose as slender, leafy cones.

Linda turned around in her seat to look at me. "This is where it happened," she said.

"What happened?" I asked.

"The accident."

"Your friend," said her husband. "Constable Walsmear. He was driving the motorcar."

"One of the few in town back then," said Linda.

"It wasn't his, of course," said Drain. "It had been stolen and abandoned."

"Gypsies, I'll bet," said Linda.

"The constable had been told to return it," said Drain. "But he'd never driven a car before."

"Imagine," said Linda. "How surprised he must have

been. To have her dart out of the garden. Into the road."

"Right into his path," said Drain.

The garden had entranced me. I wasn't really paying attention.

"Who ran where?" I asked.

"Mrs. Templeton," said Linda. "We're telling you about the accident. How she was killed."

"Templeton?" I said. "You mean this—this is the garden where the girls took pictures of— Excuse me."

I opened the car door and half stepped outside.

So this was it! No question. If there were fairies in England, this would be the spot they would gather. I imagined them dancing on every flowertop. My heart leaped at every puttering butterfly and lumbering bumblebee. What was that? And that? At one end of the garden was a vast, gnarled tree, like nothing else I'd ever seen.

"Mr. Castle," Linda called me back to earth.

"Sorry." I dropped back into the seat. "Just having a look. The garden is just as beautiful as everyone says it is. What kind of tree is that?"

"That?" Linda said. "That's Old Splendor. Oldest tree in Burkinwell. It's a walnut, I think."

"It's magnificent. All of it," I said.

"And it looks like this without any maintenance," said Drain. "Brian Templeton—he lives in that cottage—he's as lazy as any man alive."

"Now, Tom," chided Linda.

"I don't know where he gets the energy to get out on Sunday and bring the girls to services," Drain sighed. "The Templeton family owned all this land you know. The big house burned down long ago. The fortune vanished somewhere or other—"

"Lawsuits. Bad investments," said Linda.

"Brian inherited the cottage, the garden, and a little income. He's a sad creature, really. Just this side of a charity case. I wouldn't care, but those girls—"

"Darling girls."

"They deserve better. Growing up like wild Indians. No supervision."

"But they're so sweet. So innocent."

"No thanks to him," Drain said, stepping on the gas. As we passed the cottage, he stuck his hand out the window and waved. "Just in case they're looking," he said.

I turned in my seat and watched the garden and cottage get smaller. The flowers blurred and folded up around Old Splendor as the chimney and the tops of the two pointed locust trees disappeared behind a hill.

CHAPTER TEN

How I Met Esmirelda

THE STARRY NIGHT was a modest inn. Three stories. Blank stucco facade. The Rev. Drain and Linda dropped me off under its sign, a dark blue circle with the Big Dipper splotched on with a crude brush.

"Perhaps Mr. Castle could come over for tea some time," Linda suggested to her husband. "Would that be all right, Tom?"

Drain couldn't see why not. They often had parishioners over on Wednesdays for tea. "Will you be staying long?" he asked.

"That depends." I laughed. "If I'm still here next Wednesday, I'll be happy to come."

Linda and her husband bade me a jolly good-bye. They seemed to be the picture of married contentment as they drove off to return their borrowed car.

Inside, the Starry Night was divided into two downstairs rooms. There was a bar and eating room on one side. On the other side, there was a cozy sitting room. The walls in both rooms were replete with moth-eaten hunting trophies, ugly paintings, framed mottoes, and stuffed fish. A narrow stairway separated the two rooms.

The proprietor of the Starry Night introduced himself as Colin Cole. He registered me from behind a tall desk in the sitting room.

"Like the old king," I joked to him.

"What?"

"You know," I said. "Old King Cole?"

"There was a king named Cole?" he asked.

"You never heard 'Old King Cole was a merry old soul . . .'?"

"Was he?"

"Forget it."

He was a red-faced old fellow. Had a huge torso and a twisted leg.

"Broke that leg when I was a lad. Best thing that ever happened. Got me off the farm, it did. Can't work with a bad leg, can you? And—" he winked "—the ladies like it."

"Do they?"

"Blimey. Makes them laugh. I can chase them. But I can't catch them. ESMIRELDA!"

A swinging door flew open and slammed against the wall. Bits of plaster dropped from the ceiling. A hulking girl dragged herself into the room. She held a limp dishrag in one hand.

I remembered Detective Cubb's account of the Starry Night. This, I thought, must be the famed Esmirelda. She looked to be in her mid-twenties. Dark. Her scraggly brown hair was tied at the back of her neck with a piece of ordinary twine. She wore a threadbare, salmon-colored shift; no apron. The front of her shirt appeared damp, scattered with fresh stains and bits of blood.

"Take this man's trunk up to the Bachelor's Room," Cole ordered her roughly. Smiling to me, he said, "I'm putting you in the Bachelor's Room. If that's all right with you. All our rooms have names, you see. You could also have the Old Home. Or the Fairy Palace. But the Bachelor's Room is quite nice."

"That will be fine. But I'll be happy to carry my own trunk. I couldn't let a girl—"

"She don't mind."

Esmirelda was already struggling awkwardly with the heavy piece. She got it up the first couple of steps. Then she stopped. "Hoy," she said. "I ain't a'carrying this."

"And why not, you large, wretched girl?"

"It stinks."

"What do you mean? How dare you insult our guest?"

"I'm not saying he stinks. His trunk stinks."

"Well, how dare you insult our guest's trunk?"

"Can't you smell it, you daft old man?"

"My nose hasn't worked right for years," Cole snuffled. "If it did, I'd have you bathe more often."

"Limp over here and sniff it."

"Typical woman. Pick on a man's weak point that isn't even his fault," Cole said. He limped over to the stairs. "Waah!" He suddenly staggered back. "Even I can smell it now. What are you sir? A tanner? Smells like a tanner's fixings in there."

Not a bad guess.

"No, sir," I said. "I'm a photographer. Those are my chemicals. Some of the jars got broken in transit, I'm sorry to say. But I'll have the whole trunk straightened out once I'm settled in."

"You'll do it out in the stable, I'm afraid."

"The stable?"

"I can't have you stinking up my inn. I mean, with all due respect, I got other guests, too."

"It doesn't smell that bad," I said.

A man in a tweed cap was coming down the stairs. He had to jump over the trunk.

"He says it doesn't smell bad," Esmirelda said to this other guest.

"Smells like bloody embalming fluid," said the man, passing on with a broad wink.

"That's right, Mr. Parker," Cole said to his back. "That's just what I was going to say."

"But you can't—" I sputtered.

Esmirelda was dragging the trunk out through the barroom.

"Oh Jeez, what's that smell?" was among the comments from the bar. "You got a body in there, Ezzie?" "Some new kind of cheese, Ezzie?"

"Shut your fat mouths," said Esmirelda.

I watched her disconsolately. It didn't occur to me to help until she was already outside.

"Oh dear," I said.

"Don't worry, Mr. Castle," Cole said. "That one's not afraid of hard work. Your trunk will be safe. She'll lock it in the harness closet. You don't need anything out of it right now, do you?"

"No," I said.

"Well then, come on. Have something to eat." Cole winked and grinned. "I'll bet you're hungry," he said. "Am I right or am I wrong?"

"You're right."

"I know I'm right. Here now, pull up a chair. What would you like? A nice steak and kidney pie? ESMIRELDA!"

A savory pie appeared from the kitchen. I washed it down with several pints of ale.

Some locals joined me. They talked about an upcoming racing meet, a neighbor who'd been fleeced by some builders, and the railway porters' strike. One of the locals' nephews was somehow involved. Either a striker or policeman, I don't remember. But it was a chill reminder of Paolo and Shorty. It was only that morning I had been attacked, and the two were still at large.

After my meal, I enjoyed a smoke. It was provided by a genial Cole from behind the bar.

"Not much of a pub life here in Burkinwell," he said, tilting a candle flame in my direction. "Folks here stick close to home." He leaned closer and whispered. "What we get in here is mostly the strays. Lost scraps of humanity. They blow up here like scraps of paper on a fence."

Finally, I was full and tired. Wishing everyone goodnight, I went up to my room.

The room was small but neat. I saw a dormer window, a washstand, and none other than Esmirelda stretched out on the bed. The big girl didn't move as I came in. She stared dreamily at the ceiling. With one hand, she tucked a corner of the quilt around the mattress.

I coughed.

She looked up with big watery brown eyes. "Sorry," she said. "Just making the bed. I do it lying down sometimes. I get tired, you know."

Esmirelda had dark hairs at the corners of her mouth; and she was young enough for it to be attractive. She said that Cole was working her too hard; she needed her rest.

I was at a loss for a reply.

"He seems like a good man," I ventured.

"Yeah, yeah, yeah," she replied. Her voice was slow and lazy. "I can't blame him. He works me hard. I'd work me hard too. That's how you make money."

"I suppose."

"Sure. That's how you do it. I'm saving my money. And when Cole dies, I'll buy this place. I'll call it—"

"The Esmirelda?"

"How'd you know? Anyhow, I'll get my own girl. Work her to the bone. There's got to be some likely ones hereabouts."

"Local girl?"

"Maybe. I know most of them, though. Too lazy. Or too smart."

I don't know why I asked this: "Know the Templeton girls?"

"You'd have to be an animal."

"What?"

"An animal," Esmirelda sat up. "To treat those girls bad. They're good girls. Sweet girls. Not like me. Not like that minister's wife you drove up with."

"You know her, too?"

"Can you believe some of the things she wears? Do they dress like that in London?"

"Well, not every—"

"Must make the men wild. Don't know how she controls them if they're like the men up here. What do you think of her?"

"I suppose she seemed—"

"She goes down to London for her good times, she does. I'll do that too, someday. When I saved up enough. I'm saving my money, you know."

I turned my back on her. I began loosening my tie. Time to go, Esmirelda. "I suppose everything's all set up here, then?" I said.

"Yeah, yeah. Everything's fine." I heard her heavy body creaking off the bedframe. "My room's back down the kitchen." She spoke from the doorway. "The yellow door. Knock me up if you need anything. Anytime. I'm a light sleeper."

The door closed.

I flung my tie over the chair. I lay down on the bed. It still smelled like Esmirelda—a not entirely unpleasant smell. A combination of sweat, kitchen grease, and cloves or something.

Lying there, fully clothed, I began to fret. And there was plenty to fret about. Did I have enough to pay for the room? I leaped out of bed and went through my pockets and valise. I had enough money to last me a while. What about my missing valise? Some stranger could be pawing through it at that very moment. That was painful to think about. It wasn't only my underwear in the valise. There were legal papers drawn up by Sir Arthur, outlining his offer for the Burkinwell fairy photographs. Anyone reading those papers would know the whole business. Or think I was a madman. It was disturbing, as if someone were reading my love letters.

Did losing Sir Arthur's legal papers hurt my mission?

Not at all. Sir Arthur wanted me to buy the Burkinwell fairy pictures and get them out of circulation. That I could still do. But there was much more. I had plans that would make me rich. Would make Constable Walsmear rich. Would make those two little girls and their father rich.

I started to panic. Suddenly the whole thing seemed like a crazy scheme. After all, the success of my plan was based on the assumption that there actually were fairies in Templeton's garden. All I had to prove it was that one shadowy photograph. Was I losing my mind?

As I lay in that strange room, I was overcome with a sense of superfluousness. Were the fairies in Templeton's garden real? Hell—was I real? How far I was from London! From Boston! From any woman who loved me or had ever loved me! All I had here was a bit of money. No income. A few pounds away from being a tramp.

I got up and began to pace. I heard noises beyond the walls. There were strangers there. Strangers to all sides of me. Outside was a quiet town full of homes. In it, people were going to sleep behind ancient stone walls. The sheep were locked in their pens. The moon was rising over placid fields.

Now here I was, rattling; rattling through the town. Like Cole said: A stray bit of paper. Wondering what it would be like to make love to Esmirelda. Imagine that! In London, amour with someone like Esmirelda would have been unthinkable; but here I felt the need to nail myself down to that evening, and to that place. To get some weight into my being.

Not that I was ready to go down and knock on her yellow door. I stood at the casement window and looked out of the Starry Night into a cloudy night. I saw the rooftops of the town. The treetops. A church tower. Beyond all that, the sky was vague and depthless.

What brought me to this place, I wondered. What did I really think about the Burkinwell photographs? Did I think that vague image on that scrap of cheap celluloid was actually left there by a supernatural being? Or was I chasing a winking light? A will-o'-the-wisp?

Had I come to Burkinwell because it was spring? Maybe I'd looked into the clumsy constable's clumsy photographs and seen something I hadn't seen in a long time: the possibility of some other life. A new stream of vitality.

Did I seek renewal, then, amid perfumed bowers, surrounded by merry children? Did I see a last chance for my personality in a vision of Edenic village England? Did I sanctify my desires with figures from traditional folklore? Did I believe in fairies?

CHAPTER ELEVEN

How I Went to Church

THE NEXT DAY WAS SUNDAY. It had rained while I had been asleep. The sky was still a sheet of clouds. The sun glowed like a light bulb through a murky negative. Outside my window, the trees were still wet. Their trunks were slick and black. Their leaves were sloppy and dripping.

In the valise the robbers had left me, I still had my second-best suit. I put it on. I wet down my hair. One strand on the side wouldn't go down; it never does. It usually sticks out like a cockroach leg.

I could see the tower of Rev. Drain's church from my window. Gothic, but not imposing, the tower was stubby, square, and louvered. Its crockets, quatrefoils, gables, and galleries stood out with the somber detail of a daguerreotype under the sodden sky.

I followed the idiot clangor of the bells into town.

Burkinwell had grown up around a market square. From this ancient marketplace, all roads radiated in and out of town. In the "Olde Towne," clustered around the square, the stores and houses were built of a similar stone; probably from some local quarry, now long depleted. It was a rough-hewn granite; gray, with a lime-colored lichen softening the quartz-flecked chisel marks.

The Rev. Drain's was the church of St. Anastansias the Martyr, also known as Sweet Stanley's to the more irreverent Burkinwellians. (The story of St. Anastansias, a martyr from what is now Turkey, is that when the Romans pierced him with their lances, he bled honey. I learned this from the back of a postcard on sale at the Starry Night.)

St. Anastansias stood right on the town square. There was a cemetery next to it, surrounded by a crooked iron fence like a stuttering pen line. A line of fruit trees separated the church and the graveyard. The trees were in blossom just now, their pinks and yellows contrasting vividly with the church's gray wall.

Many Burkinwellians made their way toward St. Anastansias that morning. Families arrived on foot. Some country folk were arriving by horse cart. Mostly, however, people were pulling up in motorcars. These they parked in no particular order on the town square.

I didn't want to go straight into the church. I have a horror, sometimes, of being conspicuous. On the other hand, people were looking at me as I hung about outside the front steps.

I walked over to the cemetery, where I read headstones. Then I noticed that I was not alone. There was a woman over by the fruit trees, standing on a short stepladder. The top part of her body was lost amid the cloud of blossoms. I recognized the shape of her legs, however. It was Linda Drain. She was wearing a maroon dress with white piping, which covered her knees with modesty befitting a minister's wife on Sunday. A broad-brimmed white hat lay on the grass beside the ladder.

I came up below her and retrieved the hat.

"Hello," I said. "Is this your hat? You shouldn't leave it on the wet grass."

"Oh, hello, Mr. Castle. Thank you. Could you hold on to it?"

"Certainly. What are you up to, may I ask?"

"Oh, nothing in particular."

"You're just sort of standing on this stepladder?"

"Yes. No. Well, not exactly."

"Picking blossoms?"

"Not picking. Looking."

"They are beautiful, aren't they."

"Oh, so beautiful. Not many people would understand, Mr. Castle. Actually, I'm getting lost."

"Getting lost?"

"Yes. In the blossoms. I poke my head up here and—I don't know—I feel myself drifting away."

"Do you drift anyplace in particular?"

"Someplace—how do I say it? Spiritual? They all pray in their churches, but I pray out here. In the blossoms. Here, I'll get down. You try it."

"Just climb up there?" I set the hat back down.

"That's it. Don't worry, there's no bees on a rainy day. Now—inhale slowly."

I closed my eyes to do so. The scent was thick and wonderful. Joyous, like a carol.

"Open your eyes."

"All right."

It was like waking up in a Japanese print. I was under a dome of soft pastel lozenges. Jagged twigs shot through the cloud of radiant petals.

"Nice?" Linda asked.

"Very."

"Now close your eyes again."

The blossom shapes turned vivid and tropical

against the velvet of my eyelids. As I watched, they wriggled apart like reflections in a wavering pool.

"I say, do you do this often?" I said, eyes still closed. "It's really quite an interesting exercise. Prayer, you say? What an interesting concept. Have you ever—" I opened my eyes. I looked down. Linda was gone.

"Hey!"

I bent down. She was walking toward the church. The hat swung from her hand.

I jumped down from the stepladder. She was entering a side door of the church.

I did not follow, but went around to the front doors and joined the stragglers there.

Despite the crowd of automobiles in the street, the church was only half-full. Linda was in the process of seating herself up front. I took a seat in the back.

The congregation murmured and shuffled its feet. I scanned the backs of the heads, but didn't see Constable Walsmear; and, although there were children present, I did not recognize the girls from the photographs. Of course, I couldn't see everybody.

Esmirelda was very much in evidence, slouching in the corner of a pew. She wore a large straw hat bedecked with flowers. Two long red ribbons streamed down her back like ceremonial carpets.

The crowd stirred as Rev. Drain appeared on the altar. He cut an impressive figure. His was a handsome baldness; and his various surplices, chasubles, and other vestments hung well from his muscular frame.

Though I was raised a Roman Catholic, I have had the opportunity over the years to attend the services of many different religious denominations. Tedium, I have learned, is ecumenical. So it was now that, as the services began, I almost immediately drifted off into reverie. I dreamed that I was back amid the blossoms outside the church. Linda was with me, and together we floated through the pastel cloud, arm in arm; shoulder to shoulder; face to neck.

I blinked myself back into reality.

That was not the sort of thing to think about in church. According to the Law of Moses, adultery is forbidden. Jesus took the stricture even further, telling his followers that even to contemplate adultery was a big mistake. I took my fantasy no further, and instead composed myself for Drain's sermon.

His text was from Genesis: God then separated the light from darkness. God called the light day, and the darkness night. Evening came, and the morning, the first day. Then God said, "Let there be a firmament in the middle of the waters to divide the waters in two . . ."

Drain leaned on his pulpit. He stared at us all accusingly, the way people do when they want something to "sink in."

"The God of the Old Testament," he chirped, then paused, ". . . is a God," his voice swooped low, "of distinctions. He is a God who separates: light from dark, sky from water, man from animal. As the Old Testament continues past the Book of Genesis, his distinctions become ever more complex. He gives the Israelites commands that divide every facet of their lives into a multitude of fine distinctions. He is a God who, it might be said, is obsessed with differences, moieties, categories, and ultimately, genealogies.

"It is a singular characteristic. Yet it may contain the very essence of the Deity.

"What is this thing we call science? It is nothing but distinctions, growing ever more complex, between categories of phenomena, elements of matter, types of living forms. The universe began simply, and grows ever more complex. All that surrounds us is but the echo of that initial division of light from dark. It is an echo that continues to resound. The very essence of things continue to change, even as I speak.

"This may be what we experience as time: It is the lag between the infinite number of distinctions taking place at any given moment and our perception of each moment's new condition.

"Our minds: they, too, are part of this broadening, spreading tree of distinctions. Thus is time irrecoverable. Creation is growing from moment to moment. Our expanded minds of this moment simply cannot fit into the relatively narrow space of creation of only a moment ago . . ."

Fortunately for Rev. Drain, no one was paying particular attention to what he was saying. It sounded cracked to me.

As he continued, the congregation dozed, or daydreamed, or admired the simple Gothic interior of the church. Outside, the sky darkened. It began to rain. Wind lashed the panes of glass. Raindrops pounded on the roof.

This was nice. I felt my energy reawaken. I took a renewed interest in the congregation. Over the course of Drain's sermon, the people in the pews in front of me had shifted their bodies here and there. A new corridor opened up between their shoulders.

I looked. I almost started. There they were. The two little girls. What had Linda called them? Anna and Clara. Their golden hair shone out amid the dull blacks and browns of the men's coats. The taller girl wore a large red bow on the back of her head. The man with them appeared to be their father. They fidgeted. He admonished them. But the rain had stopped, and we were all fidgeting by then.

As the service drew to an end, I lost the Templeton family in the crowd. Nonetheless, I had seen them. And it was a good thing, too: My mental image of the task before me had been becoming vague. Now it was getting back to the concrete.

This was the family I had to deal with. I had to convince them to sell Sir Arthur their fairy photographs—cheap. That would be the easy part. But my plans went far beyond what Sir Arthur wanted. For them to succeed, I had to ingratiate myself with this family. Could Walsmear help me with this?

I watched the last of the congregation file out of the church. It was borne home to me that I was a stranger in this town. I was on my own. Under the clangor of bells, I joined the serpentine departure.

The Rev. and Mrs. Drain stood at the bottom of the front steps and greeted one and all, most by name. They tousled children's hair. They bent close to shout good wishes in elderly ears. They asked after the health of the afflicted, and the crops of the farmer. I supposed they were well liked, despite Drain's incomprehensible talk. He was delighted to see me coming out of his church.

"Unusual sermon," I observed.

"Ha! Yes, I hoped so," he said. "I hope it wasn't too abstruse. Maybe next week I'll take it further. Scripture talks about many distinctions. There are levels of heaven. Grades of supernatural beings."

"Like angels?"

"And demons. And much more."

"Don't get him started," Linda said. "When he

starts naming the demons, he sounds positively medieval."

"Maybe the Dark Ages weren't so dark," he laughed. "I mean, 'more things on heaven and earth . . .' All that, you know."

Some other parishioners took his attention.

Linda and I stood alone off to one side.

I leaned forward conspiratorially. "He suspected nothing," I whispered.

"What? About what?"

"That business on the train," I winked. "He never guessed."

Linda laughed. "Oh, that. Thank you so much. He would have made such a fuss. And I do hate to upset him."

"Is that all you were worried about?" I said. "Tom's peace of mind?"

Linda looked at me frankly. "Yes," she said. "That is all I was worried about. Tom hasn't always been this happy. He had some bad experiences in the war. It wasn't easy when we were first married. Night terrors. Drinking. That sort of thing. But we've found a home here in Burkinwell. Tom can exercise his mind here. And his body."

"Sounds wonderful."

"It is wonderful. For him."

"But you need more?"

"Yes. I'll get it, too—But not by upsetting Tom or his life. Do you understand what I'm saying?"

"I think so."

"Good. By the way, I wonder if you've found your friend Constable Walsmear yet."

"Not yet. No. I thought he might be in church."

"No. No. He never comes inside."

"He stays outside?"

"He's on duty. Look. There."

I turned around and looked out on the square.

The sky was threatening once more. The congregants from St. Anastansias were filtering through the jumble of parked vehicles. Little knots of people had been talking, but now they were hurrying. Almost to a one, the menfolk cranked or started the engines of their motorcars, and then tried to leave the square at the same time—each in his own direction.

The result was as when a spade is plunged into an anthill. Cars were crawling all over each other; driving up on each other's running boards; scraping fenders; locking bumpers. Drivers sat within a few feet of one another, not speaking but tooting and blaring and aooogahing their horns.

A single blue figure came speeding out the back door of a pub. It was Walsmear. He was dressed in full constable's fig, with badge, helmet, and blue coat. As I watched, he made his way toward the center of the square, climbing over bonnets, hopping on running boards, and leaping from roof to roof. Reaching his destination, he stiffly shook himself out. Then, he raised his baton in one hand, poised like an orchestra conductor. The drivers looked out of their windows expectantly. Walsmear seemed to be waiting for the downbeat. Finally, the baton came down. Cars began moving, one group to the right, one group to the left. Streams formed, and the logjam loosened. Soon the square was a smoothly flowing river of automobiles. One by one, they sheared off down the radiating streets. In the center of it all, Walsmear conducted vigorously, standing in an empty island of calm amid the traffic. I couldn't hear him, but I could see his mouth opening wide. Drivers winced as they passed him. Some mothers covered their children's ears.

Linda was now talking to some other straggling congregants. I bid her a quick adieu and ran out into the square. Dodging the last of the automobiles, I surprised Walsmear, panting up behind him.

"You!" he said, waving his baton at me.

Two drivers who'd been watching the baton immediately collided.

"The bloody idiots!" Walsmear screamed. "What are you doing?"

"I'm sorry," said one of the drivers, leaning out of his window to study his steaming radiator. "I thought—"

"You thought? You thought? Get out of here. Clear this bloody square."

Walsmear stepped between the two vehicles. With a single mighty hoist of his shoulders, he lifted and separated their two bumpers. The two drivers wasted no time beetling off in opposite directions.

Now Walsmear turned his attention to me. "What are you doing here?" he screamed at the same volume he had been using toward the traffic.

"I can hear you," I said.

"What do you mean you can hear me?"

"I mean, you don't have to scream!"

"I'll scream if I bloody want to!"

Walsmear stopped. His voice echoed off the buildings on the now-empty square. It had caught the attention of the distant group on the church steps. Walsmear grinned toward them. He tipped his hat.

Linda waved.

I waved back.

Rev. Drain looked puzzled.

Walsmear leaned in close. "What are you doing here?" he whispered to me, still grinning.

"I've come to talk to you," I whispered back.

"What about?"

"Why, the pictures, of course."

"That's all over with."

"How can it be all over with?" I hissed. "I can't just forget about them. It's far too important."

"Just to me."

"Not just to you. To the whole world. To Sir Arthur Conan Doyle."

"Don't mention his name—"

"I have to. He's offered me—er—he's offered you . . . What I mean to say is . . . he's offered money. For those photographs. And the negatives."

"What are you talking about?"

"He thinks they're very valuable."

"I don't need his stinking money."

"No, you don't. But I know some people who might."

"Beginning with you, I suppose."

"How about someone else?"

"Who?"

"How about two little girls?"

Walsmear was silent.

"Two little girls," I hissed, "who haven't got a mother."

Walsmear's hand closed around the front of my shirt. It swallowed my necktie and half my collar. "You're treading on very thin ice, brother," he whispered.

I twisted free and stepped back. When I recovered my breath, I said, "We don't have to whisper."

"What?"

Walsmear looked around. The Rev. and Mrs. Drain and the last remaining congregants had disappeared. We were alone on the square. The wind was beginning to sharpen. Raindrops were making leopard spots on Walsmear's helmet.

"You're treading on very thin ice, brother," he repeated, fully aloud this time.

"Stop thinking about yourself," I scolded, "and try taking someone else into consideration." (I might have added "for a change." Funny how this familiar phrase had popped into my head. It was the sort of thing that women always said to me.) "You're not the only one in the world, you know," I went on. "Think about those girls. You know what their prospects are."

"Mind your own business."

"I will not. You know I'm right."

"What's he offering? How much?"

"That's . . . flexible."

"How much?" Threateningly.

"A hundred pounds."

"Bah."

"Two hundred."

"Humpf."

"Four hundred?"

"Don't talk to me."

"Five hundred." I gulped. Half. I couldn't believe it. I had given away half of what I could have got from the deal.

"Go away."

"Six hundred?"

Stern silence.

"Eight hundred?"

Nothing.

"A thousand?" I squeaked.

"Maybe."

"All right, a thousand," I gasped. "But listen. There's even more. Much more. I've got a plan."

The rain was falling harder now. Walsmear looked up and held out his palm. It soon filled with water. "We'll talk about it later," he said.

"When?" I asked. "How can I contact you? I'm staying—"

"At the Starry Night."

"How do you know?"

"I know. If you want to talk, you can find me tonight."

"Where at?"

"The Gypsy camp."

"Where is that?"

"Outside of town. Three miles down the main road."

"What time?"

"Anytime after dark."

Walsmear turned and began walking across the square. The rain was coming down much harder now. I started to follow him. Then I thought better of it. If he wanted to meet tonight in the Gypsy camp, so be it. I ran in the opposite direction, taking cover under the eaves of a row of shops.

If it was still raining later, I could borrow an umbrella. Maybe Esmirelda had one.

CHAPTER TWELVE

How I Got a New Darkroom

THIN SHEETS OF RAIN swept across the gloomy little square. Where I stood was relatively dry, but just a few feet ahead, raindrops danced and puddled around the cobblestones. Separate waters combined into larger streams. All were gathered noisily by a mouthlike grate in the curb. Across the square, shops and houses squatted humbly in the dripping wet, inspiring pity like soaking cats. To my right, the stones of the church were stained with damp; brief cataracts gushed from gutters and spattered on the pavement.

With the departure of Constable Walsmear, there was not a soul on the square. As the rain diminished, however, I saw a figure in white, rising out of the churchyard. It was not an apparition. It was Rev. Drain. He was dressed in white shorts and a white singlet. With services ended, and his congregation dispersed, he was obviously taking the opportunity for a little exercise. The rain didn't seem to faze him. As I watched, he threw himself onto the ground. Then he picked himself up again, and repeated the exercise. That finished, he began running in place. He kicked his knees higher and higher. When he seemed to have built up a nice head of steam, he shot off among the headstones.

As Drain was doing all this, his wife made an appearance in the doorway of the church. She could not see him. He could not see her. She folded her arms and leaned against the doorframe. As she gazed into the rain, I was reminded of rural housewives, such as you spot from passing trains. You sometimes see them standing just so, dreaming.

Drain, meanwhile, ran several circuits of the graveyard. Then he leaped up and chinned himself on the high, wrought-iron gate. I waited for him to tire, or at least to slow down. He did not. After an appalling number of chin-ups, he dropped to earth and, without skipping a beat, shot off across the square. He ran right past where I stood. I could see his face contorted with pain. His eyes, however, glittered with pleasure. They took no notice of me. He was in a world of his own.

I looked back toward the church. Linda no longer stood in the doorway.

Soon, the rain abated; the sky glowed with pearlescence. I had a strange and sudden impulse. In obedience to it, I dashed across the square and up the steps of the church. There was no one in the dim foyer. I pushed open the doors. As I walked down the main aisle, I at first saw no one. But a brief rustle drew my eyes to the altar.

"Hello."

It was Linda. She was lying on a stack of pillows piled in front of the altar. She looked quite comfortable. There was an illustrated magazine on her lap and a box of chocolates at her side. A shoe dangled from one foot. She flipped it off her toes. It rolled down the aisle toward me. I picked it up.

"Sorry," she said. "Just showing off."

"Showing off your—legs?" I ventured, ascending the altar steps and setting the shoe down beside her.

Linda sat up straight. "I'm covered, aren't I?" She checked; she was. "I'm showing off," she said. "How irreverent I can be. Lounging on the altar. I can get away with that, you know. I'm the minister's wife. Aren't these pillows nice? I'd like to take them for the house."

"I understand perfectly," I said, sitting down beside her. "Now's the time for you to do this sort of thing. When you can be alone. It's not like any of your parishioners are going to come back in here. Imagine if they did. Seeing you stretched out here like an odalisque."

"A what?"

"From the seraglio."

"Oh—"

"No. I'm sure your parishioners have had—if you'll forgive me—a bellyful of church this morning. And so, I think, have you and your husband. He's off running and exercising. You're eating chocolates and reading magazines. You're both resting up before the cycle begins again for next week's service."

Linda looked down at where I was sitting. "You're getting that pillow wet."

"Uh-oh."

Water was dripping off my tweed coat.

"Take that thing off," she said. "And tell me why you came back to church. Prayer?"

"Uh. No. I just wondered—uh—if you knew where I could get some photographic chemicals. If there was any place in town—"

"The chemist. Across the square. He's the local photographer. I'm sure he's got some in stock."

"Ah, good."

"Got a nice darkroom all picked out?"

"Not really."

"Can Mr. Cole give you something at the Starry Night?"

"Well, he rather objects to the smell of the chemicals."

"Oh. That's too bad. So what are you going to do?"

"I'm not really sure."

"I wish we had a spare room at the vicarage. Unfortunately—say, why not put your darkroom in here?"

"In the church?"

"Yes. Down in the cellar."

"Churches have cellars?"

"This one does. Come on, I'll show you."

Linda picked herself up and led me behind the altar. I peeped out at the church from behind the candles. Backstage.

"Look." Linda bent down. There was a kind of wooden hatch in the floor, hidden by the altar from the rest of the church. The back wall came right up to the edge of the opening. A bit of rope was stuck in the hatch. Linda pulled it, and the hatch came away.

A puff of dry, stale air blew into our faces.

"Down here?" I asked, a little incredulously.

"Um hm. There's a ladder down there somewhere. Let me see. There it is. I'll go down first."

"Don't you want a light?"

"There should be a lamp down at the bottom. What I need is a match."

"I have a box. Here."

"Thank you."

"You're really going down there?"

"I've done it before. I just have to find the top of the ladder—ah, there it is—with my foot. Once I've got my foot planted . . . Here we are. All right then. Down we go."

Linda was being cheery. But she was also biting her lip as she disappeared down the hole.

"Hello?" I called down after her.

A light flared in the blackness. It dimmed, then grew robust.

"Come on, then," said Linda, in flickering, foreshortened silhouette.

"Okay."

In a second, we were standing together in a cramped little room. Its walls were of tightly fitted stone blocks.

"Oh, Linda," I said. "This is far too small."

"This isn't it," she said. "Look behind you."

She raised the lamp. Through a narrow opening, I could see another room.

"In there?" I asked.

"Take the lamp."

She handed it to me.

Feeling like I was entering the tomb of an unknown pharaoh, I squeezed through the door. Linda followed. The light from the lamp revealed a much larger room, walled with the same tightly fitted stone blocks.

"It's very clean," I observed.

"Dennis comes down here and sweeps up," she said. "Esmirelda won't come down here."

"Dennis? Esmirelda?"

"Dennis is our handyman. Esmirelda comes and cleans up the rest of the church. Maybe you met her. At the Starry Night?"

"Oh, I did. Yes. I met her. Yes. Yes, indeed. Why won't she come down here?"

"Superstitious, I suppose. She's a very simple girl. Not as simple as Dennis. But—"

"What kind of room is this?" I asked.

"No one knows for sure. It was filled with dirt for centuries. About twenty years ago, some amateur archaeologists came in and dug it out. They found some medieval pins and buttons. A pot. A few bones."

"Human?"

"Oh, I don't know."

"Why does anyone come down here?"

"Well, we keep meaning to store things down here. Someday we will. Recently, I was going to put in a potter's wheel."

"You're a potter?"

"I was taking a class. I had plans to set up a studio down here. Got it all figured out how to run the electricity in and all. But, well, I sort of lost interest. It's devilish hard, you know, making those pots."

"I can imagine."

"I know I'm artistic. I've just got to find the right means of expression."

"You've got to keep looking, I suppose."

"Maybe I should have stuck with photography. What do you think?"

I didn't answer. "This is an interesting room," I said. "But it wouldn't do for what I need. Where's the electricity? Where's the running water?"

"We've got all that upstairs. Dennis could run a wire down here. And look—" Linda walked into a shadowy corner and pulled something. A wooden panel fell down. Daylight streamed in through a barred window near the ceiling.

"Now it feels like a dungeon," I said.

"Maybe that's what it was," Linda said. "In any

case, you can run a hose with a spigot down from upstairs. It's all very simple."

"What about a drain—well, you know what I mean."

"There's a drain there on the floor."

"Rats?"

"Do you prefer them?"

"No!"

"I never saw one down here."

"It is clean," I said. "What happened to all the dirt?"

"Archaeologists are very thorough."

"I'll say. What'll you charge me?"

"Nothing, of course."

"Can I do anything for you?"

"Maybe you can teach me a little about developing pictures?"

"I'd be glad to. Will this be all right with your husband?"

"If it makes me happy, it will make him happy."

"I mean, will it be considered—you know—proper?"

"Proper?" Linda recoiled in mock horror. "Do you mean, will people talk?" She laughed. "Really, Mr. Castle. It's not as if we would be having an affair."

"No—" I sputtered. "Nothing like—that is—"

"You must be thinking of the old joke: 'Let's go into the darkroom, my dear. We'll see what develops.' "

"Really, Mrs. Drain, I didn't—"

"We shan't worry what vulgar people think," she said, pursing her lips adorably.

"I'm afraid you misunderstood me," I said. "What I meant was, would your husband, the deacons, or the verger or anyone object to using this sacred edifice for—uh, secular purposes?"

"Oh, heavens, Mr. Castle. It's Sunday. My husband is stripped down to his shorts running around Burkinwell in the rain. People are more tolerant than you'd ever imagine. So what do you say to my offer?"

"Hmmm, I'd have to—"

"Your answer is yes, yes, yes. Go back to that nasty old Starry Night and get your nasty old trunk and haul it down here as soon as you can. The sooner you do that, the sooner you can get to work. Celebrate the beauty of Burkinwell, Mr. Castle. That's what you're here for—aren't you?"

CHAPTER THIRTEEN

How I Photographed the Innkeeper

COLE STOOD BEHIND THE BAR of the Starry Night. He was the only one in the room. As I came in, he slammed his hand around the tap handle, for all the world like a railroad engineer grabbing the throttle of a locomotive. A pint glass was rapidly filled and sloshed down on the bar before me. I went for my money, but Cole said, "No, no, no." He took the rag off his belt and dabbed assiduously at the puddle of ale around the cup. "Enjoy it on me," he said.

I thanked him and took a long quaff; longer than I might have taken had I been drinking at my own expense. Besides, I needed it. I'd just shed what felt like gallons of sweat hauling my trunk from the stable of the Starry Night to the cellar of St. Anastansias. It was an arduous feat of cartage. But I didn't have to do it alone. When Cole saw me starting out, he'd ordered Esmirelda to help. She took the front. I took the rear. All the way down the road from the Starry Night to St. Anastansias, I watched her back: Her pale inner forearms were mottled with small bruises, and her haunches rolled sturdily under her thin dress. When we got to the church, I was ready to take the trunk on my back and carry it down the ladder one step at a time. Esmirelda came up with the idea of tying a rope to the trunk's handle and lowering it down instead. It was a good idea. (Without it, I might be hobbling to the scaffold tomorrow on a cane; instead I'll walk to the noose with a manly and erect bearing.)

Once we got the trunk down to the cellar, Esmirelda put her hands on her hips. "A darkroom, eh?" she said, cocking her head knowingly. "You'll have a good time here, you will. 'Step into the darkroom, my dear. We'll see what develops.' "

"I certainly will," I said, patting her hand as I slipped her a coin by way of emolument.

She looked at it.

"Is that enough?" I said, chilled. Her look was similar to that of Paolo and Shorty as they eyed my tip on the train.

"Well," she said. "We'll see what develops."

She dropped the coin down her décolletage. It slipped down her dress and plopped between her feet. With a sigh, she bent from the waist to retrieve it, then went back up the ladder.

Now, seated at the bar of the Starry Night, I could hear her creaking around upstairs.

Cole, meanwhile, leaned his thick belly against the

bar. "Yes, indeed," said the proprietor. "Burkinwell. It's a pretty little town. Quite a slice of England. And a good deal different from America, I'd wager, eh, Mr. Castle?"

I dabbed my mouth with my handkerchief. "Very different," I agreed. "Very."

"No wild Indians here," he said. "No Italians. Eh? We do have our Gypsies, though. Every place has its curse."

"I suppose."

"But Burkinwell is quite picture-eskwee in its own way. There is much that is beautiful here. A famous painter stopped by here once, did you know that, Mr. Castle? He stayed right here at the Starry Night. 'Course, I'd never heard of him. But that Mrs. Drain told me he was quite well known in London."

"Who is that?"

Cole told me the man's name. To his immense satisfaction, it turned out to be somebody I knew—or had known quite well during my early years in London.

"Yes indeed," Cole said. "I was sitting here talking to this painter chap one afternoon—just like I'm talking to you now—and he says to me, 'Mr. Cole, how do you feel about the barter system?' 'The barter system?' says I. 'That's right,' he says. 'I'd like to propose a trade.' 'Propose away,' I says. So he says 'Mr. Cole, how would you like an original oil painting of the Starry Night?' Well, I'm always looking for something nice to hang on the wall. 'Very much so,' I says. So he says, 'I'll trade you one for the price of my lodging.' 'Which you ain't got,' I says. And he says yes, he ain't got it. So what do I got to lose? I tells him to go ahead. And so he sat outside and did an original oil painting of this very inn."

I looked around the room. There were many bad

paintings there. But none in the style of my ex-acquaintance.

"You won't find it on the walls," said Cole.

"Where is it?" I asked.

"Here." Cole rolled his eyeballs downward. Then he stepped back and began clattering under the bar. Some boxes and trays hit the floor. Finally, he came up with a canvas.

"What do you think?" he asked, holding it up.

"That's his style," I said.

I grabbed my glass and drained it.

"What do they call that style?" asked Cole.

"I imagine he's got a name for it," I said. "I don't, however, know what it is."

"But it doesn't look like the Starry Night," complained Cole. "It doesn't look like anything."

"Of course it doesn't," I said, gazing wistfully into the bottom of my glass. "It's nonsense. Garbage. Trash."

"You mean it's worthless?"

"Quite the contrary," I said. "Hold on to that painting. Someday you or your heirs will get a lot of money for it."

"I thought as much." Cole gave me a canny wink. "Some of the lads hereabouts thought I'd been had. But not me. I'll just hold on to this and have the last laugh, ha ha—" Cole replaced the appalling thing in its dark hiding place "—but in the meantime, I still don't have a nice picture of the Starry Night."

"Don't ask me to paint you one," I said. "I hung up my paints and brushes a long time ago. Chaps like that fellow who did you that painting there were giving the business a bad name."

"Not a painting. A photograph. A nice, you know,

big one. I couldn't pay you. But you could drink free. What do you say?"

Fifteen minutes later, I was setting up my tripod outside the Starry Night. The sky had cleared. The early evening sun slanted through the trees. A veinlike pattern of shadows lay across the Starry Night's blank white face. Cole posed crookedly in the doorway.

"Don't you think I ought to put on my good clothes?" he said, fingering his apron string.

"Don't you dare," I said, snapping off several exposures. "You look perfect. The perfect English innkeeper. How old is this place, anyway?"

"Old enough," he said.

I was about to pack up when Cole grabbed a broom and began sweeping the flagstones. This was so 'picture-eskwee' (as he might have said) that I couldn't resist taking another series of shots.

"How old is 'old enough'?" I asked.

"Hm." Cole threw the broom aside. "Old enough for ghosts."

"Ghosts?"

"So they tell me."

"Who is 'they'?"

"Esmirelda."

"Has she seen them?"

"Oh, yes. In the rooms, she has. And out on the road."

"Out on the road? Where?"

"Why, right along here. Between here and the Gypsy camp. She says there's a ghostly rider, all pale, and shrieking, and headless. Late at night, lonely travelers have been known to come back, their hair as white as snow, unable to speak another word as long as they lived."

Oh, that's just wonderful, I thought as I packed up my camera. A ghost on the road I was to take that night. I tried to control the shiver in my spine. Cole must have noticed it.

"It's not true, of course."

"You just said it was." I exhaled to compose myself.

"It's just a story."

"Well, I'm going to be taking that road tonight."

"Then you've got more to worry about than ghosts."

"Like what?"

"Tramps. They hide in the hedges. Jump out. Knock you on the head. Take your money. Very dangerous."

"What about Gypsies?"

"Bah. They're nothing. Henpecked blokes what live in wagons. Just stay away from those Gypsy women." Cole winked. "You might end up living in a wagon yourself. Now when do I get these pictures?"

"As soon as I set up my darkroom," I said.

"Not here, I hope."

"I've got a place in town."

"Nothing personal, you know. The smell, though—the other guests . . ."

"I understand." I took my things up the stairs.

"Oh, by the way," Cole called after me. "Did you hear the one about the photographer and the lady?"

"No," I sighed, and awaited the inevitable.

"What did the photographer say to the lady?"

"I give up. What?"

"Step into my darkroom, my dear. I'll take a picture of you naked."

"What?"

"No—that's not the story. Wait a minute . . ."

"I'll be taking a nap, Mr. Cole," I said, continuing up the stairs. "I'd prefer if no one bothered me."

" '. . . Step into the darkroom, dear. Just don't tell my wife.' No . . . Wait a second . . ."

Ghosts. I was still thinking about them as I came to my room. I paused outside the door. A faint rustling sound could be heard within. Before I could scare myself through speculation, I grabbed the knob and opened the door.

Esmirelda sat on my bed. She didn't look surprised. Standing up, she went through the motions of smoothing the quilt. Then she began dusting. I folded my arms and watched. The woman's figure had been before my eyes all day, it seemed. Not that there was anything wrong with her figure as such. I mean, taken in an objective, historical context. In another era, it would have been greatly admired for its massive grandeur. Our own era, however, honors only a slim, boyish female form. Like Linda Drain's. The classically proportioned, like Esmirelda, go uncelebrated. Worse, they must wear the current fashions. These only accentuate their disparity from the current ideal.

"Oh," I said, after a moment's observation. "It's you. I thought it might be one of the ghosts."

"What ghosts?" Esmirelda lifted the lamp and polished the tabletop.

"Mr. Cole was just telling me about the ghosts that haunt the Starry Night. And the road between here and the Gypsy camp."

"He would do that."

"Are there ghosts around here?"

"Who'd be stupid enough to believe that?" Esmirelda stared at her own reflection in the newly polished tabletop.

"He said that you told him—"

"It's only stories. I tell him because, with his bad leg, he can't run from them. That scares him twice as much."

"So there are no ghosts on the road. I mean, the road between here and the Gypsy camp."

"You won't see any. If you don't believe in them, you won't see them."

"Do you believe in ghosts?"

"Not a bit of it. Don't believe anything you can't see. That's what I say." She scraped at a tiny imperfection in the tabletop with her fingernail.

"How about fairies?" I asked. "Fays, sprites, elves, and will-o'-the-wisps?"

"I don't."

"Does anybody around here?"

"Only the police."

"The police?"

"Well, one policeman." Esmirelda put the lamp back down on the table. "You know who he is."

"Michael Walsmear."

"Ask him about Bea Templeton. Brian Templeton's wife."

"But she—she died, didn't she?"

"You know she did."

"It was an accident, I heard."

"They say."

"You mean it wasn't an accident?"

Esmirelda's thick features were blank. Unreadable. "What do you want, Mr. Castle? A murder mystery or a fairy tale?"

She thudded out, shutting the door behind her.

CHAPTER FOURTEEN

How I Met a Fierce Dog

IT WAS A BAD NAP. I woke feeling out of sorts. All my sleeping and waking habits had been mixed up since Constable Walsmear had come to visit my studio. I would get up confused. I wouldn't know where I was. The sky would be red. Was it sunset or dawn? I'd wake up thinking I was a boy again; that I was back in the North End. I woke up from my nap at the Starry Night and began walking in the direction of what had been the outdoor privy behind my childhood home. I came to my senses in the Starry Night's strange hallway. Someone was peeping at me from behind a crack in the door. (It is strange: Now in prison, I wake up sometimes thinking that I'm back in the Starry Night. I leap up, thinking that I'll be able to undo what has been done; that all that has happened was only a premonitory dream. My true situation returns to mind with the cold gray light from the tiny window up near the ceiling.)

I splashed some water on my face, and got ready for my assignation with Walsmear. I wasn't crazy about the idea of walking to the Gypsy camp. But once

I was out on the road, I felt better. In fact, I felt terrific.

The crisp, rain-washed air drove the lassitude from my brain. Gazing at the last rays of sunset, I felt a soaring joy in my heart. The fall of darkness only slightly dampened my pleasure.

I didn't forget what Cole had told me about tramps. I imagined seeing them in the darkness. Any hedge or hillock could be a hiding place. They could jump out, knock me on the head, and be off—with no one the wiser. Except me.

But there were worse things out there than common tramps. And I don't mean ghosts. I was thinking of Paolo and Shorty. They were still at large. That meant they could have been anywhere. They could have been hiding along that roadside, hoping to waylay an innocent traveler. Imagine their surprise when they saw it was me headed toward them. Were Paolo's eyes still burning from the chemicals Linda had thrown into them? Could Shorty still use the arm I had stabbed again and again with that broken bottle? I knew I could expect no mercy if I fell into their power; only terrible vengeance.

With this in mind, I appreciated the sight of the occasional lighted house or cottage. I would slow as I passed each one, and hurry up through the dark stretches in between. But the dark stretches were getting longer as I got farther out of town. The road was quiet. My own footsteps seemed to thunder. Would-be ambushers could hear me a mile away. I thought it would be a good idea to arm myself. A stout stick would do. I looked around for one.

The moon was rising. By its light, I saw a fallen limb. It looked like the perfect weapon. I trotted over to where it lay. The back part was lost in some shaggy bushes, so picking up the end that lay in the road, I pulled. At that moment, there was a noise from the bushes; a deep, guttural growl.

I had come across my weapon just in time. I pulled it harder. But something had hold of the other end; something hidden in the bush. Instead of pulling, now, I gave a mighty push. I hoped to unbalance whatever was holding on.

Suddenly, a huge black shape leaped out at me. It was a giant dog. Two paws, as big as a man's fists, slammed into my chest. With the beast's hot breath in my face, I tumbled over backward. Flashing white teeth lunged for my throat. Desperately, I tried to control the furious mass of fur and muscle. My hands clung to its jaw and tore at its ears.

At the same time, I could hear a human being crashing through the bushes. A man's voice called out, "Rollo—Rollo—hoy, boy hoy!"

"Help," I gasped. "Get him off of me. Help."

"Hoy, damnit."

The speaker kicked the dog square in the ribcage. It yelped and backed off. As I stood up, I saw the man aiming more kicks, which the dog dodged, whimpering and barking at the swinging foot.

"Goddamn, stinking, swining, smelly piece of rat bait," the stranger shouted after the cowering beast. After a few more kicks, he came back to where I was standing. "Sorry, sir. Rollo didn't mean to hurt you. He's just playing. He's a good dog, basically."

"Oh, is he now?" I said, catching my breath.

"Rollo never hurt anyone."

I held my fingers out. "This far," I said. "I came this far from hitting my head on a rock. That wouldn't have hurt?"

"Well, as that's your attitude, I have to say you asked for it."

"How did I ask for it?"

"You poked him. With that stick. I saw you."

"I grabbed the stick. I didn't know there was a dog in the bushes."

As I brushed the mud, twigs, and dog saliva off my jacket, I looked the man over. He was small and swarthy, wearing an old cardigan over a dirty undershirt. He didn't look like a tramp. Perhaps it was the cardigan. I guessed that he must live nearby.

The dog came back. It bumped up against its master, panting and sloshing its tongue.

"All right, apologize to the nice man, Rollo," the stranger said. "Go lick his hand."

"Please, that's not necessary."

"All right, then. We'll be on our way. Get along now, Rollo." The stranger started up the road ahead of me. Then he paused to let me catch up with him. "Bit late to be out on the road," he observed. His accent was somewhat foreign, but I could not place it.

"Yes, it is, isn't it?"

"You're not lost, are you?"

"No. I don't think so."

"Not looking for something, are you?"

"Like what?"

"A place?"

"I might be."

"A camp, maybe?"

"Something like that."

"A camp with wagons? And fortune tellers? Men with earrings and violins? Spicy stews cooking over open fires? And girls? Beautiful, barefoot girls? Young girls? Very young girls?"

The man took a step closer. Beneath a damp mustache, his teeth shone white in a suggestive leer. A smell of uncleanliness and strange spices rose from his person.

"I'm looking for the Gypsy camp," I said, confident that I was speaking to a member of that strange nation.

"Oh, are you, now? Well, if you are, let me recommend my Grenda. My beautiful Grenda. Very reasonable. And what she will do for you, you wouldn't believe. Why, in your wildest imagination—"

"I'm looking for a policeman."

This shut him up for a moment. Then he lifted an index finger of enlightenment. "Pokey!" he said. "You're the American who's looking for Pokey. Am I right?"

"Who is Pokey?" I asked. "I'm looking for Constable Walsmear."

"Same guy," said the stranger. "Pokey's short for Hocus Pocus. That's what we call him. He does magic tricks. We taught him when he was a boy. He never got good at it. But he got a taste for Gypsy food. And Gypsy girls. Ha ha ha. But now, he's a copper. What do you call him, a flatfoot, yes? You Americans. Ha ha. Hey, I told him if I ran into you, I'd make sure you got to the camp. So come on. I'm going back there now. Follow me."

The dog seemed to read the man's thoughts. It ran through a break in the shrubbery. The man followed. I stood alone for a moment, then decided to go after them.

Both the man and the dog followed an almost invisible trail through the ragged foliage. We climbed down a culvert, then up a low grassy hill. At the top of the hill, I saw the edge of a woods up ahead. Flickering lights burned from deep inside the woods. A weird glow danced on the trees. We crossed a field. As we came closer to the woods, I could see lanterns and campfires burning within. I saw figures, a few horses, and many wagons.

It was the Gypsy camp.

It was not what I expected. My idea, like most people's, of what a Gypsy camp should look like comes from operetta. Of course, nothing in life is as it is in operetta. (Especially love. So I've learned from painful experience.) Still, I expected to see a circle of colorfully painted wagons; hearty bonfires; young women in bright scarves beating tambourines; fat men in earrings; and dancing—wild, abandoned dancing.

The prosaic look of the man in the cardigan should have prepared me. Nonetheless, as I followed him into camp, I was surprised by how dull, meager, and poor it was. The wagons were all of different shapes and sizes. None was brightly, or even recently painted. Most bore the devices of previous owners: WATSON'S PLUMBING or PURITY MILK. Tents of a sort spread out from the backs and sides of many of the wagons. They were improvised out of dirty canvas, old bedsheets, and cement sacks. Candles and lanterns glowed behind the threadbare coverings.

Though it was late, children were everywhere. They were dirty, barefoot, and dressed in rags. A very fat woman poured a basin of dirty water onto the ground. Another struggled up the back stair of an unsteady wagon, carrying a pair of sloshing buckets. She pushed open the door with her shoulder and disappeared inside.

What music I heard came from phonographs. There

must have been three or four playing; each melody clashed with the others.

The ground was a mix of mud and horse manure. It sucked my shoes under as I walked.

We approached a group of men sitting under a tree in a circle of light.

"There's your friend," the man in the cardigan said.

I saw Walsmear. He was dressed in civilian clothes—the loud jacket was slung from a tree branch overhead. Three Gypsy men sat around him. They wore ragged caps, filthy shirts, and mismatching pants and vests. They sat on boxes and broken chairs. Overhead, the tree spread its branches like a canopy.

I was about to go over to them. But the man in the cardigan stopped me.

"Before you go, you've got to let Rollo apologize."

"Really, it's not necessary," I said.

"Oh, but he's got to. I know Rollo. He won't sleep if you don't let him say he's sorry."

"Oh, for crying out loud."

The man brought a contrite-looking Rollo over to me. Wagging its tail gently, the dog proceeded to slobber all over my hand until my shirt cuff was soaked.

"There, that's better," the man said, moving on with his pet into the darkness.

There was a burst of laughter from the men under the tree. They didn't see me. They were watching Walsmear perform a card trick—badly, I presumed. He was in the midst of a flourishing shuffle as I stepped into the circle of light.

Some of the men looked at me. Walsmear did not.

It took a great deal of courage for me to speak up. "I'm glad to see more of your tricks, Constable," I said. "Apparently you've got quite a reputation."

One of the men got up and offered me his chair. The cane had been ripped out of the chair's seat, but I accepted it and sat down.

"I taught him," said one of the men. He was large-bellied, with a whiskey voice. He was also the only Gypsy man I saw with an earring: a little brass circle on his flappy lobe. "My name is Zob. What do they call you?"

I introduced myself.

"Very nice. Very nice," said Zob, shaking my hand. "But this is not good magic that he is doing here. Pokey is very bad. Very bad. Give me those cards, Pokey. Let me show him."

Zob did some tricks. He was good. No stage patter, however. And the work made him sweat and breathe hard. I could see Walsmear studying his fingers.

The other Gypsy men were not interested in Zob's tricks. One by one, they got up and left. But Walsmear and Zob got involved in a technical discussion of Zob's sleight-of-hand techniques. They went on and on. I was completely ignored.

Lanterns and torches were going out all over camp. The phonographs ground down, and a deep silence settled in. Walsmear had yet to address a word to me, or even recognize my presence. That made me very nervous. I didn't want to be on my own in the Gypsy camp. They were strange people. They had strange customs; different values. I didn't even know exactly where I was. We were deep in a woods, and I wasn't sure where Burkinwell was, or even in what direction. I needed Walsmear, I realized, if I wanted to get back to town that night.

A passing breeze made me feel even lonelier and more isolated.

"Come on now," I said. "Pay some attention to me."

Walsmear and Zob stopped talking.

"If you wanted attention," Walsmear said, "why didn't you say so?"

"I know you didn't ask me to come to Burkinwell," I said. "But you did invite me here. And now that I'm here, we might as well talk about what I came here to talk about."

"Did you understand that, Pokey?" Zob asked.

"I did." Walsmear nodded. And to me: "What did you come here to talk about?"

"The girls."

"What about them?"

"Do you want to help them or don't you?"

"Watch out," Zob leaned over and whispered loudly to Walsmear. "He looks like a tricky one."

"I am not tricky."

"Then why do you deny it?" Zob asked. He folded his arms and turned to Walsmear. "Do you see what I mean?"

"Let him go on," Walsmear said.

I could have kissed his feet.

"Let me start from the beginning," I said. "From that remarkable photograph. You don't know this, but I made two copies of prints from your negatives. One set I gave to you. The other I kept."

"Oh—what did I tell you?" Zob slapped his knee. "He's devious, Pokey. Don't trust him."

Walsmear gave a regal wave of his hand.

"Thank you." I continued, "I was impressed by what I saw in that enlargement. And I thought that you should have credit for having been correct about it. So I took a copy of the enlargements to Sir Arthur Conan Doyle."

Walsmear let out a loud snort. He poked Zob with his elbow.

"This Doyle bloke is some kind of author," he said.

"I know," said Zob. "Sherlock Holmes."

"Who?"

"Oh, Pokey, you should read more. You're missing half the pleasure in life."

"I get plenty of pleasure."

"Oh, sure."

"Will you let Mr. Castle speak?" Walsmear snarled. "Go ahead, Castle. What did he say?"

"He did not see there what we saw there."

"Ha!" Walsmear snorted. "I knew it. He's blind."

"Blind, but not disinterested," I said.

"Speak English."

"I mean, Doyle has photographs of his own."

"What kind of photographs? You mean—?"

"That's right. It's a crazy coincidence. But Doyle has his own set of fairy photographs."

"What do they look like?"

"They're a lot like yours. But they're different. They show little girls playing with fairies. But the fairies are fake."

"How do you know?"

"Trust me. They're phony. They wouldn't fool a child. Doyle will become a laughingstock when he releases them to the papers."

"So why is he doing it?"

"Well, from what he said, I got the impression he's on a personal crusade. He thinks the world would be a better place if everyone believed in fairies. And he thinks they will once they see his photographs."

"He must be crazy."

"Indeed. Crazy. But he still knows how to communicate. And he knows that to get a message across to millions, you've got to make it clear and simple and direct. You've got to hit people over the head with it. Now, for all I know, Sir Arthur may actually see the same thing in your picture as we did. But your picture is of no use to him. It's too vague. Too subtle. Too dependent on the viewers' sensitivities."

Zob sighed. "I used to enjoy Sherlock Holmes." He lit a cigarette and leaned back. "I used to steal every issue of the *Strand*, as soon as it came out. I even bought one, once. This Doyle must be a very wealthy man."

"He is," I said. "And like many wealthy men, he thinks he can control the world with cash. . . ."

Here I told Walsmear how Sir Arthur offered money to keep the Burkinwell photographs out of the public eye. I didn't mention how much money he had offered.

Walsmear was surprised. "That proves one thing," he said. "It proves that he thinks the photographs are real. I'm satisfied. That's good."

"What I'm wondering," I asked, "is if you'd be interested in selling—"

"They're not mine to sell," said Walsmear. "Talk to Brian Templeton."

"That's my next point. I was hoping that you'd help me approach him."

"Why should I help you? The photographs were real. I'm satisfied. Now I'm through with the whole thing." Walsmear gave an energetically dismissive wave of his arm. A small fountain of playing cards gushed from his sleeve.

Zob almost collapsed in laughter. I bent down and helped Walsmear pick them up.

After the interval, I took the argument on a different tack. "The girls," I said. "You're forgetting them."

"What about them?" Walsmear said.

"They could use the money."

"How do you know?"

"Rev. Drain and his wife told me all about it."

"Don't drag the girls into this."

"You're being very selfish. Do you want those girls to grow up poor?"

"They're good girls."

"Yes. But think about it. A poor girl doesn't have a choice in life. She has to crawl for pennies. She has to marry whoever asks her. And who might that be? Some crude, foul-smelling lout. A disgusting pig of a man, who would take what he wants from her, then throw her aside when he's satisfied his filthy lusts—"

Walsmear's fist shot out. It might have done to my face what it had already done to the wall of my darkroom. Fortunately, I saw it coming and ducked.

"I'll kill him—" Walsmear was saying.

I scrambled around to the back of the tree. Peeking around, I saw Zob restraining Walsmear by throwing his body in front of the enraged copper and waving his hands in his face.

"You can come out," Zob said after a few minutes. "He's all right now."

"You just watch what you say," Walsmear said.

He pointed his index finger a few inches from my nose. Foreshortened thus, it looked huge. Way down at the end of his arm, I saw his crimson face. His eyes, as they say in books, burned like coals. I had made my point all too well.

"We were talking about money," I said.

"Go ahead."

"As I said, Sir Arthur is offering money for the fairy pictures."

"It better be goddamned thousands and thousands."

"As a matter of fact, it's not."

"Then why bring the girls into it?"

"Because Sir Arthur's money is just the beginning."

"The beginning of what?"

I looked over at Zob. The talk of money made his features perk up like an alert hound. He seemed like a genial old Gypsy, and he'd certainly done me a favor in checking Walsmear's wrath; but who the hell was he, anyway?

"The beginning of what?" asked Zob himself.

I caught Walsmear's eye and nodded toward Zob.

"You don't have to worry about him," said the copper.

"I'd like to talk business," I said. "But I don't really want to cut anyone else in on this."

"Zob doesn't want any part of it," said Walsmear.

"Oh?" I said. "As far as I know, Gypsies don't take vows of poverty. Nor are they averse to a little hanky-panky when it suits their purposes. No offense, Mr. Zob, but you understand—"

"Shut up, you fool," Walsmear thundered.

"Hey, hey, hey," Zob laughed. He patted Walsmear's knee in a fatherly way. "Calm down." To me, he said, "What Pokey here is trying to say is that I don't care about money anymore. All that is past. I'm a dead man."

"I beg your pardon?"

"I'm sick. The cancer, you know. It's hopeless. The doctor says I can't be saved."

CHAPTER FIFTEEN

How I Fell Down the Hole

Zob continued, "My family, they are all sons of bitches. For them, I wish slow starvation. I have only one friend. Old Pokey, here. Ha ha ha. It is strange. All my life, the police are my enemy. Now that I am dying, I have only a policeman to bury me and pray for my miserable soul."

"I'm so sorry," I said. I felt great pity. But Zob would not meet my eyes. For a moment, we were all silent.

In that moment, I heard the slow crunch of twigs and saplings. Squinting into the darkness, I could see a car driving through the woods, its headlamps off. Zob and Walsmear paid it no mind. A man got out of the car and walked over to a nearby wagon. An old woman seated on its steps got up. The man handed her money. She motioned for him to climb into the wagon.

I had been seeing a lot of this sort of thing in the Gypsy camp. Non-Gypsy men were arriving quietly on foot, bicycle, and horse cart. I tried not to stare; but out of the corner of my eye, I saw young women roused from beneath the ragged tents and lined up for display.

I was busy with Walsmear. I didn't have time to think about it. Now, I realized: The Gypsy camp was a rural bordello. Far from being the end of the evening for the Gypsies, the night was only the beginning. The phonograph ground to life once more. The children were back, running errands for the camp's clients and girls. I felt a sick pity and revulsion. It was a drab, sordid scene. It made one long for even the shabby, artificial gaiety of city vice.

We'd had an interval of respectful silence for Zob's impending mortality. That interval was now protracting itself beyond the point of comfort. At least for me.

After a respectful nod at the old man, I went on, "Let's forget the pictures we already have," I said. "Let's sell them to Sir Arthur. We can take our own pictures. Really good, quality pictures. I'm a professional photographer, for heaven's sake. I'll experiment. Find out how to get precise, detailed photographs of whatever's in that garden. Do you realize what pictures like that would be worth?"

"Hey, Pokey," Zob said. "This fellow is looking out for himself. You look out for yourself, too. Make sure you get a cut of all this money he's going to make."

"We'll see." Walsmear narrowed his eyes at me.

"I know what's wrong," Zob said. He hauled himself up by grabbing the tree limb overhead. "We are not drinking anything here. I'm going to go get a bottle of wine. Then you can talk business."

He ambled off into the darkness.

"What I'm talking about here," I said, "is a partnership. You, me, and Brian Templeton. We'll control the pictures. We'll send them to whom we want, when we want. We'll also control the garden—if that's where the fairies are . . ."

I suddenly had a mind-boggling thought. It's a wonder that it didn't occur to me earlier. If there were fairies in Templeton's garden, we could actually capture them. Put them on display. Who knows what else?

Almost the same moment I had this idea, I rejected it. The notion of captive fairies was horrifying. Sprites in chains. Myself a kind of Simon Legree. On the other hand, it was bound to occur to others. The fairies would have to be protected, I resolved. No question. As to whether the fairies could be both protected from captivity and exploited for our benefit, I left that issue to be resolved in the future.

"Once we've proven the fairies exist," I said, "the possibilities are endless. The demand for anything having to do with the fairies will be enormous. After the photographs, we'll take moving pictures, we'll sell books, postcards, you name it. Burkinwell will become the greatest tourist attraction in the world."

Walsmear sneered. "All because two little girls took some pictures?" he said. "You'll get rich?"

"So will you. So will Brian Templeton. So will the girls."

"I don't want any part of that kind of money."

My heart sank. It was late. I didn't have the energy for any further appeal. I'd have to find a way to get to Brian Templeton myself. "So you don't want to be a partner?" I asked.

"I'll be a partner."

"You will? But I thought—"

"I don't want any money. But seeing as how you're probably going to go through with this anyway, I might as well be there to protect the girls. Make sure you don't take advantage of them."

"What about their father?"

"Brian's useless."

"Hey, what did I hear?" It was Zob. He emerged from the darkness with every shape and size of bottle known to man piled up in his arms. "Did you two make a deal or what? Hey, look at what I got. You'd be surprised what these people keep in their cars. Let's see, we got some wine here, some whiskey, what else . . ."

I looked at Walsmear. He was, after all, a policeman. Zob had stolen all the bottles of drink he was now setting up on the ground around us. Shouldn't Walsmear have arrested him? Shouldn't Walsmear have arrested the whole camp, for that matter? It goes without saying that he didn't arrest anybody. He was able to forget his job at the Gypsy camp. It is not that I didn't think Walsmear was honest. He was. But it did kind of prove what people say about the temperamental affinity between the police and their prey. It's real. It's there.

A bottle was shoved in my hand. Zob, holding his own bottle, proposed a toast to our new business arrangement.

I drank. The hot liquid poured down my throat.

The sight of bottles attracted the attention of other men. Soon, there was a merry little group of a dozen or so under the tree. Further discussion of business was out of the question. Zob had bottles in all of his pockets. I finished my bottle, and he handed me another. He was pouring drink into every proffered cup, tankard, or bowl. The crowd clamored for Walsmear to perform magic. He did so, badly. A rope that was snipped in two never came back together. Water poured into a paper funnel merely trickled out the bottom. Someone's watch—mine, actually—was hammered to pieces in a handkerchief and never reassembled. Zob leaped up and did a dance. He turned alarmingly red, then fell on his side in the dirt, where he lay panting and groaning.

After the dancing—music. A man showed up with a fiddle. Another had an accordion. They argued about which songs to play. The accordionist started playing on his own. The fiddler couldn't get in tune. He blamed the weather, the company, fate. Then he stalked off. Some women came by and pulled the accordionist away.

A tree-swinging contest broke out on a low-hanging branch. One of the men stripped off his shirt. He hooked his knees over the branch, then couldn't get down. There was discussion about whether to leave him there or help him to the ground. By the time it was over, he'd fallen on his head and was crawling around looking for his shirt.

I was enjoying myself as much as any of the crowd dancing, pushing, and shouting at each other under the tree. But my new partner Walsmear was no longer among us. Nor was Zob. We were all strangers. And there wasn't one I wanted to know any better.

"Have you seen Zob?" I asked no one in particular. "Have you seen Walsmear?" No one knew who I was talking about.

"I got a job," said one of the men. "And a damn rotten one it is."

"Not job," I said. "Zob. The Gypsy. And Walsmear. I have to find him."

"What for?"

"We just made a business deal and I forgot to shake his hand."

"Here, I'll shake your hand."

I reached for the man's hand. He pulled it away and jerked his thumb over his shoulder.

"Ha ha ha!"

I decided to leave this bunch and head out to see what I could see. I came back a second later, grabbed a half-full bottle, and headed back out into the woods.

I wasn't quite sure where I was, as I drank what was left of the bottle's strong spirits. There were figures out in the darkness. Shadowy groups could be seen here and there. Some were heading toward the camp, others were headed away from it. When I saw one of these groups, I would come up to it and study their faces, looking for Zob or Walsmear. All I found, however, were strangers; men and women. Some shrank at my approach and hid their faces; others tendered unwholesome invitations. Beyond the wagons, a huge bonfire swirled to life. The fiddler started up a strange, discordant tune. From out of the darkness came laughter and muffled cries of pleasure—or distress, I could not tell. Unable to see straight, unable to think straight, I began to panic.

"Zob, Walsmear," I shouted, running back and forth through the woods. I stopped figures, checked their faces. I looked under wagons and cars. I kicked over washbasins and lifted the sides of tents.

Where was he? How was I going to get back to town?

Sparks from the bonfire rose high in the sky, swirling like a furious constellation. The accordion wailed. A woman sang, wordlessly. The fiddle keened a weird, broken jig.

Shouting the constable's name, I crashed into wagons and ran through lines of hanging wash. Thorny branches caught my shirt. Roots sent me sprawling.

Searching through the darkness, I found naked couples, trios, quartets. Fists shot out at me. I mumbled apologies, tripped over people's limbs, spun into yet another copse and another group.

I was alone. Among strangers. In the dark. Far from home. Who would save me?

Then I saw a familiar face. Thank God! It was someone I knew. He would lead me back to Burkinwell. I approached him with my hand out.

"Don't we know each other?" I said—or my mouth tried to say. "I'm Charles Castle, I don't really recall your—"

The face of the other showed no recognition for a moment. Then its eyes filled with surprise, fear, and anger.

At that moment I recognized him, too: Paolo!

I should have run, but I was paralyzed with fear. Paolo's stockinged foot shot out and caught me in the midsection. I fell over backward onto a sapling, which cracked and broke under my weight. I thought it was my spine cracking.

"Help," I shouted. "Police!"

"Shorty," Paolo shouted. "Let's get him."

I rolled across the ground, leaped to my feet, and started running. I could hear several men in pursuit, shouting and pounding after me. I burst into the circle of revelers around the campfire. Burning brands scattered around my pumping shins. New pursuers joined the crowd at my heels. There were shouts of "Stop him, get him," and, most alarmingly, "Kill him!"

I headed away from the lights of the Gypsy camp. Soon, I was running toward the edge of the woods, my pursuers right behind me. They continued to shout as they smashed through the undergrowth. I squinted into the darkness and saw a cultivated field ahead. That would mean a farmhouse, I thought, and safety. I angled over and started running across the field. My pursuers started dropping away. I could hear their footfalls receding. Far behind, someone laughed and said, "Let him go." In time, all I could hear were the sounds of my own feet and my own tortured breathing.

Still, I dared not stop. At the end of the field I vaulted a fence and found myself in a farmyard. There were sheds and sties, troughs and chicken coops. Still running, I felt secure enough to look over my shoulder.

I should have looked where I was going.

I fell down a hole. It was a deep, funnel-shaped hole, filled with gravel. I rode a small avalanche of stones and dirt and gravel down to the bottom. There, my head struck something hard. I saw a purple flash, then nothing.

CHAPTER SIXTEEN

How I Was Roughly Treated

THE FIRST I SAW WAS LIGHT. Intolerable light. Head-smashing, eye-crumpling light. Then there was the dizziness. And uncontrollable sickness.

Someone had hold of me. He was picking me up from the front. I tried to look into his face, but all I saw was the sun. A hideous glare. Someone else seized my hands from behind. I felt a rope bind my wrists. I may have cried out. Rough hands pushed me up the side of the pit. It was not easy work. The sand and gravel gave way underfoot, and we all kept sliding back down to the bottom. I wasn't always sure which way was up and which way was down. I was that sick. The world was spinning. I was retching. Distinctions such as those between up and down, standing and falling, or living and dead were too nice for me to make just then. My captors started pulling me up out of the pit by my ankles. I blacked out again.

It was a merciful oblivion. Only a few impressions penetrated. Hands still tied, I was aware of lying on a dusty plank floor that smelled strongly of animal. The shadows of two large men, framed in a glowing rectangle, stretched out over the planking. I could hear them talking about me. Apparently, I disgusted them. I tried to defend myself through speech, which rose unintelligibly and brought with it another wave of nausea. Most uncomfortable of all was the binding that dug into my wrists. I had to lie on my side in the same position for I don't know how long. Every time I retched, the muscles of my torso seemed to tear. I could not lift my face from the rough floor. Every passing footstep was like a pounding hammer in my brain.

Many footsteps came and went as I lay there. Every so often, a foot would poke into my tender midsection, or it would assess my wakefulness by lifting my chin on the toe of its shoe. Its owner, seeing my bleary, half-opened eyes, would then let my head drop back onto the floor.

From all that had happened to me up to this point,

what lessons can be learned? What advice can I give to the young photographer, based on this experience? Well, to begin with, when traveling, always carry your darkroom equipment in a sturdy, well-padded trunk. You never know what sort of hazards you may encounter on your journey. Don't simply go with the first porters you encounter at the station. Look for some with a little spit and polish to their appearance: If they take good care of themselves, they will probably take good care of your luggage. In business, never see anyone who does not have an appointment. If someone shows up anyway and becomes violent, show them the door. Don't let yourself be intimidated. What sort of world would this be if we all caved in every time a bully raised his fist? Also, learn how to chat. Chat with people in the street, people in shops, at parties and other social gatherings. This way you will learn the social skills that are crucial to success in business. Pay your bills on time; keep an eye on practical matters; and don't leave too much of the important work to your assistants. Finally, don't be overly impressed with the notions of famous or powerful personages. We human beings are strange creatures; and the most outlandish ideas can plant themselves in our heads, taking root and bending all thoughts, dreams, and powers of judgment to the shape of that idea, until reality becomes little more than a set of vague shadows, and the idea alone stands out with vital radiance.

I didn't know how much time I lay on that filthy floor. My last impression of this scene was of the sound of many new footsteps. I heard new voices, not all of them harsh—some of them even kind. Hands fumbled at the bonds on my wrists and feet. When those ties were loosened, my whole body snapped forward like a bow, reflexively assuming that position so masterfully observed and rendered in Leonardo's notebooks: The embryonic curl. And thus I slept for a long, long time.

Book Two

CHAPTER SEVENTEEN

How I Awoke

I WAS IMMERSED IN DARKNESS. But that darkness was not complete. Luminous creatures, loosed from the pool of dreams, patrolled the deep, black trenches of my oblivion. Had these thin, lurid illusions, these inconsequential lights, been all that was left to me, the guards manning the last outpost of my consciousness might have abandoned their duty, tossed away their shakos and walked home, dragging their rifles through the snow. Fortunately, I was aware of another light, a deep, rich, pink refulgence, dawning far away, beyond the sealed, sticky rim of the eyelid. Gradually suffusing the murk with shades of gold, peach, and amber, this light drew me forward, luring me from the caverns of sleep with the promise of a new beginning, on a new ground: not the permanently scarred, corpse-strewn Cemetery Ridge of a life lived so far, but a smooth screen, across whose glowing expanse life's tragedies and confusions might slide like moving shadows—and so pass, and flicker off, leaving not the flat, meager rectangle of the cinema screen, hovering dimly behind the shoulders of a shuffling, departing audience, but a vaulting dome, blank as satisfaction is blank, shorn of the images of desire; light as light is remembered before the search for shadows, as the sun might appear to one situated comfortably in the heart of a flawless pearl in a necklace casually draped over a jewel box on a dressing table next to an open window.

I opened my eyes to find myself in a strange bed in a strange room. I lay on my back. My body was covered with a blue blanket. The hem of a crisp, white sheet peeped out a few inches beneath my chin. I was dressed in strange pajamas.

I tried to raise my head. The pain was outrageous. I let it drop back onto the pillow, and looked straight ahead over the mound of my feet. Across these foothills, I could see the room's single window—a small, mullioned square in the whitewashed wall, casting a long box of yellow sunlight directly onto my chest. Through the glass I could see trees, whose gently waving bundles of leaves outlined a V shape brimming with luminous blue sky. Clouds of flowering shrubs puffed and swelled in the middle ground; enormous red flowers growing hard by the window nosed the glass like curious fish.

It was a vision. Crisp with the hard edge of reality, yet soft, as if seen through a haze of milky luminescence. It was a vision that repaid the closest inspection not with the tattered, threadbare details quickly passed over on first view, but with richer shadows, deeper colors, and more elusive distances.

I was not such a fool as to analyze what I could see of the room and the landscape outside the window. I did not wonder or ask myself any questions, but simply lay there, enjoying where I was without doubting that I was indeed there and that where I was was where I belonged.

There was a rough, wooden door on one wall, with a crucifix nailed to the lintel overhead. As I lay there, the door opened and a little girl came into the room. She was an exquisite blond child, carrying an armload of linens toward a chair on the opposite side of the room. She did not look at me as she entered; in fact, humming quietly, she seemed altogether in a world of her own.

"So," I said, "this must be heaven. And you must be an angel." Unfortunately, this didn't come out the way I intended. My condition resulted in the words sounding something more like, "Tho, ghee muh buh habbah. Zhu muh buh an ga."

Upon hearing the sound of my voice, the girl swung around and dropped the linens. She stared for a moment; then cried, "Daddy!"

I closed my eyes. The Polish Army entered the room. Or what sounded like the Polish Army, all wearing heavy boots and stomping as hard as they could. I opened my eyes and raised my head as far as I could. No army, but only four people—three of whom I knew.

One of my visitors was Linda Drain, who quickly advanced to the side of the bed. She leaned over and maternally straightened the line of the sheet over my shoulders. Her arms, hands, and smiling face passed through my field of vision, then retreated. By rolling my eyes downward, I could see her husband standing at the foot of the bed. His arms were folded. His lips were pursed. His look was altogether one of clerical disapproval.

Behind the Rev. Drain, I could see a tall, scrawny figure that I recognized from church as Brian Templeton. His eyes glittered with an unnatural brightness as he looked down at me. A shock of pale hair stood up on his forehead, like a wisp of medicinal cotton.

The fourth visitor was a younger man who was in the process of putting a stethoscope around his neck.

"Well, well, well," he said, advancing to the side of the bed. "Awake now, are we?"

I tried to raise myself on my elbows. There was a flash of pain in my head. I collapsed back onto the bed.

Linda put a hand on my arm.

"Don't make him talk, Dr. Pride," she said. Then she looked down into my face. "Don't talk."

"I'll try not to," I said. The words came out with surprising clarity and distinctness.

The Rev. Drain folded his arms and leaned forward. "Ha," he said. "He sounds all right to me."

The doctor chuckled. "That remains to be seen," he said. "It's a head case. Possible concussion. Could be worse complications. These things never show themselves on examination. Not that I've had much experience with this sort of thing. Well, I've some experience. I want you to be confident in me, Mr. Castle. It's very important that I have your full confidence."

I had no confidence in him. For one thing, he was young—like that Detective Cubb back at police headquarters. For another thing, I could see in his nervously darting eyes that he didn't have a clue as to what to do with me.

"Here, let me look into your eyes," he said. "Follow my finger. This way, now this way. A match? Anyone got a match? Ah, yes. There's one in my bag. Never mind. I didn't know you smoked, Mrs. Drain. Here now, Mr. . . . What's your name? Castle? Here now, Mr. Castle—ouch!"

The smoking match flew from his fingers. Linda reached down and flicked it off the coverlet.

"Okay, I'll light another one," said the doctor, waving it in front of my face. "Hmmm, seems okay. But what can you say about one of these head wounds? They can be mysterious. We learned that in the war. Not that I was in the war. I was too young, really. Not that I don't know what I'm doing here . . ."

I sensed it was dangerous to lie passively in this man's care. So despite the fact that it was painful, I tried to raise myself to a sitting position. I did so by degrees. Everyone protested, but I was determined. Linda helped me each step along the way, raising the sheet and gently repositioning the pillow under my head.

Down at the end of the bed, Rev. Drain stood immobile. His arms remained folded. The look of disapproval on his features deepened. I threw him the best smile I could under the circumstances, as his wife plumped the pillow under the back of my neck. He took my smile as an opening: "The shame of it is," he said, "is that you're so young."

"Oh, Tom," his wife said remonstratively.

"I mean it," Drain said. "To abuse a young, healthy body that way. It's a sin against God's creation. Our body is God's gift to us, and it's our responsibility not to dissipate that gift. It's bad enough among us Englishmen; but I never expected it from an American. I always pictured the American as vital, energetic, strong. This weakness surprises me."

"Aren't you jumping to conclusions?" Linda said.

"It's difficult not to," Drain said. "But I'm prepared to be corrected."

He looked at me. But I was in no position to correct him. What had I done? How had I got there? I was fully prepared to believe that I had committed some scandalous act subsequently knocked out of my memory.

"I don't remember much," I said. "But I apologize for anything I might have done, if I've done anything. I only hope no one was hurt, or if they were it was not serious. By the way, where am I?"

"You are in my home," Brian Templeton said as he stepped forward.

He had a curious voice to go with his tense, etiolated face. It was a high, strained, wheezy voice. He didn't always have his teeth clenched, but it seemed that way.

"I am Brian Templeton," he said. "The Rev. and Mrs. Drain have arranged for you to stay here."

"Thank you," I said. "So kind."

"Don't thank me," he said, waving a boney white hand. "I'm being paid for it."

"Who?" I tried to sit up further. Once again, the pain pulled me back down.

"Don't worry," Linda said. "The church is taking care of everything through St. Anastansias's Wayfarers' Fund. It dates from—what was it, Tom? The sixteenth century? It pays for sick or injured travelers to be taken care of in a parishioner's home while they recover. You and Brian are the first beneficiaries in over a hundred years, I think."

Rev. Drain nodded. "You can thank Linda. The fund had been more or less forgotten. Lucky for you, she came across the charter a few months back while she was going through some old records."

"I thought of it immediately when I heard you were tied up in the Klempers' barn."

I waved my hand for her to stop. "How," I asked, "did I get tied up in the Klempers' barn?"

"That's what we hoped you'd tell us," Drain said.

"He doesn't have to tell us anything," Linda said. "Mr. Castle's private affairs are his own business."

"I don't remember too much," I said. "Who are the Klempers?"

"A farmer and his son," said Linda. "They were not very pleased with you."

"What did I do?"

"They found you at the bottom of a hole they'd been digging for a—ah, cesspool. Apparently, however, you weren't the first. They've been having trouble with trespassers. Drunks from the Gypsy camp. Not that I'm saying you were drunk. Or that you were coming from the Gypsy camp."

I didn't address those points in reply. "How did I get here?" I asked.

"The Klempers called the police. Constable Walsmear went out there and retrieved you. Then he called us. Somehow he knew that we knew you. I suggested that he talk the Klempers out of having you sent to jail, and I suggested to Tom that we use the Wayfarers' Fund to help you."

"How long ago?"

"You've been lying here unconscious for two days."

"My God. But I feel like I've barely slept. And my head—"

Here the young doctor interrupted. "I'm sorry, everybody," he said. "But I'd like to perform a more thorough check of our patient here."

"Come, let's leave them alone," said Drain, leading his wife and Brian Templeton out of the room.

The physician hummed and clucked as he gave me what appeared to be a comprehensive investigation. Various parts of my anatomy were poked and prodded.

"Nothing wrong with you, old boy," he said. "Just a bad hangover, I should say."

"A two-day hangover?"

"Could have been worse, you know. Much worse. Those Gypsy girls will rob you of everything. Even your clothes. My advice is to go with a group. That's what I do. You can have your fun and there's safety in numbers." He winked, stood up, and loudly cleared his throat. "If anyone's still out there, you can come back in."

Templeton, Drain, and Linda re-entered. Linda came over to my side. She smiled down at me, briefly showing a matronly double chin.

"Well, how is he?" Drain demanded. He sounded impatient. I suppose he wanted to get out and run in the fine weather. I didn't blame him.

"He is fundamentally sound," the doctor announced. "But there is that nasty bump on the head. So I recommend that he not be moved or agitated for a few days. Time alone will tell us if there is a concussion."

"Should he be given anything?" Linda asked.

"Bed rest," the doctor said.

"Voilà," said Linda. "And what about changing that bandage?"

Bandage? I reached up and touched my head. A bandage was wound around my forehead. So where was the bump? I felt around the back of my head. Ouch! There it was.

"I'm not going to do that," said Templeton. "I'm not a nurse. You're just paying me to keep him here and feed him. Not change his dressings."

"Oh, for heaven's sake, Brian," Linda said. "I'll come round and do it."

"Won't need it for but a few more days," said the doctor.

"All right then, now that we know that Mr. Castle is all right, we can go." This from Rev. Drain, who took his wife's arm and patted her hand.

"Of course," smiled Linda. "I'll look in on you tomorrow, Mr. Castle."

"Thank you so much for everything," I called after them as they left the room.

Brian Templeton alone remained. He stood there unsteadily, looking down at me out of his pink-rimmed eyes. He grabbed his hair and pulled upward—a habitual gesture that guaranteed the continued presence of his erect forelock.

"This is so very kind of you," I said.

"Not kind," he wheezed through clenched teeth. "I'm being paid. I told you."

"I'll be paying them back, of course."

"Who?"

"The church," I said. "I can't accept charity."

"And I can? It's all right for me to accept charity?"

"You're not accepting charity," I said. "You're providing a service and you're getting paid for it. But if you see it that way—"

"Don't move." He waved his long, thin fingers.

"Don't get up. The doctor said not to get up." Templeton's voice rose to a near-shriek.

"I don't want to insult you."

"No, no, no," he said. "I'm sickly myself, you see. I'm not always balanced. You needn't worry. We'll take good care of you. The girls will nurse you. They have nursed me for so long. Yes. For most of their lives this has been a house of the sick. I'm a very sick man."

Looking at him, you couldn't argue with his self-assessment. With his sickly gray face, and rheumy eyes, he was the living suggestion of hospitals, sanatoriums, and other places of wasting and decay.

"My cook will bring you your meals," he said. "We will see that you are well taken care of." He passed a weak hand over his forehead. "I see you are tired. I'll tell the cook you'll be having dinner." He turned and dragged himself out of the room.

For my part, I could not think about what he'd said. Nor could I meditate on my situation. My head throbbed like a steel press. The pain obliterated everything but the desire to sleep. The moment he left, I turned my head to the pillow and invited oblivion.

And that was the pattern for the next several days. I'd wake up; then I'd get a huge headache; I'd drink some tea; eat some bread or sip broth; I'd feel better; sleep; and wake once more to the pain in my head. In time, the periods of being awake stretched themselves out. The pain in my head was no longer a furry, monstrous thing that slopped over into every aspect of my existence. It shrank to a small, manageable knot. And it was getting looser every day.

The doctor continued to prescribe bed rest. I got better in the proportion that I enjoyed it.

Brian Templeton remained his irritable self in my presence, but I got the impression that I was not an entirely intolerable burden to the household. For one thing, he was getting a little money out of the deal. And having to take care of a strange invalid had brought a salutary order and sense of purpose to the little household. From various impressions, including the gabbing of the friendly old cook, I guessed that the Templetons were leading a fairly aimless life before I came.

For example, the girls were accustomed to staying up until all hours of the night. With me in the house, however, they couldn't make noise after eight. This requirement made their evenings so dull that they started going to sleep when I did, and waking early when it was time for my breakfast. And since they liked taking their meals with me, they also acquired regular mealtimes as an added benefit. Out of chaos, order.

For all his self-proclaimed sickness, Brian Templeton spent a lot of time up and about. He even took the girls into town and bought them new frocks. They burst excitedly into my bedroom to model them. St. Anastansias's Wayfarers' Fund was changing their lives.

One day, when the doctor came in to check on me, I asked him about Brian Templeton. (I was well enough to sit up in the chair by this time.)

"He keeps saying he's a sick man," I said. "What exactly does he suffer from?"

"Ho, ho, ho," the doctor laughed. "That sort of information is confidential. I can't talk about my patients."

"Oh, so you're treating him?"

"No—not really. Actually, he treats himself. Gets some kind of exotic medicine through the mail. Mostly narcotic."

"So he's not your patient?"

"Never has been."

"Then you don't even know what's wrong with him."

"Oh, everybody knows what's wrong with him. You can hear that down at the Starry Night." The doctor snapped his case shut. "No, sir," he said as he was leaving. "You won't hear from me that Brian Templeton suffers from syphilis."

"What stage?"

"You won't hear anything from me." The doctor stepped aside to let Anna and Clara run into the room. "See you next time, Mr. Castle."

"Read to us, Mr. Castle," Anna begged, dropping a copy of the *Journal of the Edinburgh Philosophical Society* onto my lap.

"Oh, I don't think you'd enjoy this," I said. "It's very dry stuff."

Both girls reached over and felt the pages, solemnly assessing the journal's apparent moisture content.

"Could you read it better if it was wet?" Anna asked.

Templeton's promise that Anna and Clara would "nurse" me was fulfilled inasmuch as the two helped bring me my meals and put fresh flowers by my bed. They kept my water pitcher irregularly filled. Plus, they gave me all the company I needed.

Anna was the oldest. She was a tallish, dreamy girl, who stared out of the window a lot and drew pictures on any piece of paper that came to hand. Clara was a little fireball. Shorter and squarer than her sister, she liked noisy fun that involved running, and games that let her dress up and show off.

Now, for my part, I usually don't get along well with children (I had no brothers or sisters myself); but just as Anna and Clara had enchanted me in their photographs, so they captured my heart in person. I was charmed by their innocent receptivity to everything around them. And though I know I am sometimes an overly stiff and formal person, the Templeton girls had no trouble bringing me on to their level and making a suitable playmate out of me.

About the only "adult" role I took was reading to them. (They were both repelled and fascinated by my accent. Clara said I talked like a duck—if a duck could talk.) They brought me all sorts of things to be read. In addition to the *Journal of the Edinburgh Philosophical Society*, the girls at various times wanted to be read from Coote's *Principles of Motion*, Wald on taxation, and volume three of Richardson's *Clarissa*. They took no heed of my advance warnings that a particular book would not interest them. It was only after I read a page or two that Clara would reach on to my lap, wordlessly slam the book closed, throw it aside, and hand me another.

The stories they liked were the ones you'd expect them to like. Cinderella. The Little Match Girl. All the old favorites. I even extemporized my own stories. I did my own version of the Brer Rabbit stories I remembered from my own childhood. And, of course, Tom Sawyer's trip down the Mississippi on a raft with Injun Joe—which I know by heart.

Every so often, amid all this storytelling, the subject of fairies came up. It came—and it went.

I never grilled the girls about the fairies, their garden, or the photographs. I know it is difficult to believe, since this was my purpose in coming to Burkinwell, and fairies were the secret pulse of my most ardent desires. But I felt a strange, almost moral compunction about introducing the subject around the girls. Sometimes I would upbraid myself for this absurd, under the circumstances, delicacy. I would make up my mind to question the girls as fully as possible about the fairies at the very next opportunity—indeed, to create such an opportunity. But the moment the two girls would come into the room, my determination would falter, as I'd see their faces, so full of trust and ingenuousness.

I think the manner of my coming into their house determined the character of our relations. I was a guest there (even though, technically, the church was paying). When I was in London, planning my strategy, I had hoped to establish a different sort of relationship with Brian Templeton and his girls. A more businesslike relationship: mutually respectful, but a little exploitative on both sides. Now, however, while I was enjoying their father's hospitality, I could not in good conscience pursue my profit motive. Later, I thought, when I was out from under their roof and back at the Starry Night—that would be another matter.

Only once while I was staying at Templeton's did the subject of fairies flit up and sail out of the fictional context. It was on a day I found myself feeling stronger of mind and limb than I had for a long time. I was sitting up in a rocking chair, fully dressed, reading an old romantic novel. The girls came imperiously up on either side of me and slapped an illustrated magazine over my book and ordered me to read it aloud. Happily, as always, I complied, following their orders to read everything, including picture captions, girdle advertisements, and the contents page. We came across that advertisement for Tomilson's Chocolates, the one that shows a slender, dragonfly-winged girl in gauzy clothing whispering "Tomilson's" into the ear of a ritzy-looking lady.

"And this fairy is saying 'Tomilson's' to this lady," I half-read, half-narrated.

I went on to read the next page—something about a hunting party—but the girls began discussing the advertisement.

"She can't talk," said bold Clara. "That's not true."

"Yes, it is true," said Anna. "It's in the magazine. It's true."

"Who can't talk?" I asked.

"Fairies can't talk," Clara asserted.

"It's in the magazine," Anna said, appealing to me with her eyes.

But my answer disappointed her. "Not everything in a magazine is true, Anna," I said. "Especially in advertisements."

"Maybe some fairies can talk," she said.

"They don't talk," Clara insisted. "Not to people."

"Maybe," Anna said, "they talk to each other."

This exchange resulted in a moment of silence; Anna and Clara stared at each other across my knees.

I decided to prod the subject a little. "Perhaps," I said, "they talk the way cats and dogs talk to each other."

This perked the girls up.

"Cats and dogs can talk?" Anna asked.

"Not with their mouths. But you've seen cats and dogs, I'm sure, sort of bump into each other and sniff each other's noses."

"That's not talking."

"It's communicating," I said. "Or take bees, for instance. They communicate by touching each other's antennas and bumping into one another."

"Let's talk by bumping!" Anna said, coming around the back of the chair and falling on top of her sister.

"I'm a bee," Clara said, lowering her head into Anna's chest.

They collapsed giggling onto the floor.

I tapped Anna on the shoulder. "Pretend you're a fairy," I said. "How would you talk?"

"Nooooo," she said. "I'm not a fairy."

"No fairies in the house," Clara said.

"Why not?" I asked.

"Houses are for people." She made a fist and struck my arm. "Don't you know?"

"Couldn't a fairy come in by accident?"

"How?"

"Maybe one could stray through an open window. Like a bee."

Clara suddenly grew very serious. "A bee came into the kitchen," she said, laying a hand on my wrist. "It was looking for jam. That's what the cook said. It was flying around the table."

"How did it get in?" I asked.

"Through the window."

"What happened to it?"

Clara didn't answer. She just looked very serious.

"Papa killed it," Anna answered.

Clara gave a slow verifying nod.

"He had to," said Anna. "It would have stung us."

"Oh yes," I said, helping the two girls to their feet. "He did the right thing. No question about it."

Later that day, I decided that the time had come

for me to leave Templeton's cottage; it was time to get on with things. I came upon Brian Templeton out in the garden. He was seated in a wooden chair, shaded by a tattered umbrella.

"There's no reason for you to move back into the Starry Night," he said, in reply to my proposal of moving out. "You can continue on here."

"But the church fund—" I began to protest.

"Was not being used for anything else," he snapped. "It hadn't been used for two hundred years. Finally, it's helping people, instead of just moldering somewhere."

"Money?" I asked. "Is that what it's all about?"

"Don't get high and holy with me about money, Mr. Castle. I know why you're here. Walsmear told me everything."

This was distressing.

"Oh, I'm sorry to hear that," I said. "I'm very sorry. I'd wanted to present my ideas to you myself. I think you'll—"

"A very dubious proposition. Very dubious. Still, no cause for you to move out just yet—"

"I can't abuse the Wayfarers' Fund for your benefit."

"Mr. Castle." Templeton clipped his words. "The girls—"

"What about them?"

"They'd miss you."

He turned and called, "Anna! Clara! Come here. Mr. Castle wants to leave us."

The girls came running around the corner of the house, golden curls streaming behind.

"No, no," they said, pulling on my arms. "Don't leave us."

I melted.

Templeton smiled.

"But Mr. Castle is feeling much better," he said, tousling the girls' heads. "So we're going to have a special dinner in his honor tonight."

The girls clapped their hands with glee.

It was the first dinner I had eaten seated at the table with Brian Templeton and the two girls. For Anna and Clara, it was fascinating. They folded and unfolded their serviettes and stared at the silver candelabra in the center of the table. After the girls had gone noisily to their bedroom, Templeton and I had cigars and brandy in his study, just like two civilized men in a story.

The dinner seemed to function as a formal declaration of my recovery from the injury to my head. And Templeton's indirect acknowledgment, that if the Wayfarers' Fund was helping anyone now, it was himself, seemed to put us on an equal footing. I felt free to discuss many things. Most important, my purpose in coming to Burkinwell.

"Fairies," he sniffed. "Come, come, Mr. Castle. I've seen you out walking in my garden. Have you seen any fairies there?"

"No," I answered. "And believe me, I've studied every square inch of it. What we're talking about is a phenomenon that shows up only on film."

"Like spirit photography?" he said. "Is that something you believe in?"

"I don't," I said. "But some people do. Sir Arthur Conan Doyle, for instance."

"Perhaps one of the world's most gullible fools," he said.

I was sitting in an overstuffed chair beside the cold fireplace. Templeton was standing up and leaning on the study's somewhat ornate wooden mantelpiece. There were various knickknacks on the mantelpiece, including a brass idol—an ugly little trinket from the Far East. He flicked the idol with his fingernail. It pinged.

"People believe what they want to believe," he said. "They won't face reality."

"I grant you, some people want to escape the harsh—"

"I face reality, Mr. Castle. I have no choice. I'm talking about death, in case you didn't know. But I'm sure you already know what I—"

I coughed in embarrassment.

Templeton went on: "An affliction such as I have can be the product of a lifetime of vice. Or it can be the unfortunate effect of a single lapse. I leave it to your goodwill to guess which it is in my case. However it may be, I have two things to look forward to: insanity, followed by a painful death. It is not a pleasant prospect. And it is not one from which I can be distracted by fantasies of fairies."

"You don't necessarily have to believe—" I said in a quiet, respectful voice.

He waved away my words. "Yes, yes, yes. I know, I don't have to believe in fairies to sell those photographs to Arthur Conan Doyle, or to let you crawl all over my garden with your camera. I'm not arguing with your proposition, Mr. Castle. Let's get on with it. I use expensive medicines, you know. And Anna and Clara—well, I want to leave them something besides this cottage. If there is money to be made here, let us make it. You said Doyle gave you contracts to sign. Well, the photographs and negatives are locked in my desk. Where are the contracts?"

"Ah," I said. "They've been stolen. . . ."

I explained that the contracts from Sir Arthur were in the valise that had been taken by Paolo and Shorty.

"What I want to do now," I said, "is take new photographs."

"New photographs?"

"New photographs that will be owned jointly by you, Walsmear, and myself. New photographs that will be worth a fortune, Sir Arthur or no Sir Arthur."

"Worth a fortune? Then what are you waiting for? Why aren't you taking them!" He threw up his hands and abruptly left the room.

I poured myself another brandy.

Templeton's shriek seemed to echo in the air. But that, as I said, is the way he always talked.

CHAPTER EIGHTEEN

How I Photographed the Garden

TRANSFORMING THE CELLAR of St. Anastansias into a darkroom presented no insurmountable difficulties. As I was still technically a convalescent, Linda directed the church handyman to do most of the heavy work. My main worry about using the room was that dust might fall from the ceiling onto my prints and negatives. Linda suggested I tack a rubberized sheet over the ceiling to catch any particles that might fall. I thought this was a good idea. But where would I get a rubberized sheet? Fortunately, Linda had one. She brought it over from their house. She brought Esmirelda along as well. Esmirelda had been hanging around the town square, trying to avoid some task at the Starry Night.

You wouldn't think Linda and Esmirelda had much in common, but Linda, as the wife of a minister, could talk naturally to anybody from any class. She and Esmirelda chatted easily as they helped me tack up the sheet.

They talked about fairies. They spoke names that meant nothing to me: Dab Swallowfoot, Busky Debaree, Kip-Kip, Pin, and Pupkin. They discussed which fairies lived under tables, which drank from bowls of milk, which could be bought with gold, and which ones scattered curses and sickness over houses.

Linda noted my expression of bewilderment.

"Don't you have fairy stories in America?"

"Oh, yes. Yes, we do," I answered. "I never went in for them much. I rather liked pirate stories better."

"Then you missed out on some great stories, didn't he, Esmirelda?"

"Yes, m'um."

"The British Isles are full of wonderful fairy stories, Mr. Castle," Linda went on. "Every brook, hillock, and tree has some little fairy or elf associated with it. And the kitchen—the larders, cupboards, and stoves are just overrun!"

"What brought this subject up?" I asked.

"You did."

"Did I?"

"Yes. When I was leaving to get this sheet. I lost my key, and said that some sprite must have stolen it. And you asked me if I believed in fairies. A strange question from a man, if you must know. Don't you think it's a strange question, Esmirelda?"

"I don't know, m'um. Some men believe in fairies." Esmirelda gave me a look. I could not, however, fathom its meaning.

"Well, I'm always throwing off comments," I chuckled. "I guess I don't even remember them."

We were standing on boxes holding the sheet up against the ceiling. I was about to hammer a tack into it when the hammer slipped out of my fingers. I jumped down to get it. The sheet dropped down around Linda. She stood there with her head covered by the sheet, looking like a tent post.

We all had a good laugh, and I apologized.

"I suppose I haven't thought about fairies in years," Linda said, as I helped her out from under the sheet. "They're sort of cheap now, aren't they? Like Father Christmas. Advertising things, and all that. Children can still enjoy them, though, can't they? There are some wonderful books. I know if I had children . . . Well, enough of that. Mr. Castle was being whimsical, Esmirelda. Don't you think he was being whimsical?"

"What's that mean, m'um?" Esmirelda took the hammer out of my hand. She started tacking up her end of the sheet.

"Whimsical?" Linda looked on as she did so. "It means light and charming and childish."

"Then I wouldn't know."

"Why not?"

"She's not a whimsical person," I answered for her.

Since Esmirelda said nothing, Linda thought Esmirelda assented to what I had said.

"Oh, you must have whimsical thoughts," Linda said. "We all do. We only have less of them as we get older. That is, I can't believe in fairies as a grown-up. But I remember what it was like. Being young. Those were the best years, really. Years of trust and simple belief. When you're a child, you can create a whole little world in your imagination."

"Like the Templeton girls?" I asked.

"Exactly. Playing with fairies in their garden. Photographing them. Isn't that precious? It's a kind of ecstasy, isn't it? We cast it aside in order to grow up. Then we spend the rest of our lives trying to get it back. We look for it everywhere; love, books, religion—"

"You think believing in God is the same as believing in fairies?" I asked.

"Maybe."

"Strange words from a clergyman's wife."

"No one cares what I think about religion."

"Lucky for you."

"You think so?"

"Yes, people might talk. Look at me, for instance."

"What about you?"

"You have been very kind to me. Both you and your husband."

"I've been much more kind than my husband."

I raised my eyebrows.

Linda went on, "My husband is very suspicious of you."

I gulped.

"He thinks you're here on some mysterious business," she said. "Land speculation or something. He says he finds you 'maddeningly vague,' whatever that means. You aren't listening to this, are you, Esmirelda?"

"Not my business, m'um."

"And why do you think I'm here?" I asked Linda.

"I don't care why you're here," said Linda. She'd climbed up on a chair to help Esmirelda. Now she climbed down. We stood face to face. "I'm just glad we met," she said. "I'm happy you're here."

I backed off a little. I don't know why. I wasn't thinking. I could see in Linda's face that this gave her offense. I was sorry. I coughed. "I'm very glad, too," I said. "Burkinwell is a beautiful little town."

It was no such thing, really.

Linda ventured a step closer. "I hope you'll be staying awhile," she said.

I found myself backing off again. "I hope so too," I said. "So much to photograph here. That reminds me, I'm supposed to go back to Templeton's at half past. I'm going to photograph their wonderful garden today."

Linda folded her arms. She turned away. "It's past that," she said. "I'm sure."

"My God, I've got to go," I said, grabbing my hat and camera bag.

I hesitated before running out. Was Linda offended? If so, how deeply? And if so, why? It was all so confusing.

Noting my hesitation, Linda turned around. She was all smiles and brightness. "Off you go, then," she said. "And good shooting."

"Thank you."

I studied her face for a moment. Her expression was that blank, cheery look the English have a patent on. I turned and climbed up the ladder.

Trotting down the aisle, I passed through the church's gloomy vestibule and burst out into the sunshine.

Why do people worship in church? I wondered. God is out here, in this airy, blue-vaulted temple. My mind was crowded with thoughts of God, man, and nature as I made my way through the town and out to the road that led to Templeton's cottage. These thoughts passed. Soon I was sweaty and tired. My arm ached from carrying the heavy camera case (containing my Hapling "Omnic" field camera, extra celluloid film magazines, a tripod, monopod, light meter, and spare folding reflex camera). I was relieved when I got to the low rise just down the road from my destination. I paused there for a moment before going on.

Below me was Templeton's cottage. Low and broad, with a mighty chimney, it was a place I could not help loving. There was something exceptionally pleasing about it. Maybe it was the tiny, square windows; the sturdy stone walls; the way the tiny front door hid behind the aprons of the squat shrubs. It was almost a fairy-tale cottage. How thankful I was to have spent the days of my recovery there! How wonderful it was to have enjoyed the hospitality of Brian Templeton and the Rev. and Linda Drain—and to have enjoyed the company of Anna and Clara. How unworthy I was of it all. I determined then and there that whatever I did concerning the fairies in the garden I would do with care, courage, and probity. I would bring glory on us all.

With joy in my heart, I picked up my camera case and hurried down the rise. Around the back of the house, I met the scowls of Templeton and Walsmear. The two men were seated side by side. Walsmear had his watch in hand.

"Not in any hurry, are you, Mr. Castle?" he said.

"Sorry I'm late," I said.

"Not very considerate," sniffed Templeton.

"Not like he has anything else to do," said Walsmear. "Makes a lot of fuss for everyone, and then what?"

"Where were you, anyway?" asked Templeton. "The way you rushed off this morning—"

"I assure you," I said, "what I was doing was an essential part of this project. I've been setting up my darkroom in the church. And a very nice darkroom it will be."

"I'll bet," Walsmear sneered. "With you and Mrs. Drain down there."

I ignored his remark.

"You've worked your way into this town pretty well, haven't you?" he went on.

Before I could answer, he'd turned around and started clapping his hands.

"Girls!" he shouted. "Anna and Clara. Come along now."

The two little girls came around the corner of the house. Vigorous little Clara was in the lead. Anna came dragging along behind.

"We made tarts," Clara said, holding out a mud pie to Walsmear. "Will you pull a shilling out from behind my ear?"

"Not now, girls, not now." For all his uncouthness, Walsmear was genuinely gentle and affectionate with Anna and Clara. To them, he was a familiar old gargoyle; they did not hesitate to climb over him, play with him, or ignore him. "We're going to hunt for fairies now. Just like we talked about. Out into the garden. Come on."

With Walsmear's hands on their backs, the girls started toward the garden.

"Remember, girls," I said, "I want you to be perfectly natural. Don't pay any attention to me or anything I do with the camera. Pretend I'm not here, all right?"

Walsmear turned around. "They're not stupid, you know."

"I'm just saying—" I followed them down the three steps to the garden, which ran alongside the road, spilling over the edges of a long narrow lot between two low, stone walls. It began at the back door of the cottage, and petered out around Old Splendor, the venerable walnut.

Old Splendor was a remarkable tree; vast, seamed, and rippling. Its trunk twisted upward like a torso drawn by Michelangelo, sending thick, muscular branches skyward in a hundred dramatic gestures. On its lower levels, it spread broad, benedictory canopies of leaves, in whose shadows nothing grew. Roots like great gnarled knuckles clung to the earth and spread in a circumference almost as wide as the branches.

From the shadow of Old Splendor, a path paved with mossy, green flagstones ran to the back door of the cottage. To either side of the path was a narrow strip of grass (which somebody appeared to have recently mown—perhaps Brian Templeton took more care of the garden than people thought) onto which the flowers spilled over. Thick tiers of blossoms, billowing shrubs, and spiky stalks poured down on either side of the pathway.

It was the picture of profusion; and more than a little heady. I had spent many hours there during my recovery, and every time I walked down the path, I discovered some new flower—either a weed, or a cultivated blossom—configuration of leaves, or fascinating tangle of vines. Will heaven be like this? I suppose I'll soon find out.

Beyond Old Splendor, past the cultivated part of the property, there was a grove of brilliant green ferns that grew as high as a man's waist. There was something fresh, almost prehistoric about this grove. The earth underfoot was blacker than in the garden. The trees around it were younger, smoother, and more slender.

If you looked beyond the ferny grove, you could see some redbrick walls. These were the outbuildings of the ruined factory, which was itself about two hundred yards back, hidden by saplings.

I set my field camera up on its tripod in the middle of the pathway.

Walsmear stood on one side of me. Templeton stood on the other. We stared at the girls. The girls stared at us.

"Well?" I said.

Templeton clapped his hands briskly. "Come, come, come, girls," he said. "Go do whatever it is you do with the fairies."

Anna and Clara huddled in the path.

"Don't watch," Anna said.

"We're not watching," Templeton said.

"Just be natural," I urged once again.

"Come on," Templeton said to me and Walsmear, "let's not watch them. See girls, we're not looking. All right now, let's talk."

Templeton put his arm around Walsmear's back; the two turned away from the girls. I made as if to adjust my camera and blow dust off the lens. Anna and Clara walked slowly toward Old Splendor. Then they broke into a run. A few minutes later, they were shouting and playing a hide-and-seek game around the tree's mighty trunk.

Still not watching, Walsmear and Templeton talked about the crops and the condition of the roads. I turned the camera and took some shots of the cottage and the tiny clouds sailing overhead. Walsmear detached himself from his friend and came up behind me.

"Oh, by the way, Castle," he said. "Your suitcase turned up."

"The one that was stolen?"

"It appears so."

"My God, do you have it?"

"No, no, no. I don't have it."

"Is it at the police station?"

"No."

"Then who has it?"

"An old Gypsy woman. She purchased it. Innocently, of course. Old gal didn't know it was stolen."

Strange as it may seem, up until that moment I had forgotten all about having seen Paolo and Shorty that confused night at the Gypsy camp. Perhaps the blow to my head had driven it from my mind. Now I recounted the fact to Walsmear. The constable affirmed that the police were aware that the two were in the vicinity that night. (And were the police aware that *he*—Walsmear—was in the vicinity that night?)

"Why don't they catch them?" I asked.

"It's not up to me. Unless they come into my patrol area. Then I'll do my duty." The Gypsy woman, he went on to inform me, would be bringing me the valise the next day. "I hope you'll have something for her," he said.

"Money?" I said. "I have to buy back my own suitcase?"

Walsmear shrugged. "She didn't know it was stolen when she bought it."

I doubted that it was official police policy to make me pay to get my suitcase back, but I decided to go along with it. I wanted to stay cordial with Walsmear. And I wanted my property.

The girls, meanwhile, busied themselves among the flowers. I saw them crouch at the end of the pathway. They were intently regarding one particular stalk of blossoms.

"What is it, girls?" Templeton shouted in his thin, irritating voice. "Is there something there? Do you see something?"

Clara turned around and mouthed the word *fairies*.

With clattering of tripod and upsetting of benches, we grown men leaped up and scrambled down the pathway. Hurriedly, I set up the camera, and Templeton demanded of the girls, "Where? Where? Where are they?"

"Right there," Clara said, solemnly pointing to a single pink flower.

"Hold still," I said, taking a shot of the girl pointing to the flower.

"There's one over here," said Anna, who'd moved a few feet into the flowers. I dragged my camera over. "In the black-eyed Susans," she said. "Oh look, she's standing on Susan's face."

I took a shot of the little patch of flowers and several shots of the flowers around it just in case.

Behind our backs, we heard Clara shout, "Here's more," and we ran halfway back up the pathway. The shorter girl was pointing to a flowering shrub. "They're dancing. There's a fairy dancing on every flower."

"I don't see anything," Templeton wheezed petulantly.

Clara looked frightened.

"Show me which flowers," her father demanded.

Walsmear stepped between them. "Get back out of the way," he said. "Let the man take his pictures. You wouldn't see the fairies anyhow. Only the girls see the fairies. That's the point. Do you get it? If you or I could see them, we'd see them every day."

"I expect to see something," Templeton pouted. I moved around the bush, taking shots from two angles.

Now the girls had run back down to the far end of the garden, where we saw them whispering conspiratorially around a fat, red tulip.

"What is there?" Templeton said, walking toward them.

"A little man," said Anna.

"He's trapped in the tulip," said Clara.

"What do you mean he's trapped?" Templeton asked.

"He can't get out."

"What does he look like? What is he wearing?"

The girls exchanged a look.

"He's got a jacket on," said Clara, staring up at us to measure our reaction. She looked back at the tulip as if referring to something inside. "Oh, and he's got shoes. With little buckles. And a belt. And stockings. And a pointy beard."

"And he's got yellow hair," shouted Anna.

"No, he doesn't," Clara disdained her sister's contribution.

"Yes, he does."

"No, he doesn't. You can't see his hair. He's wearing a little cap."

"No, he's not," said Anna.

"Yes, he is."

"You don't know anything," said the older girl.

Templeton said, "What is he doing in there? You said he was trapped."

"He's getting honey," said Clara. "But it's too slippery and now he can't get out."

"He doesn't want to get out," Anna said, defiantly. "He's hiding." Then she turned her back and ran around the back of the shrubbery. A moment later, we heard her shout, "Oh look. More fairies. Lady fairies. In beautiful clothes. And they're wearing crowns and brand new shoes."

Walsmear and I looked at each other with expressions of dubiety.

Templeton was still absorbed with the problem of the tulip. "Let's have a look at this little man in his jacket," he said. Bending low, he brought his face down to within an inch of the flower. Suddenly, he let out a sharp cry. Leaping back, he stumbled over a tripod leg and onto his back. A bee, in its last mortal throes, spiraled away from his face.

"I've been stung," he said, staggering to his feet. "Oh, oh, oh." His features were a watery mask of self-pity as he patted his nose. "It just flew out and stung me."

"Oh, stop crying and we'll put some mud on it," Walsmear said, taking Templeton by the arm and leading him toward the house.

While they did that, I dutifully carried my camera over to where Anna had just reported yet another fairy. The two girls looked a little frightened at what had happened to their father.

"Where are we looking now?" I asked quietly.

"Nowhere," Anna said, gently.

"Where is the fairy?" I asked. "The one with the crown?"

"She's gone."

"Where has she gone to?"

Without another word, the two little girls went running back toward the house with Walsmear and their wounded father.

I stood alone by a tall flowering bush. Quick, darting yellowjackets sailed back and forth before me. Bumblebees bobbed from flower to flower. The scents of a thousand blossoms mingled in my nostrils. Where had Templeton, Walsmear, and the children gone? I did not care. Standing there beneath the perfect sky, the waving trees, surrounded by the gently swelling and falling fabric of flowers, high, frozen jets of blossoms, still, exploded sprays of pink and lavender, blue and yellow, amid petal textures of velvet, crepe, flesh, and japan, I had the unmistakable feeling that I had reached some kind of goal, or come to the end of some quest that I had been only vaguely aware that I was pursuing. But what was it? To experience one perfect moment in the middle of an English garden? Was that my compensation for what loomed ahead as years of penury, loneliness, and shame?

I left my thoughts in question form and contemplated the bee. Now here, I thought, is a magical creature. How meager is the fantasy of the fairy compared to the reality of the bee.

Templeton's sting was a rebuke from nature. While we search the garden for tiny, imaginary versions of ourselves, we miss entirely the more fantastic creatures that crowd there, more mysterious and impenetrable than any parallel universe of floating fays.

And so I stood perfectly still with folded arms, allowing my eyes to receive the tracery of apian flight, so like curling silver strings in the air. White butterflies, faint as powder on a mirror, yet imbued with the mysterious force of life, hovered and flitted, half-powered by their own efforts and half-carried by the breeze. That all these creatures, and all these plants and dirt and blossoms, from the earthworms to the dung beetles, to the rhododendrons, catnip, delphinium, clematis, lupine, campanula, and bearded iris should all come together here in this spot to create this wondrous place seemed a fact beyond all possibility of mere fortuity, betokening some kind of marvelous providence having the sense of an artist and the mechanical persistence of an inventor.

The girls seemed to have made fools of us.

CHAPTER NINETEEN

How I Scared Myself

IT WAS LATE AFTERNOON of that same day. I came into the town square. It was almost deserted. A lone shop owner could be seen locking up and hurrying off. Some flat clouds, blowing up from the west, kicked up a breeze. A piece of paper blew across the square and into the graveyard.

I looked at the church as I walked toward it. Again I remarked the plainness of this structure. It was like a great stone shed with Gothic ornaments attached, the way decorations are stuck on a wedding cake. But there was no question that it was old. You could tell by looking at its walls. Every stone was hewn by crude tools. The surface had the rough texture of time.

What about that room underneath the altar? I wondered. My new darkroom. How old was that? You sometimes heard about English churches built over the sites of pagan ceremonial sites. What if my darkroom was built on a thousand-year-old place of human sacrifice? What horrible spirits might roam the utter blackness I would occupy during the developing process?

I scared myself. It helped to get my mind off my problems.

Coming up along the graveyard side of the church, I saw a tall figure coming out the side door. It was Dennis, the church handyman. Linda had introduced me to Dennis when he was helping to build the darkroom. His powerful, forty-year-old body housed the mind of an unspoiled nine-year-old. A sweet fellow, and quite handsome, he took an almost canine pleasure in meeting and greeting.

"Hello, hello, hello," he said, bobbing his head—indeed, his whole body ducked with each hello.

I gave him a huge slap on the back. "So, Dennis, you've been working, eh?"

"Yeah, yeah, yeah. I been working. Up there. I mended that window."

"Way up there?" I gasped in a tone I wouldn't even have used with Anna or Clara. "My, that's very high up."

"Oh, I had a ladder."

"Still, you must be very brave to climb that high."

"Oh, ho, ho. I must be brave."

"I wouldn't climb up that high."

Dennis shrugged. "Huh, huh, huh," he laughed.

"I'll bet you're not afraid of anything," I went on.

Dennis's face grew serious. "Sometimes," he said, "I'm afraid of the dark."

"Afraid of the dark?" I said, with exaggerated astonishment. "Why, there's nothing to be afraid of in the dark."

"Yes, there is."

"What? Tell me one thing there is to be afraid of in the dark."

"Ghosts."

"Ghosts? Bah. Dennis, I can't believe I'm hearing this. And from a big fellow like you."

"I know." He pouted and kicked at the ground ashamedly.

"You don't see me being afraid of the dark, do you?" I said. "I'm going in there right now. Into that dark cellar under the altar. I'll be under there for hours in total darkness."

Dennis looked up at me. Admiration shone from his clear blue eyes. I couldn't help but go on, "That's right, total darkness. And yet, who knows what kind of room that is down there? Maybe it's an old tomb. Or an ancient dungeon. Or a torture chamber. Think how many lost souls may have died in agony between those very walls! Why, the stones may reverberate to eternity with their ghostly cries of men hung from chains, torn on the rack, or lashed with a cat-o'-nine-tails."

Dennis's mouth hung open.

"Ghosts?" I laughed. "Why, look over there, Dennis. The graveyard comes right up to the side of the church. That means, when I'm down in my darkroom, only a few feet of stone and earth stand between me and a hundred buried corpses. Imagine what spirits could seep through as I stand there in the total darkness. Skeletons could come dancing through the walls, I could see luminous riders on horseback . . . pale maidens in flowing gowns . . . gibbering centurions in long winding sheets . . ."

"And you're not scared?"

"Not a bit."

The simple fellow gazed upon me with awe; and for a moment I knew what it felt like to be a hero.

"So," I said, "if I'm not afraid of the dark, why should you be afraid?"

"I don't know," he said.

"Then you won't be, will you?"

"No," he shook his head. "I won't be."

"So there you go. You're cured."

"I'm not afraid!" he said, bobbing his head again. "Not afraid!"

Now it was Dennis's turn to slap me on the back.

"Not afraid!" he shouted.

Then he abruptly turned and walked off across the square—smiling and humming to himself.

I was sorry to see him go. Very sorry. For although I'd cured Dennis of his fear, I'd managed to scare the bejabbers out of myself. With a last, wistful look at the outside world, I pushed into the church. A puff of chill air greeted me on the other side of the door. Rows of hushed pews stretched out in the darkness. A smell of dust and sandalwood hung over the stone and woodwork. Wan light glowed in the high windows, gleaming dully off the brass altar rail far below.

Skipping up to the altar, I nervously essayed a whistle. The note echoed through the vast empty space like the breath of a ghostly organ. I whistled no more.

Behind the altar, I pulled away the wooden hatch, lit the lantern, and lowered myself down the ladder. A dry wind seemed to play at my ankles. Humming "Dixie" under my breath, I hopped to the ground and made my way to the darkroom.

I turned on the electric light. It shone slickly on the ceiling where Linda and Esmirelda had finished tacking up the rubber sheet. On the table below I saw spread the tubs, chemicals, towels, tongs, clips, and other tools of my trade. It was like running into a group of old friends in a strange neighborhood. My fear gave way. Pleasurable anticipation filled my bosom. I was ready to work; ready to get my hands wet and throw myself into the familiar routines. No more nonsense. It was time to develop pictures.

Of course, I didn't expect the pictures to show fairies. At least, not where Anna and Clara had pointed. But who knew? The lens may have inadvertently picked up some fairy splotches elsewhere in the frame. To work, however, that was the important thing now; the getting busy and getting on with it. Total darkness did not cow me. The wraiths and optical phantasms I saw there were familiar acquaintances from other darkrooms; the smell that filled my nostrils was not the stink of death, but the lively, acrid odor of chemicals busily suffusing inert celluloid with images of light, life, and vitality.

My energy and exuberance were strong as I worked in the darkness. But when I turned on the red safelight, the uneasiness returned. Why should this be? Because in the light, I saw the strange room, and the little doorway off to my left. I kept seeing things in that doorway out of the corner of my eye. Flickering shadows. I would quickly turn. Nothing. My imagination. Or was it?

There was a noise. From upstairs in the church. At first I thought it was nothing. Then I was sure—someone was up there. I could hear footsteps and the sound of something being dragged across the flagstones overhead.

I checked that the negatives were safe. Then I lit the lantern and went up the ladder.

"Hello?" I shouted over the rows of empty pews.

No answer.

I came down off the altar. I walked up one aisle then down the other, all the time peering along the pews to make sure no one was hiding there.

No one was.

Was the front door locked? I crossed over and tried it. Unlocked. I locked it now and tried it. Secure.

The sound, I guessed, had been in my imagination. Shrugging it off, I walked back down the center aisle toward the altar. Halfway there I stopped. Someone was standing in front of the altar. A thin figure, draped in black. As I gaped, it raised a bony finger in my direction. A shovelful of ice seemed to have been dropped down the back of my shirt.

A voice croaked: "You . . ."

I might have said something; all that escaped my larynx was a croak.

The voice spoke again: "You . . . lost . . ." was all I could make out.

"Wh-what do you want?" I stammered.

The voice spoke more clearly now. "You the fella that lost the suitcase?" it asked.

All became clear. This was the Gypsy woman Walsmear had told me about. The one who'd recovered my valise. She wanted four pounds for its return.

"But I didn't even pay that much for it," I protested.

The old woman shrugged. "If you want it," she said.

"Why, I could just take it now," I said. "It was stolen from me in the first place."

She shook her head. "You wouldn't. I can tell. You're not the type who'd fight with an old woman. Would you?"

"No. Anyway, you'd probably have Gypsy men find me and beat me up for it."

"Gypsies aren't like that," she said. "We don't hurt anyone. Food, and song, and wine. That's all we want. Look here, I only got two teeth left. But I can still chew salami."

"How impressive. But before I pay you for this, how do I know there's anything in it. Are my clothes still there?"

"No."

I sighed. "My shoe-polishing kit?"

"No."

"How about the papers? There was a folder with some papers."

"Still there."

I handed her the four pounds. She handed me the suitcase. I opened it. The papers were there.

"By the way," I asked as I watched her count the bills, "is it bad form to ask how you came by this property of mine?"

"Bad form. Very bad. But I'll tell you. I got it from a couple of fellas I calls the fairy men."

"Why do you call them the fairy men?"

"Because they asks me, 'Granny, what do we get if we catch ourselfs a fairy?' Grown men they was, too. So I says to them, 'If you catches a fairy, and she can't get away, she has to give you a wish.' And they says, 'Anything we wants, Granny?' And I says, 'Anything you wants.' And they was happy as could be to hear that, I'll tell you."

"Is that true?"

"You wouldn't believe it, would you? Two grown men—"

"No, no. I mean about the wish. Is that true?"

"What, you, too? You're prize gulls! I just made it up."

"Well, what made them think they could catch a fairy?"

"I dunno. They thought there were fairies about. In Burkinwell. Ahh, if I was younger. I'd give you fairies. You don't find gulls like you lot every day, you don't." She winked a glittering, black eye.

I asked, "Was one of the men tall, and the other one short?"

"Mmmm. Could be. But don't ask me no more. And I won't tell you no lies."

The Gypsy woman waddled down the steps of the church. I locked the front door behind her. Her words had filled me with new distress. I no longer feared the supernatural. I feared two all-too-real criminals: Paolo and Shorty. The two must have read the legal papers that were in the stolen valise. Returning to the darkroom, I studied the papers themselves. They were covered with palm prints and cup rings. I reread the documents. They were full of references to photographs "purporting to show fairies in Burkinwell" and "fairies to be found in the garden of Brian Templeton." The criminals wouldn't understand exactly what was going on from reading the documents; but they would know something was up—and that it involved fairies in Templeton's garden.

Were Paolo and Shorty following me? Is that why

they were in the Gypsy camp that night? Perhaps they were lurking outside the church even now. Or maybe they were haunting Templeton's garden? Perhaps the girls were in danger.

The girls—I returned to the darkroom and finished developing the photographs I had taken that afternoon. I didn't expect to find fairies in those photos, and I didn't. There were no fairies in any of the prints: No prettily dressed and modishly coiffed fairies, like Sir Arthur championed; no faint, blotchy, blurry fairies, such as I had seen in Anna's and Clara's photographs. No fairies. Period.

What were the results of the morning's labor? A few inartistically pretty shots of Templeton's garden; and many not-very-candid shots of two little girls looking guilty and confused—as well they might, leading their own father, an officer of the law, and a distinguished visiting photographer on an embarrassing wild-goose chase.

CHAPTER TWENTY

How I Discovered the Minister's Strange Secret

THAT NIGHT IN THE DARKROOM under the church wasn't the first time I had scared myself. I've been doing it since I was a little boy. I used to do it most often at midnight—the hump of the evening. Midnight always struck the symbolic note of evil in my heart. Its twelve chimes signaled an end to things; the fullness of hours; a crowding of spirits.

Death.

I recall the approach of midnight when I was a child. Lying in my bed, in my little room over my father's North End shop, trembling beneath a quilt lovingly sewn by a grandmother's hands, I would stiffen as the Old North Church chimed the quarter hours after eleven; the hands of its black-faced clock inexorably crawling toward "the witching hour" (a phrase heard once, and destined to echo forever between my ears).

How to hold in abeyance the terror emanating from midnight and all its implications? I would strain my ears toward the street outside, hoping to soothe myself with some prosaic sound of ordinary life: the clop of a passing cart horse; the laughs of late-night revelers; distant train whistles; the wheels of the rubbish cart grinding against the paving stones. Unfortunately, as I did this, I heard other sounds: I remember the mournful wind, rushing in off the bay; a blast from the trackless Atlantic off beyond Cape Cod, sounding like a chorus of moans, and picking who knew what horrors from Copp's Hill burying ground a few blocks away and delivering them square into my little room to terrorize me in my bed.

My terrors would last for a full hour, from midnight until one o'clock. Lying awake, I would stare at the door, expecting it at any minute to creak slowly open and admit the shrouded, scythe-bearing figure I had seen in magazine illustrations labeled "Death." It was fortunate for my sanity that this condition of fear was clapped in such constricting irons of time. By one o'clock, the witching hour had ended. At that moment, terror abated; the remaining hours of the night were marked by short, sweet chimes from the Old North Church, each hour marking an orderly stage in the march from darkness to light.

We can never shake off certain childhood notions. At least, I can't. So it was with some relief that I noted the time as I emerged from the cellar of St. Anastansias. It was one o'clock exactly. The witching hour was over. I could walk back to Templeton's cottage without fear of the supernatural. From there on in, merrier spirits owned the night. Even as I clapped my watchcase closed, the wraiths and spirits were fleeing back to their graves (I did not glance toward the graveyard), while Puck and his minions began their revels amid the streams and forests.

As I crossed the town square of Burkinwell, I forgot my personal disappointments. The silence of the night was like a charm. How different this was from my life in London, where I might have equal disappointments, but not under a sky so full of crisp, bright stars; a stellar display so long forgotten by me, but which has been burning on, cool and steady through the years of my "exile," and will continue to do so long after my death tomorrow.

Under the hard glare of the constellations in the night sky overhead (and the motes of stellar dust between them) I saw my situation with a rare clarity. I saw the breathtaking folly of my having come to Burkinwell; the comical foolishness of my believing that there were "fairies" to be photographed there. That I had been willing to do so said something about my character, both good and bad. On the good side, it showed that I was open-minded and imaginative; on the bad side, it showed that I was unable to face reality, and would chase after the most incredible delusions rather than do so. I foresaw that my financial ruin was inevitable and unavoidable; and I foresaw the pain it would cause me. But I also saw that I would survive somehow, and that the world with all of us on it would go on spinning.

The prints I had just developed were packed in my newly returned valise. As I walked along, I swung the valise in carefree vagabond fashion. Soon, I passed out of the "town" portion of Burkinwell. Fences began to lengthen. Gardens became fields, yards became lawns; and lawns shaded into pasture. Through the landscape, I moved in a bubble of reverie. Now the bubble suddenly burst.

I had been quite alone with the night ever since I had exited the church. Suddenly, outside of town, I heard footsteps charging up behind me. My heart quickened. I turned and looked down the road.

Nothing.

But something was coming around the bend. I could hear it getting closer: pat-pat-pat.

I had the valise, I thought. I could swing it as a weapon. But would it be any good against Paolo and Shorty—or any novel criminals that might be abroad in the night?

I chose discretion over valor and hid in the bushes.

The pat-pat-pat grew louder. Holding myself still, I peered out between the leaves. I saw a man in athletic costume, slowly trotting around the corner.

It was Rev. Drain. Out on one of his runs.

Indeed, I thought, England's tradition of eccentric clergymen is well upheld here. But then who could blame the Rev. Drain for being out on such a beautiful night? Not I. I had just been enjoying the night myself.

For a moment, I thought about jumping out of the bushes and hailing the running minister. Then I thought better of it. The man would probably be frightened out of his scant britches. His face wore a look of pained self-absorption; and it was not an expression that invited fellowship. So I stayed hidden, and he passed in a puff of sweat smell and body warmth. When he had gone some distance, I came out of the hedge.

Down the road, I could see his white shorts and singlet bobbing far up ahead. As I followed with my eyes, he made a sudden turn off the road. He leaped over a fence and took off across a field. There, he was swallowed up in the darkness.

Even as I followed this image with my eyes, another image crept into my mind. I pictured Linda. She was lying in bed—alone. I saw her stretching her limbs beneath the cool sheets, enjoying extra space in bed while her husband was off on his midnight run. I wondered how often this happened. How many nights did she spend stretching and sliding and thinking in the darkness? Perhaps she didn't wake when he left the bed. Perhaps they didn't share a bed, or share a room.

I realized that I knew very little about their relationship. Or anybody's relationships. Or anybody's anything. What can we know of another? Only that he is very much like us, but entirely different.

I continued walking. Dogs barked in the distance. I guessed Drain was passing their farmyards. He certainly seemed to enjoy his running. I wondered if it was a practice I could enjoy. As an experiment, I decided to run some myself. With a hop, skip, and a jump, I was off. The valise was hard to carry, and after only a few yards I staggered to a stop, breathless, weak, and exhilarated.

It was good to feel exhausted. Walking on, I looked forward to a long sleep in the comfortable bed. I imagined how, after a long, dreamless slumber, I would awake upon a plump pillow, with sunlight tunneling into the room through the ivy outside my window. I rounded a bend; and there, up ahead, was Templeton's cottage, where that very bed and pillow awaited me. I could see the silhouette of its rooftop, flanked by tall, pointed locusts making black gashes in the starry sky.

I was going to go into the cottage through the garden door, but before turning off the road, I heard a swish and rustle from off to my right. I stopped and gazed out over the farmer's field across the road. I saw a running man, who proved, again, to be Rev. Drain. He was headed toward the road where I stood, but he did not see me. As I watched, he slowed to a trot. About thirty feet away from where I stood, he crossed the road. Then he disappeared into the cluster of trees beyond the far end of the garden. I could see his white clothing capering like a spark between the trunks. Why would he go back there? I wondered. Surely, the ruined factory was no place to run.

Now I was sorry I hadn't hailed him, as it would have been awkward to do so at this point. It occurred to me that Rev. Drain might actually appreciate knowing that there was some other mortal abroad in the night. I chuckled as I imagined what we might say to one another: some banal commonplace, like the highly charged civilities of Stanley and Livingstone.

I decided to go and find him. Walking as quickly as I could with the valise, I followed him into the trees.

Regarding what I saw next, it is as I stated in court: not a thing I am proud or eager to recount. It gives me no pleasure to tell what I saw of Rev. Drain that night. That I told it at all was only in an attempt to save my own life. And I do it now only as part of this more personal exculpation—made on the eve of the moment when I shall have to answer for all my sins; not in the assizes of men, but in the court of He who knoweth and seeth all; on Whose forgiveness rests my only hope for eternal life—and thus, I hope, forgivable in the eyes of civilized men.

Still, I must pause. I must struggle against my unwillingness to unveil a moment cherished by a fellow creature in the dark privacy of a wooded night. Never, never would Rev. Drain have dreamed that his pleasures would be observed by even one other living being, much less known to the millions of London newspaper readers who smacked their lips over it during the trial.

It is indeed . . . Let me gather myself and go on.

I will describe the ruined factory. It was a long, shedlike building. Brick. It had mostly fallen down. Charred timbers angled into the interior. Saplings grew up between them. Shards of broken glass hung from tall, empty window frames. Piles of bricks and mortar lay in weedy piles under the stumps of fallen chimneys. It looked like a paradise of rats.

I saw Drain up ahead of me. He had stopped in front of an empty doorway leading into the factory's main building. As I watched, he looked about him. He seemed to be making sure he was not observed. I froze where I stood, enshadowed by trees. He did not see me. Satisfied that no one was watching, he ducked into the dark factory.

I realized that Rev. Drain would probably not be happy to meet me at that particular moment, but I was consumed with curiosity. So I took a few steps forward. Again I froze. Drain had reappeared. I saw him framed in the doorway. He was stark naked.

I dared not breathe as he picked his barefoot way past me (it was a warm night). Each muscle in his body stood out in tense articulation. His eyes glowed like a hunter astalk.

Time to go, I thought to myself. Whatever Drain was going to do, I didn't want to see it. A man's own business is a man's own business. Whom among us would care to be judged by what we have done under no one's eyes but the Lord's?

Unfortunately, I couldn't figure out how I was going to get away. I had to get back to Templeton's. But the garden stood between the factory and the cottage; and Drain was headed for the garden. There was no way of slipping around him: all routes involved the possibility of discovery, either by noisy traversal of thickets or passage through open spaces. I decided the best thing to do would be to follow him at an inaudible distance. He was choosing his path carefully; I could wait until we got nearer to the cottage before I made my move.

Silently, I crept from tree to tree. I could see Drain's pale shoulders up ahead. I stopped when he reached Old Splendor, the thick, gnarled tree presiding like a wise eminence over the far end of the garden.

Drain stood on one of Old Splendor's mighty roots. He folded his arms and gazed down into the garden. Stepping out from beneath the tree, he lowered himself to his haunches. His posture was attentive. He seemed to be waiting for something—for the right moment. After a few minutes, he got down on all fours. Had the right moment come? He began creeping along the grassy strip beside the garden path. Then he got down on his elbows and started to crawl on his belly, like a Red Indian. His fingers dug into the sod and his toes pushed against the grass. Finally, he reached the spot he apparently wanted, beneath a bush of the variety known as bleeding heart, whose branches hung low, freighted with underslung blossoms like tiny crimson bells. Drain raised his arms and rolled over onto his back. Starlight sparkled in his eyes.

With slow, silent footsteps, I had made my way to Old Splendor. Now, I hid behind its roots. As I watched Drain's strange behavior, I was desperate to escape. But I was also transfixed.

The man is playing. That's all I could think. Just like a little boy, he's playing out some very detailed fantasy.

I almost envied him the ability. What other man of his age and station—Then I had another thought: Perhaps the man is having an epileptic fit, or at least the early stages of one. For though his face was calm and his jaw slack, his fingertips shook ever so slightly. And as I watched, a distinct spasm traveled up his leg and into his torso, where it caused his arm and shoulder to tremble. On his other side, his knee twitched. A pectoral rolled. Suddenly, he let out a loud gasp. His back arched, and he rose onto his elbows. A shudder passed down his frame, like a mild electric shock.

I started from my hiding place; I thought perhaps I should restrain him, or place something between his teeth to keep him from biting off his tongue. Then I stopped. There was something fishy about Drain's "fit." His convulsions seemed too—delicate. His body twisted and bent, but he seemed to be decidedly relishing the experience.

I moved back behind the root. Peering over it, I saw that Drain was indeed in control of his movements.

His hands stroked his torso, then moved down toward his groin. There, they hovered, and he seemed to be gathering some invisible substance in the air. He did not touch his member, but as he made his gathering movement around it, it achieved a condition of straining engorgement. I turned away, sick with disgust.

So this was the nature of Drain's "play." I tried to block the image of what I had seen from my mind's eye, but I could hear the clergyman's breathing: It followed a pattern, rising to stertorous peaks then catching ecstatically and collapsing into little gasps.

I crawled deeper into the shadows behind the tree. A deep melancholy overcame me. Why was I so sad? I tried to understand my feelings, as perhaps a psycho-analyst might.

Perhaps, I thought, I was being too narrow-minded—probably because of my New England upbringing. My family was of old Puritan stock. It was the pinched, censorious ways of my ancestors that had made the name Boston a byword for prudery among progressive people. It was my sort of sexual small-mindedness, I reflected, that destroyed the sensitive young cleric in Hawthorne's *Scarlet Letter*, as well as countless other New Englanders who, in real life, were guilty of no greater sin than that of expressing their own natural instincts and desires. And, heaven knew, I had lived in London long enough to become worldly in such matters. I knew of the stream of filth running beneath the surface of respectable life. What Drain's behavior deserved from me was an urbane chuckle, not pursed-lipped disapproval.

Now it was myself I condemned. But at the moment that my self-condemnation grew most severe, another image popped into my mind: Anna and Clara.

Drain was lying in the very spot where Anna and

Clara would be playing only a few hours hence. It was the spot where the two girls enjoyed their richest childhood fancies; the place where they imagined fairies, racing and tumbling between walls of flowers, singing and shouting with their angel voices.

I peered back at Drain. He was stretched on a rack of pleasure. His eyes opened and closed. His body writhed. But his hands—they were strangely inactive. I couldn't help thinking that Drain was not actually doing anything to himself; but that he was, in fact, having something done to him. It was eerie. I didn't like it. I didn't like any of it.

I grabbed a stone.

Drain's breath started beating like a pulse. His whole body strained toward the obvious climax.

You bastard, I thought; and as he reached his jetting goal, I hurled the stone at his head. Not waiting to see if I'd hit him, I dived around to the other side of a tree.

Drain gasped and hopped to his feet. He passed where I was hiding as a kind of blur, making fleet passage for the factory. For my part, I grabbed my valise and took off through the garden, headed for the house.

It was a moment of total confusion. But thinking back on my run through the garden, I now recall a peculiar sensation that perhaps I didn't make enough of at the time. It was this: As I bounded through the place where Drain had been lying, I felt a kind of soft patting against my face. The feeling was like that of running through a flock of weightless birds. As I could see nothing, I presumed it was a cloud of midges or mayflies; reflexively, I closed my lips so I wouldn't breathe them in.

The sensation passed quickly. And before I had time to give it much thought, I got another shock. Bounding up the steps of the cottage, I ran smack dab into Brian Templeton.

He screamed and clutched his chest.

I shouted and stumbled backward. "What are you doing out here?" I asked, as I saw who it was.

"What are you doing out here?" he wheezed. He looked even sallower and more sickly by the wan starlight.

"Why, I was—running," I said, no doubt looking guilty and confused.

"From what?"

"I was running here to—to show you these." I held up the valise.

"What's that?"

"It's the prints from the pictures I took this morning," I said. "I've been developing them all evening and I wanted you to see them."

Templeton's eyes lit up. "You've found something? The pictures—do they show . . . ?"

I tried to give a smile that hinted at something wonderful. At the same time, I looked back toward the factory. What had happened to Drain? Did he get away? Was he hiding someplace, listening to Templeton and I talking? Or had he hightailed it off in the opposite direction without waiting to learn who had observed him?

"Are you being followed?" Templeton asked. "Have you brought someone here?"

"Oh, no, no, no," I said. "I'm just—well, we can look at these pictures inside. Shall we? After you."

Templeton led the way into his library. I had never been in this room. Not that anyone had forbidden me;

but it was a filthy, disorderly room that did not encourage a visit. I had to step around small tables piled with yellowing newspapers, mold-encrusted teacups, and old pipes with wads of gray ash spilling out of them. A desk, piled high with litter, stood in one corner. Templeton turned on a small lamp and cleared a space on the blotter.

"Well," he said, challengingly. "Let's see them."

"All right now." I balanced the valise on my knee and removed the stack of prints. "I'll hand them to you one at a time and you can—"

"Just give me the lot," he said. "If there's anything to see . . ."

I handed him the pile. He lay it on the blotter and began turning over the prints.

I coughed nervously.

"They're nice studies of Anna and Clara," I lied; actually the girls looked sad and uncomfortable.

"But no fairies," said Templeton, peering down at a shot.

"They're much better than studio shots of the girls would be. Studio shots can be very forced and unnatural. I get so tired of that."

"But no fairies," Templeton went on.

"I think the natural light does particularly well in bringing out the clearness of the girls' complexions—the highlights in their hair."

"But no fairies," Templeton concluded.

"No," I said. "No fairies. I didn't really expect—"

"What's this spot here?" he asked, pointing down at one of the prints.

"That's a speck of dust," I said; for that's what it unmistakably was.

"And this spot over here, on this one."

"Another speck of dust."

"Are you sure?"

"Positive," I said. "These spots don't look at all like the specks that were on the photographs Walsmear first brought me. The ones Anna and Clara took. The ones you—I think—have here in your desk."

"I do have them here in my desk," Templeton said, opening a drawer and pulling out an envelope. From this envelope, he removed the prints Walsmear had brought to me in London two weeks (and to me an eternity) ago.

We compared that morning's pictures with the earlier shots. The dust specks on the newer pictures were nothing like the glowing splotches on the originals.

Templeton made a noise of disgust something along the lines of "Bah!"

"Hmmm," I responded. "I suppose we have to take stock of where we stand now, and plan our next course of action."

Templeton folded his arms and shook his head. "There will be no next course of action," he said. "This charade is finished."

"What do you mean?"

"I'm tired of this silliness. I've only gone along with it for the sake of my old friend—not that I owe him any such consideration, but that's friendship for you. In any case, it's over. I'm out of the game. And so are you."

"Wait a second." I waved my hand. "You're out of what game?"

"Walsmear's game. His fairy—thing."

"I'm sorry. Could you be more explicit?"

"Why should I? The whole situation is ludicrous in

the extreme. My dear Mr. Castle, there are no such things as fairies. Not in my garden. Not anywhere."

"Did Walsmear show you the enlargement? The one with the figure in it?"

"Yes. And I saw nothing."

"You must think we're mad."

"I don't think Michael is mad—exactly. His conscience bothers him. He killed my wife, you know. In an accident. I was able to get over it. He wasn't. Now he's seeing things. And he's using you."

"I'm not easily used," I said, trying to sound—I don't know—tough.

"Yes," Templeton said in reverie. "She died in that very room you're sleeping in. Walsmear carried her in. She was broken. Broken and bleeding. Battered beyond repair."

Now here was a tough man. Templeton talked about his wife's accident without a trace of emotion. I wondered if he had "gotten over" his wife's death, or simply never faced it. Being able to make this penetrating observation made me feel superior to my host. I needed it, too. I felt hopelessly at sea. A minister cavorting naked in a moonlit garden. A constable consumed with guilt. Syphilitic Templeton. Crazy Castle. Anna and Clara. Lonely Linda. My head injury began to ache.

"What sad men we are," Templeton said, tracing a design in the dust on the mantelpiece.

"Some of us are sadder than others," I said. "But you, at least, have Anna and Clara."

"They won't remember our sorrows. And the world will crush them, too. The way it crushes us all."

Templeton looked up at me. His eyes had milky highlights. The skin hung in pouches beneath them. I pitied the man. I hadn't guessed it, but he was pitying me in turn.

"And you're the saddest of us all, Castle," he said. "An opportunist without an opportunity. I suggest you move out tomorrow. Go back where you came from. This fairy business is—" Templeton waved his long, bony hand "—over."

CHAPTER TWENTY-ONE

How I Discovered the Policeman's Strange Secret

MICHAEL WALSMEAR MAY HAVE BEEN an unconventional policeman, but he did subscribe to one of the great traditions of his calling: He was never around when you needed him.

It was the next day. I had bidden farewell to Anna and Clara. Then I left my valises behind the bar at the Starry Night. The innkeeper seemed to know all about where I had been and what I had been doing. Actually, my adventures seemed to be a subject of which he was already tired. But—wiping his hands on his apron—he was happy to step outside and direct me to the Burkinwell police station. Perhaps he anticipated some new wrinkle to my story.

The police station was a gloomy little house that did not reflect the majesty of the law. The door creaked as I pushed it open. I found two uniformed functionaries inside. One was a senior officer. He was giving directions to the other man, who was pecking out words on a typewriter.

"Get that spelling right," the senior man said, bending over the other's shoulder. "It's Walsmear. W-a-l-s-m-e-a-r."

"Walsmear?" I stepped up to the railing without introducing myself. "I happen to be looking for Constable Walsmear. Do you know where I can find him?"

The two men looked up at me.

"No," said the senior man.

Then the two went back to their work.

"Only one L," the senior man admonished.

"Know it well enough," the other fellow said.

"Are you sure this is the right form?" said the senior man.

"I believe so, sir. Says right here. 'Disciplinary—Form 117 dash K.' "

"Never had to do one of these," said the senior man. "But, I suppose there's a first time for everything."

"Excuse me," I interrupted. "I can't help but hear that you're talking about Constable Walsmear. And I'm looking for him myself."

"So are we," said the senior man. He gave me a sly look. "American, are you?"

"Yes," I said.

"You're that one who's been staying at Templeton's, eh? Had a little trouble over at the Gypsy camp? Been spending time in the church basement with the minister's wife?"

"Are you accusing me of something?"

"Not I. No, sir. Not I. Some things are not the business of the police. Not unless you start frightening the horses, stop the chickens a-laying, or otherwise disturb the peace." He laughed. "But tell me," he said, leaning casually against the railing . . . "Where is Michael Walsmear?"

"I just asked you that question," I said. "I've been looking everywhere for him."

"Have you tried his house?" asked the senior man.

I had.

Walsmear lived in a rundown little house with a morose dog tethered out front. The helpful old lady next door informed me that "Little Mikey" had grown up in the house, with his mother—dead long about a decade now. Mikey wasn't about much these days. And as she had for years, she fed the dog when he was away. No, he didn't tell her when he was going. The dog would start to yelp after a few days, and she'd know to feed it. Did she know where he went? No—but he was always partial to the Gypsies. Maybe he was out there. They were a bad lot, of course. One or two she'd met were all right; but you have to take your friends where you find them in this world, and Mikey can't be faulted for wanting to be by his friends. . . .

"Yes, well." The senior man picked up some papers to rattle while he spoke. "These behavior cases can be tricky. After all, when a man's served on the force for as many years as—well, you owe him some consideration. But how much? Eh? How much? There's some things you just can't allow. Just can't allow an officer to wander off duty in the middle of the day. No, sir. Can't have it. Can't have him walking around in half a uniform. Or none. And earrings? No, sir. Out of the question. No officer can be permitted to stroll about wearing a Gypsy earring. It's just not proper."

"So you can't help me?" I said.

"I'm sorry."

"And you can't find him either?"

"If you should learn anything, let us know. That's a good fellow."

Back at the Starry Night, Cole informed me that my old room awaited. "First we got to clean it," he said. "Gave it to a man while you were gone. Salesman, I think. He ate crackers in bed. Left crumbs everywhere."

I went upstairs and found Esmirelda attacking the crumb problem with a broom. I dropped into the chair and watched. She swept with slow dreamy strokes, like a punter. Her hips and shoulders rolled; her cheap, ill-fitting shift clung in all the wrong places.

"I'll be sweeping this floor for weeks," she said in her slow, singsong contralto. "There'll be another man sitting in that chair. Then another. I'll be sweeping up the crumbs that've hidden from me now."

"Can't get them all, can you?" I pleasantried.

"They hide, you know. They fall down in the cracks and under the table legs. They get down into the yarns of the rug. People walk over them and they work their way out. For months, they'll be working themselves out, these crumbs."

"Hard to find, then?"

"Who?"

"I beg your pardon."

"Who's hard to find?"

"I didn't say who. I said 'what.' I meant 'what.' "

"You're looking, aren't you?"

"Looking for what?"

"Him."

"Who?"

"The Gypsies."

"What? What about them?"

"They're not like you."

"What do you mean?"

"They don't judge him." She continued to sweep, broad, steady strokes. "That's why he goes to them."

"You mean Walsmear?"

"Whatever."

"Do you know where he is? Is he out at the Gypsy camp?"

"I wouldn't chase after him there. Remember what happened to you last time."

"I'm not chasing him anywhere."

"Bah. You and the likes of you. You and that Brian Templeton. You'd torture him, you would. For one mistake."

"I'm not sure I—"

"Well, you needn't bother. He's been torturing himself. Plenty. For ten years."

"How am I torturing Michael Walsmear?"

"His little dreams of fairies. You'd smash it, wouldn't you? It would solve all his problems and you'd just smash it. You're just like all the rest."

This was too much. Standing up, I walked over and grabbed the broom from her hands. She wouldn't look at me. I took her hands in mine. "Esmirelda," I said, trying to catch her averted gaze. "Please, please tell me what you are talking about."

Her deep, liquid brown eyes lifted and searched my face. "You know," she said, though her tone utterly lacked conviction.

"I do not know. What is Walsmear's little dream of fairies?"

"Mrs. Templeton."

"He killed her. I mean, he accidentally ran her down."

"She ran under his wheels."

"Yes?"

"Use your head. A grown woman? She don't know how to cross the road? Some say she did it on purpose."

"Suicide?"

"Some says."

"Remorse."

"About what?"

"Sin."

"What sin?"

"What other sin? A woman. Married. Out there in that little cottage. Not many sins she can commit. Just murder and—"

"Adultery."

A thrill passed from Esmirelda's fingers to mine. At that moment, I knew I should break our physical contact. But I didn't want to break her flow of revelations.

"I never knew her," she whispered. "But they say she was a good woman. Look at the faces of her children if you don't believe it."

"I believe it."

"If something happened between her and another man, one of her husband's friends, say—her husband's only friend, say . . ." She was silent for a moment. Then: "She might not be able to live with that."

"Walsmear? Walsmear and Templeton's wife?"

"Things happen between people."

Esmirelda's slightly sticky hands crept from my fingers to my forearms until she held my arms by the elbows. She was a big girl, and her eyes were almost level with mine. An image of the small, four-paned window swam in her sable pupils.

"What," I asked, trying not to blow breath into her face, "does that have to do with fairies?"

"What if she didn't just happen to run under the car? What if something was chasing her?"

"Fairies? Chasing her out of the garden?"

"Michael never told me. But he told the board of—of—the men, who sat at the big table—"

"The board of inquiry."

"He told them she was acting strange as she ran out. She was grabbing at the air. Like she was being chased by a swarm of bees, maybe."

"Maybe she stumbled onto a hive."

"No one ever found the hive."

Esmirelda's dreaminess seemed to be catching. I felt like we were talking about persons who didn't exist, like characters in a book, whose most mortal dilemmas could be pondered and tossed about for inconsequential amusement and reflection.

"I have another explanation," I said, with thoughtless dispassion. "Maybe he killed her. Perhaps they quarreled. He jumped in the car. She tried to stop him. He ran her down."

Esmirelda shook her head. "You don't know him," she said.

Her arms slid under mine. She spoke into my clavicle, for to look into my eyes now would bring her lips close, so close to my face. At that moment, I realize now, I should have withdrawn. By not doing so, I joined her in an implicit compact. Together, without consciously admitting it to ourselves, we had ascended a peak. We were tempting gravity. Now it would draw us down. Together. We would not tumble down, to land bruised and battered atop a mound of rubble. It might have been better if we had. Instead, we floated down on a cloud. So easy. We closed our eyes and launched ourselves into the air. And when we opened them, it was a different world. The peak was far beyond us, and nevermore accessible.

"But the fairies," I said.

"Suicide or accident, Michael still has to live with himself. Let him think it was fairies chasing her out of the garden. Let him have some peace."

I murmured some assent, as her lips slid up and down over mine, and we simultaneously sank onto the bed. My senses were filled with Esmirelda's pale olive flesh, and the mixed odors of the kitchen and cleaning closet, blending in her hair with the sweet sweat of her temples. The bed groaned beneath us, and now and again there was a scraping and shuffling outside the door, as if someone were listening there, or peeping through the keyhole. From the ceiling came a creaking, as though someone were pacing irritably. A burst of coarse laughter rose from the bar.

CHAPTER TWENTY-TWO

How I Learned the Girls' Strange Secret

I MIGHT HAVE CONFIDED EVERYTHING to Linda Drain. As it was, I'd told her nothing, not thinking, or only half-considering, that absent accurate information, people simply form their own wild suppositions. I should have told her the whole situation the next afternoon as I perched on the edge of the uncomfortable sofa in her sitting room, sipping tea from a delicate cup and gazing into her extraordinarily sympathetic smile.

"Mrs. Drain," I should have said. "Linda—may I

call you Linda? Thank you. I can't tell you how much I've appreciated your kindness and consideration. You've helped me set up a darkroom. You haven't asked any probing questions. You've accepted me and let me go my own way in Burkinwell. But I can't believe you really accept the story I gave you about why I am here. I wouldn't blame you. I don't even remember what it is myself.

"Let me put your mind at ease. Let me explain everything. I've come here to Burkinwell to save my business. I need money and I need it soon. I'm not planning to borrow the money I need. Nor am I really prepared to earn it. My plan is to come into sudden riches through a farfetched, unlikely scheme only an idiot would consider feasible."

(Linda would probably try to reassure me here, as her eyes grew wide with empathic wonder. The essence of her remarks would be that I was surely not an idiot—an insulting form of reassurance that I would have brought upon myself.)

"Wait," I would have said, "until you hear the scheme. You see, your constable, Mr. Walsmear, came to me with some photographs showing the two Templeton girls sporting with sprites, playing with peris, basking with brownies—that is to say, consorting with real, live, actual, and existing fairies. Silly, you say? Perhaps. But Arthur Conan Doyle didn't think so. Yes, the famous author and spiritualist. He had his own set of completely different fairy pictures. And he wants ours off the market. Do you understand?"

Here, she might have nodded, but her sympathy would have grown less earnest.

"Thank you, Linda, for bearing with me so far. Here,

then, is the essence of the business I am on in Burkinwell. Doyle wants to destroy our pictures, as they are rivals to his own. He is willing for me to acquire the pictures from the Templetons and make them disappear. And he is willing to pay me for this service. I intend to do just that and gladly pocket the money.

"But here's the good part. I have a little trick up my sleeve. I will destroy the pictures Doyle wants—and then take my own fairy pictures. These pictures will be the true, authentic fairy pictures. I will own them. I will control them. The whole thing will be worth a fortune. And not only to me, but to Walsmear, Templeton, Anna, and Clara—you, even, if you like. We'll be rich, rich, rich!"

As it happened, I said none of it. Linda and I spent a pleasant afternoon talking about America, religion, books, and photography. From overhead came the occasional rustle of Rev. Drain, working on a sermon or something at his desk. Twice he called down for tea and biscuits to fortify himself. Outside of that, he left the two of us alone.

In conversation, Linda was stimulating and surprising. I could imagine her making an impression far beyond that prettily decorated but barren sitting room. She might (and still might) shine in London or New York. Before and after that afternoon, I will admit that I imagined myself selling my studio and supplies, paying my debts, and convincing her to run away with me on some wonderful adventure to Paris, New York, or San Francisco. Across the short expanse of hooked rug between us, we two were like the tines of a tuning fork, vibrating (I thought) in extraordinary sympathy. One of us, it seemed, could not say something to the other without provoking the most marvelously unpredictable, yet perfectly agreeable, response in the other.

As we tripped lightly from one topic to the next, I felt our two spirits merging and rising out of the little sitting room and coming together on some plane not precisely exalted, but surely sweet nonetheless.

Protracting such a delightful visit would have been to risk spoiling the weightless perfection of its tone, so I forced myself to rise and take my leave somewhat in advance of my true inclinations. As I stood at the foot of the stairs, saying good-bye to Linda, a door opened above and the Rev. Drain finally appeared, wearing slippers and an open-collared shirt.

"Well, well, well." He descended the steps, somewhat stiff-jointedly I thought. "You must think me very rude, Mr. Castle. But I've learned over the years that it is fatal to break the spell when the fever of creation is upon me."

I must have looked at him quizzically, for he explained, "Writing a sermon. New one. Might be good. Might be a disaster. That is what I'll learn once the fever subsides."

"I'm sure it will be wonderful, dear," Linda said, taking his hand.

Seeing the two of them at the foot of the stairs, gazing at each other's eyes in what for all the world appeared to be genuine connubial coadmiration, I recalled the scene in Templeton's garden the previous night, savored the still humming pleasure of the conversation just completed, and grew almost dizzy with the heady advantage I had over both mortals standing before me. Though neither Linda Drain nor her husband had anything to do with my purpose in coming to Burkinwell, fate had somehow cast them into what—had I chosen to exercise it—could only be called my power.

Of what use was this "power" to me? I was attracted to Linda, but outside of my fantasies I had no desire to abduct her from this airy parsonage and chain her to my uncertain fate. And though I was sickened by Rev. Drain's solitary nocturnal orgy (for reasons that seemed somewhat obvious, but which may not have borne close scrutiny), it could not benefit me in any way to destroy his career by exposing him to public obloquy.

To bear this kind of power and not to use it can bring about a certain pleasurable intoxication, which I thoroughly enjoyed as I backed, nodding agreeably, out the door of the Drains' parsonage and bounced out through the gate and into the road.

Perhaps it was an excess of tea, or some residual effervescence from my conversation with Linda, but I felt a surge of energy and high spirits as I walked back through Burkinwell toward the Starry Night. It was late Saturday afternoon: The pocket of the weekend. Housefronts, walks, and gardens—the very air seemed pervaded with an air of relaxation and freedom. I passed neighbors chatting on doorsteps, children swinging lazily on gates, and girls walking arm in arm with warmly scented baskets of fresh bread. Hearing a rattling on the stones behind me, I stepped aside and was passed by a group of Gypsies, their wagon loaded with town provender.

Should I hitch a ride with them? I wondered. If Walsmear was at their camp, now was as good a time as any to seek him out. But I rejected this activity as far too heavy for my mood, which was one for the flourishing of happy plans and carefree imaginings.

Here, now, what was next for me? I imagined. Perhaps I could gather up my equipment from the church, pay my bill at the Starry Night, and return to London tomorrow. Bury this bizarre little episode in my life behind me in Burkinwell's not-likely-to-be-disturbed obscurity. I could face my economic dilemmas with courage and cheer, and survive to fight another day with many still-vigorous years of manhood ahead of me. Running alongside the plan was another, completely opposite scheme. Why, I wondered, should I ever leave Burkinwell? Wasn't that small town a kind of paradise in its own modest way? I would surely never get rich there, and the company (aside from Linda) would hardly be sparkling. But I could survive by supplanting the town's resident photographer, with his ancient camera, moth-eaten bellows, frayed, dusty backdrop, and overfondness for drink.

So many choices! Savoring my mood, I did not head directly for the inn, but took a wide circle around the town, strolling down as many unfamiliar ways as I happened upon. At one point, I found myself angling a little farther into the countryside than I had intended, and so began circling back through a field that, at first, I didn't recognize, but while I was in its midst realized was the field adjoining the Templeton cottage. Rather than passing the cottage directly, I backtracked a little, and hopped over the fence onto the road where it curved around beyond the factory.

Once again, I was on the bend around which Michael Walsmear drove his motorcar on what the penny dreadfuls might call "that fateful afternoon" when he struck Mrs. Templeton. Walking around the curve now, I imagined what it might have been like for him, high up in the driver's seat while the motor putted ahead of or behind him, the leaf springs creaked beneath, and the wind blew around the glass and through his hair. Perhaps he was admiring the view from his bouncing perch, the gray stone walls, neat fields, and lush treetops swelling like hills above the scattered rooftops. Perhaps his eye was taken by the pointed sparkle of broken glass from the ruins of the factory, or the more sinuous reflections of the little stream that tumbled for a while alongside the road.

Whatever pleasant thoughts occupied him as he approached the far end of Templeton's garden, the very place I was now walking toward, they must suddenly have been overwhelmed by the awful, horrible helplessness of those who witness fate hurtling along its path at a pace too rapid and inexorable for intervention. And so he must have seen her disappear under the front edge of the bonnet, must have rocked with the ba-bump, ba-bump as the wheels passed over her body . . .

This is as it might have been, I thought, passing the scene, if the policeman's story was true. On the other hand, if, as was possible, Walsmear purposefully ran her down in a moment of passion and anger—what terrible, dark, and malevolent currents would have been flooding his soul as he passed this way!

The thought gave me a kind of chill that had nothing to do with the temperature. I actually hugged myself as I stopped beside the garden to let it pass. To the west, the sun was lowering toward the treetops. Skylarks, dark as commas, sailed above the tallest branches, and from leafy rooms, an easy, desultory twittering announced the coming dusk. I looked down at the garden to admire the effect of the slanting sun on its colors. To my surprise, Anna and Clara were there, playing amid the wands of blossoms.

I had not seen them at first. And they had not seen me. The reason for the latter, I guessed, was their deep involvement in some sort of imaginary sport. In solemn silence, and with faces possessed by a still absorption, they appeared to be chasing some thing or things down the path and through the byways between the flower beds. I recalled myself at their age chasing squirrels across Boston Common, or going after butterflies outside my aunt's house in Quincy. What were these girls going after now? Midges? Fireflies? Fairies?

My pulsebeat suddenly roared in my head. Oh, why didn't I have my camera?

They had to be chasing fairies. It made perfect sense. Whatever charm brought the fairies out would not likely operate when adults like myself, Walsmear, or Templeton were about. Otherwise some one of us would have seen them earlier. It was when the girls were alone and—I imagined—the air was charged with the full magic of their innocence that the fairies came out to play.

I almost dared not move lest they see me. But to observe them better, I had to take slow steps toward the fence. As I did so, all question of their playing a game of the imagination vanished. Their little eyes were both focused on something real. Sometimes the pupils of both would converge on the same precise spot. Other times they would diverge, clearly being led by things that flew before them. Moving points in space that they alone could see.

What would they do when they caught a fairy? I wondered, if indeed they were trying to catch fairies. An unsatisfactory answer came to me as I watched the younger girl, Clara, suddenly stop and put her hands together as if holding something between them.

Stopping my breath, I watched her quickly shift the

invisible thing to the fist of her left hand, while giving a sharp twist over it with her right. At the end of this quick operation, she opened her hands, gave them a little shake, and went on pursuing another invisible point. Anna, standing a little way off, stopped and did almost the same thing: holding whatever it was in her left hand, then giving a twist with the other, almost as if she were taking the lid off a jar.

Astounded, and totally mystified, I took a moment when both their backs were turned and dropped to my haunches. Quietly and painfully, I duck-walked toward a portion of the garden wall overhung with a tall shrub where I might more comfortably hide and observe. Over the course of about ten minutes, I saw the girls appear to catch whatever quarry it was they pursued many times. And each time, they gave that little twist of the wrist before opening their hands and resuming the chase.

Never had I seen children so exhaust themselves in play. Yet the sport seemed utterly without merriment. Damp strands of hair flipped about their faces as they ran, stopped, crouched, and pounced through the flowers. Clara stopped at one point and began blinking and rubbing her dark-circled, red-rimmed eyes with her fists. Stretching, she squinted up into the sky as if waking from sleep and walked slowly toward the wall behind which I hid. Searching the ground around a certain low shrub, she crouched, then stood up again holding a small flower she had apparently plucked from the ground. Listlessly, as if performing an onerous duty, she stuffed the flower into her mouth, stem, leaf, and all. The moment she did so, she spotted me peering at her over the wall.

"Hello, Clara." I smiled cheerfully.

She didn't answer, but impassively spat the flower out of her mouth.

"Is that good manners?" I said.

"Mr. Castle!"

The shout came from her older sister, who came running over, apparently glad to see me. The younger girl stepped back.

"Now what are you girls up to?" I asked. "Eating flowers?"

"We're saving them," Anna said.

"Saving the flowers?"

"No," Anna said, confused for a moment, then giving forth a weary giggle. "Not the flowers."

"What's he say?" asked Clara.

"Not the flowers." Anna confused the girl further. To me: "The fairies."

"You're saving the fairies?"

"From . . . from . . ." the younger girl tried to name something for which, it appeared, there was no name.

"The little men," Anna chirped. She turned to Clara. "The little men."

"What are the little men doing?" I asked.

"They're . . . they're . . ." Clara began again.

"Hurting them," Anna said. "They're hurting the—"

"Hoy!"

There was a shout from the cottage door. It was Brian Templeton, calling the girls in for their evening meal (it seemed that their new domestic regularity had survived my absence). Spotting me, he came walking over as the girls obediently ran inside.

"Just taking a last look, I hope," he said, folding his arms as he approached the wall.

I nodded. "I'm considering going back tomorrow."

"A very good idea. The best thing for all, I think."

"I think so too," I said, a little irritated by his manner. I wanted to goad him a little. "Of course, there's nothing that truly compels me to go back there. You know, I might just settle down here in Burkinwell. I could set up a studio here. Maybe combine it with a camera shop and gallery. I think that kind of life might just suit me."

"That would not be wise, Castle." He frowned at me steadily. "This is not the American West. You can't simply plop yourself down wherever you fancy and set up a life. The names in this town go back centuries. You have to be known to be accepted here. You have to be known or liked. If the people are against you, you don't have a chance."

"Well, thank you for the advice. I'll keep it in mind."

With a wave of my hand, I set off down the road. Glancing back, I saw him watching my departure, as if to make sure I was well and truly gone. From a stranger, to a guest in his home, to the man who might make him rich by photographing fairies in his garden, I had finally become for him a kind of enemy, it appeared. Or, at the very least, I was a discomfort and persona non grata. As far as I could see, I had no cause for self-rebuke in this becoming so. The status of my relations with Templeton had always been outside my control, his emotions clearly being steered by winds loosed in tempests long past.

The sun, the air, and the freedom of the day left me Saturday-afternoon tired by the time I returned to the Starry Night. The public room was crowded with strangers, in town for some commercial reason. I sat among the group for some time, listening to the talk and stories, but not really participating in the company. My mind was not held by the topics of motorcars, horses, crops, or the weather. Nor was I preoccupied by thoughts of fairies, or, curiously, the mysterious activities of Anna and Clara and the "little men."

Almost to my own surprise, I found my mind crowded with a single image. It was an image that filled me with a terrible longing and sense of my own loneliness. It was the eyes, face, lips, hands, waist, and curving lips of Linda Drain as I had gazed upon them amid the plush and tea things of the afternoon.

I was aware that I myself felt strongly toward her almost from the moment of our meeting in the railway carriage. And it was no vain fancy of mine to believe that she in her turn was not indifferent to me. But up until now, I had felt myself constrained. I had put a limit on how far I would allow myself to dream of Linda Drain. She was, after all, married. And married to quite a decent fellow, as far as I could see.

My discovery of Rev. Drain's nocturnal ramble, however, had changed my opinion drastically. I wasn't quite sure what I had seen, but I was certain that it was "faithless," in some serious way, to Linda. The man had, as the jazz singers might put it, "done her wrong." To be writhing in sensual frenzy, alone, in a dark garden, while a woman such as Linda, ripe, eager, and narrow-waisted, lay alone amid the cold sheets, was, to my mind, a kind of senseless criminal act.

Therefore, I felt free to admit my feelings. And those feelings were simple. I loved Linda Drain. I desired her.

Of course, it was insane. Adolescent. But as I admitted these feelings to myself, I realized that I would not be leaving Burkinwell for London the next day. Or the day after. The thought that Linda Drain might be close would be enough to hold me in that little town. To weight me with longing, to confuse my ambitions, and probably to drive me to despair.

It was with an incredible melancholy that I dragged myself up the stairs to my room. I was, of course, spiritually prepared to love Linda in secret forever, to endure the hidden torture of my soul, and to go to my grave with her name seared in cipher on my exhausted heart. What I could not endure at that moment, however, was the impossibility of any physical union with the woman I loved.

My sense of physical longing became particularly acute as I entered my room where, as Esmirelda had predicted, the crumbs were still working themselves out of the floorboards. I had, in fact, a very rich sense of Esmirelda as I stood by the bed recalling the feel of her voluptuousness beneath the threadbare quilt. Where was she at that moment? I wondered, and then spotted a piece of paper protruding from under my pillow. It was a note. In a crude scrawl, it read, "We cannit meet here. Meet me jympsee camp. Tonit—Esmirelda."

Yes, I thought, I will meet her. I will discharge my longing there, even as I despair that the great, low, inarticulate girl is not another. The body, if not the heart, shall have its release.

It was dark as I left the Starry Night, set out down the road, and went looking for the Gypsy camp. It would not be the experience I most wanted, I thought, but it would be good. Very good, in its own way.

The Gypsy camp, however, proved elusive. It was not in the wood where I had visited it before. Searching for it through grove and dale, I spent the evening chasing lights, shadows, fluttering bats, and lumbering cattle across the shadowy landscape.

By midnight, I had given up in despair. Wishing I had at least borrowed a bicycle, I set wearily off on foot back toward the town, wondering how to get myself readmitted to the inn without the unpleasant necessity of waking Cole.

From the place where I had decided to return, the most natural route took me, once again, down the road past Templeton's. For the second time in twenty-four hours, I found myself rounding the bend toward the cottage; and as I did so, I had a queer fancy, seeing the darkened structure emerging from behind the wood.

The cottage, I fancied, looked like a sleeping man. The windows on the upper story were the eyes (now shuttered); the two large windows on the lower floor were the spots of two large, rosy cheeks; and the door was a squarish kind of mouth. Beneath what would be the cottage-face's chin, the garden began and spread out in a great rectangular square like an enormous bedspread covering a vast recumbent sleeper.

This notion that the cottage was a sleeping face and the garden its blanket was, as I said, merely a notion or fancy. But it was so striking as to make me stop and enjoy it for a moment. Indeed, the rounded rooftop (tiled in the shape of its thatch predecessor) might have been an old-fashioned sleeping cap, and the chimney a—what?—a tall feather or a pipe tucked behind the ear. While I was pleasing myself with this view, I noticed some movement in one of the cottage's cheeks.

Squinting into the darkness, I observed the shutters of the lower right hand window slowly push open from within. As I had done earlier that day, I hastened over to the garden wall and hid myself behind it.

Peering over the edge, I saw a small figure draped in white emerge from the window and drop to the ground. This was followed, a moment later, by a second figure, similarly garbed, who, as the first had done, ran for the garden the moment she touched the ground.

It was, of course, Anna and Clara. With their nightclothes billowing around them, they sped down the pathway to a spot not far from where I was hiding. There, I saw them bend and each pick a tiny blossom from the same spot where I had seen Clara pick one earlier that day. And as Clara had done then, both did now, each popping a flower into her mouth.

Not caring to be observed, I ducked down as Clara turned in my direction for a moment, chewing with a slightly pained expression on her face. I could hear the girls rustling out amid the flowers, whispering inaudibly between themselves. When I again looked up, I saw them grimly pursuing the same business I had surprised them at earlier. There were chasing some invisible things and occasionally catching them. And when they had caught one, they made that jerking, twisting motion with their hand, and went on to capture some others.

I could not imagine what the girls were doing, and Anna's explanation that they were "saving the fairies from the little men" was not very helpful as I could see neither fairies, little men, or anything else in the moonless night.

Behind a wall in more ways than one, I wondered if the girls were under some kind of spell. In fairy lore, I recalled, there was something called the "glamour," which was a kind of trance into which the fairies struck mortals to make them do their bidding.

As I was wondering this, I found myself creeping alongside the wall toward where the girls had picked their little flowers. Another part of my mind had seized on the flowers as perhaps offering an answer, and the rest of my too-contemplative self was somewhat surprised to be dragged along by its purpose. Soon, however, my whole self was acting in concert. It was beyond question that the girls were eating the flowers for some good reason, and I intended to find out what it was.

Waiting for a moment when their backs were turned, I bent over the wall and fished through the plant life around the shrub on the other side until my fingers closed around a tiny flower. After shaking off the loose dirt, I stuck the flower into my mouth and chewed.

Sitting back against the wall, facing the deserted road, I slowly masticated the rough vegetable matter. The flower had an initially sour, weedy taste followed by a distinctly sweet note. As I licked the remnants off my teeth, I noticed a kind of mist rising far out on the other side of the farmer's field directly across from where I sat. It was a little like the fog that forms along country ground in the early morning; but morning, I knew, was a long way away. What struck me about the mist was that it didn't lie over the ground in a normal way, like a cloak, but seemed to move with a sinuous undulation, like a ribbon waving slowly in the breeze.

Staring, I noticed that the mist seemed to run off around the distant tree trunks, where it curled around their roots and—I almost didn't admit it to myself—glowed. Yes, it glowed! Or how else was I able to observe it so clearly from such a distance on such a dark night? As I rose onto one knee to observe the phenomenon more intently, another strange thing happened. The mist disappeared! But then when I stopped moving, it appeared again. There was some kind of optical phenomenon at work that allowed the mist to become visible when I held my head still, and caused it to be imperceptible when my eyes were in motion.

It was all very curious. I couldn't imagine what I was seeing. Was it really a glowing mist? Or was it some kind of illusion, swamp light, or will-o'-the-wisp? I stood up, determined to walk across the field and investigate. As it had before, the mist vanished as I moved my eyes, but became vividly clear when I stared. Indeed, standing up, I had my best view yet. The mist seemed even more ribbonlike than before. It even had a rather crisp edge.

I wondered if the girls had seen me yet. I did not care to frighten them, and so turned around to call their names and announce myself. But as I did so, what I saw in the garden struck the words from my lips.

CHAPTER TWENTY-THREE

How I Met the Fairies

THE GARDEN WAS ALIVE with misty tendrils. Glowing ribbons of light curled and flowed through the flowers and over the pathway. Here, they bent in long, looping folds. There, they tapered off into baroque curlicues. They flowed from the trunk of the massive old tree like streamers from a maypole.

My first thought was that all the streamers in the garden were emanating from the massy, creviced bark of the old tree itself. But a look beyond disclosed other, corollary streams flowing down in gauzy rolls and curls from the vicinity of the factory and the grove of ferns.

In my eyes, these were the impressions of but a second. The mist grew vague as I physically moved, or jerked my head even slightly. So it was that much of it vanished as I began scanning the garden for Anna and Clara, to see how they fit into this phenomenon.

The girls, however, had seen me first. They were standing near the trunk of the great tree, staring at me, their hands clasped apprehensively at their waists. As I stared, I saw the mist again, rippling and waving around them.

"Anna, Clara," I said in a loud whisper. "Don't be afraid. It's me. Mr. Castle. Tell me, do you see it? Do you see all this?"

Clara took a few steps toward me. "We don't mean to," she said, mysteriously. "But they're hurting them, Mr. Castle. They're hurting them."

"Hurting who? Who's hurting who?"

"The fairies, they're—"

"Fairies? Where? Tell me, Clara. Where are the fairies?"

Clara looked from side to side with a slightly confused expression, as if she didn't know quite what was expected of her. Then she stepped back, as if to get out of the way of something, and a tendril of mist parted around her back and rejoined in front of her. This streamer curled to within three feet of me, and as I stared at it, it began to flicker and waver. For a fraction of a second, the mists vanished, or re-formed somehow into what appeared to be a rippling frieze, covered with human figures. In the next fraction of a second, the figures became round. Where there had been a misty, flat ribbon, there now danced a group of perfect little female homunculi—each not more than ten inches tall. Smiling, laughing, even. Stark naked and curling their little fingers delightedly.

I blinked, naturally. And jerked my head in surprise.

Suddenly, I was overcome by a physical sensation I had never before felt. It was a thrill of fear I had previously only experienced in dreams of falling. The sensation was one of near-total disorientation. My mind had grasped that what I saw were indeed little people disporting in the air, that they were real, and not an illusion. But it also knew that this was impossible. And that if this impossible thing were real, all the things it had taken for real in the past might not be real. My rationally constructed view of the universe collapsed in that moment, baring the most ancient foundations of the human soul. My bowels loosed. And like a terrified, unreasoning animal, I ran.

Exactly how far I ran down the road, I do not remember. A mile, at least. And as my fearful sinews heated with exertion, my mind cooled and collected itself. Fear vanished. I slowed to a walk, and felt a new sensation overtake me. This was the sensation I should rightly have felt from the moment I saw the homunculi: a magnificent ecstasy; the thrill of discovering a new universe. As quickly as I had run away from the garden, I now ran back to it.

This time, I leaped over the wall and ran up the center walk.

"Anna, Clara," I said, coming up to the children and kneeling down between them. "Do you see them? Do you see the fairies?"

"Do you see them?" Clara asked.

"Yes, yes, yes. You dear girls. I ate the flower."

Clara reached out and touched my cheek. There were tears running down my face. I grabbed her little hand and squeezed it in mine.

"Where are they now? Where—?"

Seeing the fairies, I was learning, required a peculiar set of optical gymnastics and constant attention to the act of observation. I had to both look and to *not* look: to stare hard out of the corner of my eye, to swoop in with the full pupil, then look away and swoop in again at the last possible moment. With practice, this paradoxical way of seeing became easier, and soon I was able to fix the fairies one by one in my eye. At this moment, I descried some ten to fifteen fairies in my near vicinity. That it was late at night and very dark did not at all prevent their being seen with full clarity, given that one performed the optical exercises described above. The fairies "glowed" (for want of a better word) with a light of their own. It was not a vulgar, electrical sort of light, nor had it the sharpness of the firefly's cool beacon. The fairies' was a subtle luminosity, for which I can think of no parallel in nature, but which resembled somewhat the images thrown from a dim magic lantern.

Since I am describing the fairies' light, let me describe their walk. They did not appear to walk as we do, flat-footed and hip-heavy; nor did they walk precisely on the tips of their toes, like a corps de ballet. Instead, they stepped with a weightless bounce, as if they were underwater. And they were by no means tied to the ground, seeming to have access to some kind of invisible aerial walkways on which they ascended and descended over and around the shrubs, pathway, and beds of flowers. I cannot say for certain, but the topography of these walkways roughly corresponded to the curling ribbons of mist.

As I knelt between the girls, I watched a fairy come toward us. Gliding to earth on the flagstoned path, she stopped and appeared to be looking at us with the same corner-of-the-eye movements with which we were watching her.

As we faced each other on the path, I marveled at the perfection of her tiny body. Like all the others, she was ten or so inches high, slender-hipped, bare-footed, and buck naked. Whether she was old or young I could not tell. There was no hair at all on her body, except for the head, where it was fair and very long. It floated down around her shoulders and her back obeying the very languid gravity in which she moved. Though neither brown nor white, her skin could not be described as a single color. Like a beam of sunlight, she was all colors and no color at all.

Observing this creature and her fellows gave me a visceral delight. She was so cunningly formed in every detail. So like a perfectly animated doll. And when she gave her head a quizzical little tilt, as if she were wondering what kind of creatures *we* were, a little sob of pleasure caught in my throat.

Wishing this fairy to come closer, I held myself perfectly still, as I would trying to coax a squirrel to take a peanut from my hand. But fairies are not squirrels, and the two girls simply ran up and held out their arms to the fairy, who rewarded them with a smile and a little skipping, bobbing dance. Ducking under Anna's legs, the fairy pulled herself up the little girl's nightdress and circled up around onto her shoulder. There, she braced one leg on Anna's collarbone, grabbed a strand of the girl's golden hair, and swung around until she was directly in front of her face. There, she bent forward and gave Anna a kiss on the lips, before bounding down her arms and toward the branch of a nearby bush. From there, she flew into a bed of yellow yarrow and vanished.

(Here, let me add one more item to what might be a huge and contradictory rulebook of fairy visibility. To wit: When a fairy stops moving, it disappears.)

While watching this single fairy, I could not help being aware of the other fairies nearby. The movements of one seemed to affect them all. And since the fairy with whom I was interacting seemed to have the most intentionality in her movements, it was hers that seemed briefly to rule the others. There was no purpose to this elaborate minuet, and I can only state that when this one fairy jumped up on Anna's arm, I sensed that the others in the vicinity adjusted their movements in concert. I was reminded of a flock of birds, all turning in unison, linked by some unknown telegraphy.

Now other fairies were skipping, sailing, and bouncing toward us and past us. Where were they going? I wondered. It was difficult to tell, owing to the fugitive glimpses by which they were of necessity observed. They seemed to be coming from the direction of the great tree, and bounding toward the house, or the end of the garden, past which they were no longer to be seen.

Anna and Clara both had two or three fairies sporting through their hair, running up and down their arms, and balancing on their outstretched fingertips. Would the fairies do the same to me? Lowering myself to the grassy verge between the pathway and the flowerbeds, I leaned on one arm and waited. A second later, a fairy bounced and sailed and came to a stop on the ground directly in front of me.

She was looking at me, into my eyes, trying to understand me, I think, even as I was trying to understand her. Once again, I felt frightened and disoriented. Here was this creature from another world, a scientifically unknown dimension of the universe, trying to determine if I was real or an illusion, even as I did the same to her. A second later, I ceased to question the reality of both of us as the little creature danced onto my ankle and laughingly curled up in the crook of my knee. I could feel the slightest pressure from her tiny body through the cloth of my trousers and hose. Then, with an acrobatic little twist, she jumped up and onto my hand, which lay open at my side. I dared not move, though the sensation of her touch was chilling, outlandish, and totally overwhelming.

Now I felt the pressure of her toes on the backs of my fingers, one, two, three, as she hopped along. Though she weighed no more than a leaf, every nerve in my body prickled; a chill spread up my back and out around my shoulders; and the two points where her toes rested tingled with sensitivity.

Would she sail off if I turned my hand? I dared to do so, and was delighted to see that she stayed on. In fact, as I turned my hand further, she began to treat it as a game like rolling on a log, silently laughing all the while. Now she slid into the palm of my hand. Some reflex caused me to close my fingers gently around her hips. She slid out and upward a few inches, balancing one foot on the tip of my index finger. I made another tiny motion as if to grab hold of her, and she again bounced away, coming to rest on another finger.

Soon, we were engaged in a teasing game where I would ever so softly snatch at her, and she, with clear signs of delight, would evade me by dancing across my hand.

As we played this game, I could feel her arms and fingers and ankles brushing against my palm and fingertips. I found myself almost laughing out loud with the sheer, uncanny delight this caused me. As I finally did so, I found myself almost covered with fairies. They danced on my nose and cheeks, sported on my chest, and raced up and down my legs. Laughing ridiculously, I lay back on the ground and felt their pattering footsteps up and down my body.

Being touched by the fairies was an experience that was so far unlike anything that I had felt before, my mental workings had trouble finding their accustomed channels. As the fairies pattered over me, I felt myself being blown along as if by a fresh breeze. This splendid zephyr seemed to whisk away the accumulated experience of my adult life like so much dust, baring what lay beneath: that delightful childlike state where fascinations succeed one another without stopping, where curiosity aches and is satisfied and renewed with every glance.

As I felt this very literal touch of wonder, I delighted in the range of fairy shapes and sizes and the range of expressions they displayed. There was not one fairy "type." Each was an individual. Some were slim of hip and slender of shoulder. Others were riper in limb and hip, and rounder in bosom. Although faces were less easy to capture in the eye, it was clear that variety obtained there also. Some of the fairies had noses longer, flatter, or wider than others, with cheeks, chins, and foreheads corresponding. And these features were not for a moment passive. They were every moment expressing some emotion, whose sources, I'm sorry to say, were more mysterious to me than not. One second a fairy might be smiling (you could see their little teeth), and the next second she would be looking quizzical, wondering, or abashed. They might have been going through an emotive drill, like an actor, but there was nothing false or actorish in their manner.

As to their age, you could tell nothing by their skin or features; but some of the fairies displayed a whip-cracking energy I could not help associate with youth, while others moved with a measured grace I could not help attributing to greater age and maturity.

As I enjoyed observing the fairies and feeling them dance over me, my first feelings of wonder and curiosity gave way to a certain slackness of mind. This grew into a kind of torpor. The constant exercise of the eyes required to keep the fairies in sight left me somewhat confused as to what was of the fairy dimension and what was not. One moment, it would seem that the fairies were the only things that were real, and that the house, garden, and trees were all a flat mural painted around me. The next moment, the fairies would vanish and things would resume their ordinary roundness.

I grew sleepier. My limbs went slack, and I felt one arm rise from the thigh where it had been resting. Looking down, I saw that it was in fact being lifted by two of the fairies.

What could they possibly be doing? I was curious, but had not the energy to speculate or resist. As I watched, several other fairies came around and began lifting my elbow. My consciousness was overwhelmed by something I can only describe now as a kind of enchanted sleep, and I was aware that a whole troop of fairies had gathered around me. As my body dropped into the attitude of slumber, I had the impression that at the same time it was being lifted off the ground and carried floatingly along. A golden haze filled my mind and the velocity of my transportation seemed to accelerate. I was being motivated at an alarming pace. As I went faster and faster, my heart began to race, my stomach seized up, and all my muscles grew disobedient in their dread. Then, when it seemed like I had reached a truly awful rate of speed, I crashed. It was like slamming into a wall. There was a horrible, sickening second of unconsciousness. Then I awoke.

CHAPTER TWENTY-FOUR

How I Met the Little Men

I HAD NOT MOVED AN INCH. It was still very dark, and there were no fairies to be seen. Sitting up, I saw the girls over by the great tree. Though I could no longer see the fairies, they apparently could. I guessed, therefore, that the effects of the tiny flower were only temporary. Staggering over to the shrub where both the girls and I had been getting our flowers, I searched around and found another, which I picked and ate.

Recovering from both physical and mental exhaustion, I sat down against the wall and rubbed my eyes. I recalled how earlier, when I had eaten the first flower, and sat against the other side of this same wall, I had seen the fairy mist off on the other side of the neighbor's field. Now I stood up and looked again and, indeed, there was a long patch of fairy fog off across that field, near the edge of the wood.

And where else, I wondered, might I see the fairies if I walked this night with a pocketful of the little flowers? Were there patches of fairy life all over Burkinwell? All over England? Where did the fairies come from? And where did they go? I saw before me the outlines of a great architecture of knowledge yet to be discovered: a natural history of fairies that would keep generations of scholars immersed in study. Somewhere walked the man who would be our Darwin or Humboldt of fairies. There was much to think about. Much to do.

Turning back to the garden, I saw the tendrils of fairy mist reaching through the purple columbine and tall, white peonies. All thoughts of what the fairies meant to the world at large fled, and I felt an absolute hunger, a joyous need to look upon them once more, to be the object of a fairy smile.

Without getting up, I turned to a tendril of fairy mist that ended atop the wall about a foot from where I sat. Oscillating my head, I focused on the periphery of my vision and tried to bring the fairy or fairies into view. As I had known it would, a figure became visible. But it was not at all the type of figure I had expected. Instead of the lithe female forms with whom I had been playing, I now saw before me a grotesque little man. Like the female fairies, he was not much larger than ten inches. But his neck was almost nonexistent, and his head was nearly as wide as his shoulders. A rough beard hid most of his face beneath the eyes, and seemed to merge with the short, curly hairs that covered his chest and the rest of his body. The only parts of his body that lacked hairs were his outsized hands and feet and, oddly, his large, knobby genitalia.

I stared at him, and he stared at me. Then, unexpectedly, he bared his little teeth under his beard. Startled, I gave an involuntary jerk and momentarily lost sight of him. When I had got him refocused, he had begun to run, or at least to make a distinct running movement. For though his arms and legs were pumping, his actual rate of speed was slow, floating, as he appeared to be, through the same ether as the female fairies. As I watched, he made his way off the wall and down into a stand of purple baptisia.

I myself ran over to the two girls, who were crouched in anticipatory postures by the great tree. They were waiting for something. Waiting like two hunters in a blind. Anna shushed me as I approached.

"What are you waiting for?" I whispered.

Suddenly, a thick wave of fairy mist broke around the great tree, and ribbons and curlicues spread out from it in great profusion. Tendrils arched high under the branches and fell precipitately, quivering and pulsating with a nervous sort of agitation. Individual fairies were difficult to pick out amid the mist, as the pulsating ether produced an effect much like viewing a landscape from a fast car through an irregularly slatted fence.

What glimpses were possible revealed female fairies soaring through the mist's arcing tracery, motivating with graceful running, swimming movements. With hair flowing around their shoulders, they came in twos and threes, looking back over their shoulders, eyes wide and mouths making circles of apprehension.

They were clearly being chased. But by whom? I found out a moment later, when hard on the females' heels came the male fairies—I'll call them elves. The elves moved more firmly through the ether, their arms grasping and snatching at the females. For their part, the females managed to stay just beyond the elves at arms' length. But though they ran in earnest, they did not do so evasively, nor did they take advantage of such cover as the leaves and shrubbery might have offered.

All this, I repeat, was gathered from flickering, pulsating images such as were visible amid the agitated mist. And so also did I see what followed only in little bits and pieces: a flash of an image here and there, a brief glimpse of a key action, and long looks at unimportant movements.

Grasping and reaching, the elves finally began catching up to their quarry. When an elf came close enough, he grabbed a fairy by her long, flowing hair, which he wound around his fist. This seemed to be a kind of signal for the fairy to cease flight and allow herself to be pulled back toward the elf. Here the elf took her gently from behind, and locked in copulatory embrace, the pair tumbled to earth. What happened then was impossible to say, since they vanished before hitting the ground, like water droplets turning to steam over molten lava.

Once I gathered what was occurring, I looked about me and saw that the air was filled with fairy couples. They rolled, spun, and floated about me like weightless seed cases, or snowflakes slowly revolving in a souvenir paperweight.

As my first gasping moment of wonder passed, I suddenly became concerned for the girls. This sight, as natural as it might be for the fairies, was nothing for a human child to witness. These were, after all, not mating dragonflies, but creatures cast from a mold similar to that of the human beings around them. Gathering the girls around their shoulders, I suggested that perhaps it would be best if we left the fairies alone just then, that what we were seeing was probably very private for the fairies, and that someday the girls would understand, although now it might seem very confusing and alarming.

The girls, however, didn't even listen. Wriggling from my arms, they ran over and each grabbed one of the fairy couples. I could not stop them both, and as I took the fairy couple from Anna's hands, Clara rather expertly separated the male from the female of the couple she had taken and let the female trip away. The elf was not so lucky. Though he pumped his arms and legs, and worked his mouth in fierce expressions, he could not free himself from Clara's hand, which held him fast about the waist. Heedless of her captive's writhings and strugglings, Clara reached up and took his large head between her thumb and the first three fingers of her free hand. Then she gave it a sharp little twist, quickly and neatly breaking the elf's neck. Opening her hand, she let the lifeless body flop to the ground, and immediately reached for another.

Shouting a protest, I lunged for Clara, inadvertently freeing Anna, who proceeded to perform the same fatal operation on the male of another fairy couple.

"What are you doing?" I shook Clara by the wrist. "You're killing those little men."

Clara looked up at me confusedly. "They're hurting the fairies," she finally blurted. "The little men are hurting the fairies."

"No," I said. "It's not—not what you think."

"They're hurting them," she whispered, looking back at her sister.

How could I explain? Nature and the supernatural both perpetuated themselves the same way, it appeared.

"Take my word for it," I said, giving her wrist a shake. "Please go inside. Go back to bed."

Gathering Anna, I knelt before them both and explained that it was late and that their father would worry if he knew they were both out in the cold night air like this. Having seen what the girls had done to the elves, I was actually a little afraid of them at that moment. But they could not resist the authority of an adult voice. Meekly, they allowed me to lead them back to the window they'd come down from. I released them and watched them climb back inside. What I wanted to do next was go back into the garden and learn more about the fairies. I wanted to try to communicate with them, to find out where they lived, where they were going, what they ate. I knew they copulated. But where were the babies?

Study proved impossible. I was suddenly overwhelmed by an utter weariness. It was a fatigue such as I had never experienced. Was it the effect of the flower? I wondered. I still do not know. Whatever the cause, I lost all initiative for further pursuit of fairies that night. I was worried that I might simply drop off to sleep right there outside Templeton's cottage. I did not want to be discovered that way in the morning, so I dragged myself back to the Starry Night. There, I slept like a drunkard.

CHAPTER TWENTY-FIVE

How I Returned to the Garden

I AWOKE NEXT MORNING to a cold, damp wind blowing through the window. Esmirelda heard me stirring. She came into the room and closed the door behind herself. Her disappointment was manifest when she saw I was already up and about.

"I have to go out," I told her, and asked if she had an overcoat I could borrow. She went down into the cellar and came back with an enormous, tweed, raglan-sleeved monstrosity that had been left behind by a previous guest. The skirts of this garment flapped around my ankles as I headed out the door. I almost tripped over them as I chased Brian Templeton down the flagstone path of his garden.

"Brian," I shouted. "Stop. Don't waste—"

I grabbed him by the collar.

There were three of us there. Myself, Templeton, and Walsmear, who'd had a fight with his superiors. He was now an ex-constable. All three of us were shouting at once. Anna and Clara stood in the doorway of the cottage. They seemed to be cowering.

Amid curtains of clammy mist, we three grown men stamped through their flowers. We argued. We slipped. We turned the earth into mud underfoot.

"There's got to be more," Walsmear bellowed. He kicked a shrub. A shower of pink petals flew into the air. Some stuck to his muddy shoe.

"Stop, stop," I said. "We can't just crash about."

Templeton was in a snarling mood. "I can do what I want in my own garden," he said.

He stood there before me, staring furiously. In his fist, he clutched a single tiny flower. It was the kind the girls ate to see the fairies. We had been able to find no others in the daylight.

"How many of the flowers were there last night?" Walsmear angrily demanded. "How many did you see?"

"I hardly counted them," I said. "It's just a wildflower. There's got to be more."

"There isn't more," said Walsmear. "How do we know you haven't picked them all? How do we know you're not hoarding them?"

"Why would I tell you about the flowers if I was only going to hoard them? Anyhow, I was in no state of mind—"

"What state of mind were you in?"

I thought about it. "Have you ever," I said, "been terribly drunk?"

"Don't ask a stupid question."

"I mean," I went on, "so drunk that you felt sober?"

"You mean you were drunk last night?" Templeton raged, waving the fist that held the flower.

"No, no, no," I said. "I mean—oh, never mind." I was exasperated. "Listen," I said, "we've got to work together here. This can't be the only example of this flower in all of England. We'll find more. But we've got to go about it methodically. Right now, we're just damaging the garden. We could be stepping on fairies or elves right and left."

Walsmear jumped uneasily.

Templeton clutched the flower closer to his chest. "Whatever we do," he said, "whatever you find on my property is mine. And that includes this flower here and any others you might find. Do you understand that?"

"Of course I understand," I said.

"I don't want anything of yours," Walsmear said.

Templeton gave his old friend a lofty look. "Oh?" he drawled.

"Don't start, Brian." Walsmear shook his finger at him. "Just don't start."

"Start what?" Templeton asked. "I'll start anything I want. In fact, this is just as good a time as any to start something. If you're trying to start something."

"Stop, stop, stop," I said. Standing between them, I held out my arms. "Listen to me, gentlemen. We have to establish our next move. There's a great deal of work ahead. Please. Settle down. Don't spoil everything by fighting."

"I won't spoil anything," Walsmear scowled.

"I've got the flower." Templeton flared his nostrils. "And I may just eat it. Someone's got to find out if all this is true."

"No, no, no, hold on to it," I abjured. "Before anyone eats it, we have to record it. We have to sketch it. Or photograph it."

"Where's your camera?" Templeton asked. "Didn't you bring it? How convenient."

I ignored his barb. "We'll hold on to it for now.

Someone can go to the library and get a book on wildflowers. We'll find out what kind it is. We'll find out where they grow. Once we know where to look, we've got to go out and collect as many as we can while they're still in season. Then we can store them. Or we can give them to a chemist and distill their essence. But we've got to keep them secret, just as the girls did."

"But if it's a wildflower, anyone can pick one," Templeton said.

"So we've got to control that information. That's all we have to keep the fairies from becoming public property."

"Why not form a corporation or limited partnership," Templeton sneered.

I, however, had been contemplating just that. "That may be the only way we can profit."

"What an absurd notion. Fairies, Limited. It's a farce, that's what it is."

"You shut up." Walsmear stood in front of Templeton. "I got no job now, Brian, and I could use a little money. We've got to protect our property."

"Our property? This is my property you're standing on. All of this. Fairies and all. Don't come on all communal with me. It is all mine."

Walsmear seemed to guess that Templeton was getting a little frenzied. And for the first time since we met, I saw Walsmear attempt tact.

"Now, now," he said, trying to sound soothing. "Brian, you know we've been friends for a long time."

"Friends?" Templeton stood back and bent forward in anger. "Now that there's profit to be made you throw friendship in my face? After what you've done?"

The mist was gone, but the rain had gathered into

a steady downpour. I huddled under my giant coat and watched as Walsmear moved forward and stuck his nose right into Templeton's. Water streamed down their faces. They stared at each other from a distance of mere inches.

When Templeton spoke, his voice was quiet and husky. "She died right there," he said, pointing to the house. "I forgave you for that. Long ago. But what happened then won't happen again. What's mine is mine, Michael. Not yours. Not again."

Walsmear answered through clenched teeth. "Damn you, Brian. You know nothing. You understand nothing. Don't stand here—don't make a fool—don't make a fool of yourself."

Templeton laughed. "You made me a cuckold. Then you made me a widower. But I'll make a fool of myself if I please. Yes, damnit. I will make a fool out of myself."

It must not have been simple for Walsmear to be tactful and appeasing toward his old friend. Now he dropped all pretense. His face reddened and his fist shot out as if sprung from a box. It glanced off Templeton's shoulder and struck him on the chin. More stunned than injured, Templeton stumbled backward. Quickly recovering, he opened his hands and leaped for Walsmear's throat. Gripped about the neck, Walsmear pulled Templeton to the ground. There, they struggled through the flower bed. They tore at each other's faces. They pulled at each other's clothes. They threw punches that did not land. And they churned great portions of the garden into a morass of mud, pale green broken stems, and mangled blossoms.

It was Templeton who finally ended the hostilities. After being pushed into a bush, he decided not to get up and push Walsmear back. Instead, he rose (with branches crackling and snapping beneath him) and simply walked back toward the cottage. He did not look back.

Walsmear followed him at a distance of a few feet, shouting, "She didn't kill herself. I won't stand it anymore. She didn't. She loved both of us, Brian. Both of us. It was an accident, Brian. Don't you see, Brian? She ate one of these little flowers. She saw the fairies. She was frightened. She ran out into the road . . ."

He went on until Templeton gathered the girls (ashen-faced witnesses) and slammed the door in his face.

Esmirelda had told me that Walsmear believed the fairies had chased Mrs. Templeton out of the garden. It was that belief that had brought him and the photographs to London. But I hadn't thought much about the likelihood of the theory being true. Exactly why Mrs. Templeton ran out of the garden in front of Walsmear's motorcar would always be a mystery. At least as far as I had been concerned. Now, I gave the whole theory another pass through my mind.

The key for me was recalling what I had done when I first saw the fairies. What I recalled gave me a turn. When I had first sighted the little homunculi, I had been very afraid. I was so afraid that I ran. Blindly. If there had been a motorcar coming down the road just then, I would be dead now.

Walsmear stood for a moment staring at the cottage door. Then he turned angrily away and began walking down the road. He did so without a word or look in my direction.

I ran after him. He still didn't look at me. He didn't even acknowledge that I was there. Trotting alongside, I told him what I had just been thinking about my first reaction to the fairies. I told him how an instinctive fear had made me run.

"There was no thought behind it," I said. "My legs acted of their own accord. I heard it was like that in the war. During a bombardment. You wanted to run, didn't you? You couldn't help it. You just wanted to get up and run."

I still didn't know if he had heard me. He continued walking silently, face expressionless. I was about to give up and let him go on. Then he said, "Of course she was afraid. I was in the war. And that's what it was like."

"Yes," I said. "I was frightened because they were different. So different from everyday life. The mind rebels. The body follows. The same thing would have happened to Mrs. Templeton. Imagine if she had idly put one of those flowers into her mouth. Or if it had been on the back of her hand and she'd rubbed her hand against her mouth."

"Don't go on about it," Walsmear said, still not looking at me. "You don't know the whole story."

"I know some."

"Esmirelda."

"What about her?"

"Esmirelda?"

"She does talk," I said. I was embarrassed, but I didn't know why.

"That's not all she does."

"I beg your pardon?"

"I know what she's like."

"How is that?"

"You've been to bed with her."

I was silent.

Walsmear asked, "Do you love her?"

"Love her? I, well, no, I can't—"

Walsmear swung around to face me like a great door on hinges. "I *do* love her," he said.

I looked down. His thick finger lay against my chest.

"And you're going to be the last. I won't kill you. But you can tell everyone else you meet at the Starry Night that you were the last. The next man who goes to bed with her, I kill. Things are different now. I'm at peace. I know what happened and I'm at peace."

I guessed aloud that he meant this: He was at peace about the death of Mrs. Templeton.

"I'm glad if I helped," I said.

He nodded. "I'm going to marry her," he said. "I'm going to get on with my life. I'll go to Canada. Australia. Where you from?"

"Boston."

"I'll go there."

"Well, I wish you luck."

"Luck? What about our agreement? The photographs? Arthur Conan Doyle?"

"That's still on. But there's a problem."

"What's that?"

"Templeton has the pictures. And the negatives."

"That bastard."

"We can reason with him."

Walsmear spat. "I'm not reasoning with that bastard."

"What should we do?"

"You stay out of it."

"Me stay out of it?"

"I've got a plan."

"What kind of plan?"

"The less you know the better."

"What? Is it illegal?"

"I suppose breaking and entering are illegal."

"You can't do that. You're a policeman."

"Not anymore. And I don't plan to do it myself."

"You're going to hire somebody?"

"I know people. Experts at this sort of thing."

This was crazy talk. But I did not argue with him. In fact, I doubted that he really wanted to go through with it. Walsmear was now in possession of what he had wanted all along: Peace of mind. Now I was sure he would forget about the whole fairy episode.

I, too, was ready to forget. I was ready to put the whole Doyle business behind me. I had an idea of what my own next step should be. It did not involve thievery, exploitation, or overnight riches. Walking down that road in the drizzle, I felt a sudden urge to act morally. To do what was right, not just expedient. I felt what might be described as a spiritual rebirth. I don't know why, really. Maybe it was watching Templeton and Walsmear wrestle in the mud. It made me want to cleanse myself.

CHAPTER TWENTY-SIX

How I Almost Got Arrested

WALSMEAR WAS SILENT all the way back to town. In the square, he took his leave with an offhand wave.

I did not see where he went. I'm not even sure of the direction he took. My thoughts were occupied elsewhere. I was thinking about the flower. The one you ate to see the fairies. That tiny wildflower was the key to everything.

I had conjured an image of the little blossom in my mind. A perfect, crisp image like you might find in a botany textbook. And I was committing that image to memory.

Templeton had the only specimen. While walking along the road with Walsmear, I had been scanning the roadside for another; but apparently it was not a roadside plant. However, that did not discourage me. There is a big world out there, I thought, and it's full of wildflowers. I would eventually find another specimen. Many others. I would pick them. Cultivate them. I would build up a bank of the little flowers or their essences. Then I would dole them out to the doctors, natural scientists, and anthropologists who would soon be clamoring to study the fairies. I would make sure the studies were done with proper consideration for the fairies and their feelings. I would be the fairies' protector, as well as their discoverer.

So much to study! My heart beat faster just thinking about it.

There must be fairies throughout England. But what about the rest of the world? What about the South Pacific? America? Africa? China? Were there different fairy races? Did Africa have black fairies? Did Alaska have Eskimo fairies? Could the fairies speak? Could they write? Were there fairy books, poems, epics? Or were the fairies no more than animals with human form? Perhaps the sprites did no more than flit about the flowers, mate, and die like so many mayflies. What

I saw of them myself made me suspect that this was true. But perhaps there were different types of fairies. What if the fairies I had seen were simply a particularly primitive tribe? Maybe they were savage fairies. Other fairies in other parts of the world might look down on the fairies of England. All sorts of strange fancies came into my head. Maybe the fairies of the civilized human nations were the most primitive, and the fairies of the most savage human nations the most advanced.

Communicating with the fairies was going to be a challenge. We had to have patience. We couldn't rush anything. Just looking at them would be hard enough. And could they even hear us if we spoke? Sound is carried on air. But did the fairies live in a world of air? Did they live in our world, or another? What was the ether they moved through?

I suspected that we and the fairies occupied different realms of the natural world. Could they, I wondered, enter our realm? And could we enter theirs? I knew it was possible to be touched by the fairies. I had felt them. Our skin apparatus could register their weight. But not fully. You didn't feel pressure when a fairy landed on you. You felt a sensation that seemed to go deeper than the skin. You felt slightly permeated. And if we humans squeezed hard enough, we could touch the fairies to the extent that they could be injured—fatally, even, as the girls had done.

Back in my room, I sketched the flower from memory. If only I had been able to photograph it! But I hoped that what I was able to recall of its petals (short, purplish red, spiky), the single yellow tuft that protruded above them, and the sharply serrated leaf edges would be enough for me to take to the Kew Gardens library for comparison. I was prepared to leave for London on the morrow to do just that.

Moving just as strongly was another urge: I wanted to go back to Templeton's garden and have another go at photographing the fairies. After all, this time I knew for certain that they were there.

IT WAS THE DAY FOLLOWING Templeton's and Walsmear's battle in the rain. Fat little clouds marched across a blue sky. While some parts of the garden were still calmly and luxuriously intact, other parts lay in whorls of muddy ruin. I got off several shots before Templeton spotted me. I heard an upper-story window creak open. Then I heard Templeton's creaky wheeze.

"Go away, Mr. Castle. This instant."

I turned around and saw Templeton's shaggy thatch through the open window. Beneath it, I saw the two heads of the little girls pop up through another window.

"Hello, Mr. Castle," they shouted.

"Hello, Anna. Hello, Clara."

"Castle, I'm warning you. Get off my property."

"Shush," I said, snapping another shot. "This is not your property."

"By the devil, it most certainly is."

"Not where I'm standing now. I checked the town property records. As long as I stand right here by the road, I am not on your property. So I can stand here and photograph your garden all day. I'm perfectly within my legal rights."

My intention was to methodically map the garden by photograph. Standing on the verge of the road, I shot the garden from the great tree right down to the door of the cottage. I took close-ups of the flower beds and of all the flowering shrubs. Even if I didn't get a single fairy image, I'd at least have a comprehensive record of the garden. Somehow I felt this was a good, scientific sort of thing to have.

But I was very certain that this time I would capture the fairies on film. It was only a matter of persistence, I was sure as I went about my work.

The policeman who tapped me on the shoulder was one I had never seen before. He must have been Walsmear's replacement; a polite young man.

"Move along, sir," he said, not bothering to dismount from his bicycle.

I took another photograph before answering.

"I'm sorry, officer, but this is a public road. I've looked into it. I'm perfectly within my rights to take photographs from this spot."

"That may be, sir, but the man in that cottage doesn't like it."

"Well, that's too bad, isn't it?"

"You've got to show some consideration, sir."

"I'll only be a few minutes longer, anyway. I'm almost finished."

"You'll finish right now."

Through the lens, I saw the policeman's palm loom up. Then I saw blackness.

"I beg your pardon?" I said. "Do you know what you're doing, officer? What's your name? I think I'll report you. What's your name?"

The policeman grinned and told me his name, which I've forgotten. "And feel free to report me," he said. "But until then, I think you'll have to move on."

"Oh yes. I'll move on. I'll move on, all right. But if you think you can push me around, you're mistaken, officer. You're awfully mistaken. You'll hear about this Mr. [whatever his name was]. You'll hear about this."

I heard myself talking and couldn't believe my ears. I sounded like some rough type being shooed off a street corner in the North End. On the other hand, I felt fully as self-righteous as I sounded. I thought I was special. Maybe it was because I knew about the fairies; I knew their secret. Because of this, I was given some special destiny. The ordinary rules of humanity didn't apply to me.

After giving the policeman a piece of my mind, I began scornfully sauntering back toward town. Behind me, I heard Templeton's voice. He was out on the road now.

"Yes, officer," he was saying, "I know him. His name's Charles P. Castle. An American of some sort. I was charitable to him once. I let him stay at my house after he'd injured himself in a drunken debauch. Now he won't go away. I'm afraid for the safety of my daughters, if you must know."

This was too much.

"Where does he live?" I heard the policeman ask.

"He has a room at the Starry Night, I understand," said Templeton.

"He won't stay much longer, I think."

"I hope not."

"Please give me a call if you see him hanging about again."

"I most certainly will."

"Ha!" I shouted back over my shoulder. I didn't care what they thought of me. I had seen the fairies. They could all go to blazes.

For the next few days, I had similar prickly encounters with almost everyone I met. Whipped into a high emotional pitch as I was, I was ripe for making some terrible mistakes. And that's what I proceeded to do.

Returning to the Starry Night, I felt possessed by a strange, restless energy. I might have swept the floors if there had been a broom nearby. I could have raked the yard, weeded the garden, or cleaned the stable. That was what I could have done. But what I really desired, what was really at the heart of this sudden surge of energy was—and by luck I entered the dining room just as Esmirelda came clunking heavily up from the cellar. She was dragging a broom behind her.

"Ah, Esmirelda," I said with quiet, eyebrow-bobbing heartiness. "I'm going upstairs to my room now. You might want to come up and tidy if you like. I mean, you won't be in the way, if you know what I mean."

As I stood there grinning and rubbing my hands, Esmirelda set her broom against the wall. Then she took one step forward, made her hand into a fist, and swung it full at my face.

I jumped back, expecting to be struck. But Esmirelda's fist stopped just short of my nose and hovered there. I gathered that I was supposed to look at it for some reason. Then I noticed the large diamond glittering on her grimy ring finger.

"Me and Michael," she said.

"Walsmear?"

She nodded. "We're thinking about a Christmas wedding."

"Gosh. That's . . . well . . . congrat—best wishes—I mean . . ." I uttered other confused phrases as the big girl brushed past me. She left behind a cloud of her earthy scent.

Nobody ever really requires an alcoholic beverage, but "I need a drink" was the first thought that came into my head. Fortunately, the means of getting one were near at hand. I stepped over into the bar. There, I found a larger than usual crowd. Cole seemed in particularly good spirits as he hobbled back and forth to serve them.

"Here's another one to join the party," he said, seeing me come in.

"Party?" I asked.

He filled a glass to foaming and slid it under my nose. Grabbing the glass, I gratefully raised it to my lips. Quaffing deeply, I scanned the crowd from over the rim.

Beside me was a balding man in an apron. His hair and shoulders were flecked with sawdust. I guessed he was a carpenter.

"To her good nature," he said, raising his glass.

On the other side of me was an older man. He smiled, showing a single tooth. "Her nature," he said, "was like Mother Nature's."

"She was like a forest," said a third man from the crowd. "Or a mountain. She was the Matterhorn."

"But a hell of a lot easier to climb," laughed the carpenter. "What about you?" He nodded toward me.

I lowered my glass and licked my lip. "What about me?"

Cole filled another glass. "He's one of the fraternity," he said. The crowd cheered. "He's from the American branch."

There was laughter. Someone slapped my back.

"She was international in scope," said a younger man in a fedora.

"You going to write that up in that newspaper of yours?" said another voice.

"I certainly am," said the man in the fedora.

I gazed across the faces of these dozen or so men at the bar. Their cheeks were flushed with drink and fits of laughter. I knew, of course, the object of their little *fête galante*. It was Esmirelda.

The men seemed to be from the whole range of social classes. My God, I thought. What diseases might I have caught?

"We'll miss her," sighed the man in the fedora.

This man appeared to be somewhat younger than myself. He was, it turned out, a reporter from the local newspaper. He and I got to chatting. In the back of my mind was the thought of how astonished this young fellow would be if he knew what I knew. About the fairies, that is.

I suppose I got a little drunk. I let slip that I might have a big story for him someday.

"How big?" he asked, somewhat drunk himself.

"Maybe too big. Too big for your newspaper, perhaps. Say, you don't know anyone at a big London newspaper, do you?"

"If I had contacts in London," he said, "do you think I'd be working in Burkinwell?"

He turned away with a bitter look.

I realized that I had handled him badly. If I was to make the most of this fairy business I would have to cultivate better relations with the press. That, I guessed, would come with practice.

I would gladly have stayed longer with that crew and helped them celebrate Esmirelda's impending removal from the list of local amenities. But I had some other tasks to accomplish.

Whisking out the door of the Starry Night, I hurried to the chemist's. He was straightening up his store prior to closing for the evening.

"Could you sell me a bottle of mineral oil?" I asked, standing at the counter.

The chemist assented, whereupon I heard another voice.

"Charles."

It was the voice, followed by the face and form, of Linda Drain. She came out from behind a rack of combs.

"Oh, hello."

"Not feeling well?" she asked.

The chemist laid a bottle of mineral oil before me.

"I feel very well, thank you," I laughed.

"You know, we have a very good doctor," she said. "The one who treated you after your—fall. He's very good with colds. My husband, you know. He gets so many colds."

I'll bet he does, I thought.

"Thank you so much," I said. "But really, the mineral oil is for the darkroom."

Linda bought a comb. We walked outside together.

"You know, since you've been here, I've been reading up on photography," she said.

"Really?"

"Just the technical side. I can't seem to find anything about the artistic side. You know, the beauty of photography. That's the part that interests me."

"That can't be taught," I said. "The technical side, however, can be. And that's a good thing."

"Why is that?"

"Because it's the technical part that makes the beauty part possible. Without a sure grasp of the technical, aesthetic skills are useless. If you can't control your medium, you can produce beauty only by accident. You know, like these abstract painters."

"Oh, I like abstract painting. But it is all so very hard, I do understand that." She sighed. "I wish playing the piano were easier. But everything is so difficult. I get so discouraged sometimes."

"Don't get discouraged."

"I'm not discouraged about photography. I think that's something I could understand. Now, what about this mineral oil? What do you use this for?"

"The mineral oil keeps down the dust."

"The dust?"

"Yes, dust, tiny bits of skin. You don't want them to get on the negative if you're doing very fine work. Like I'm doing now."

"You put mineral oil on the negative?"

"No, no, no. You put it on yourself. Spread it on your skin. It's an old photographer's trick. Actually, this will be the first time I've tried it."

Linda laughed. "I've swept up enough rooms," she said, "to know that you can't keep all the dust down. Dust will fall from the ceiling. Bits of lint will fall off your clothes."

"Oh, you take off your clothes," I said, realizing as the words left my mouth how odd this sounded.

"All of them?"

"Well—"

"Don't you get cold?"

"I've never done it before, as I've said."

"Sounds Greek."

"Beg your pardon?"

"All oiled up and naked. Sounds like ancient Greek sportsmen, doesn't it?"

"I suppose it is rather Greek, now that you mention it. Sort of like being in some kind of aesthetic Olympiad."

"What a striking thought," said Linda.

She was still musing as I parted from her in front of the church.

Once inside, I made straight for the altar. Again I met the simple handyman, Dennis.

It was a pleasure to see this innocent soul. He expressed such uncomplicated joy in meeting. He asked nothing, required no acknowledgment, but simply beamed and uttered a loud syllable before moving on. When we were running the electricity and water down into the cellar, I had had the opportunity to admire his overall handiness and the clever way he solved small problems. It struck me as tragic that this cleverness did not go hand in hand with conventionally recognizable verbal and social skills.

The setting sun shone gold through the church windows. Magnificent buttresses of light angled down onto the pews. I paused to admire the scene before lifting the stone and descending the ladder into the cellar. At the bottom, I struck my toe on something hard and wooden with sharp corners. Holding the lantern, I could see that it was Dennis's box of tools. The fellow was obviously forgetful as well as simpleminded. I made a note to tell him about the tools the next day as I set down the lantern and began removing my clothes.

Standing naked in the flickering light of the lantern, I felt cool and unfettered. As I rubbed the mineral oil over my whole body, I watched my shadow on the wall. I fancied myself a Red Indian warrior preparing for battle. I imagined that the lamp burned buffalo oil and the wall was reindeer skin. Outdoors was the wild darkness, alive with bears, cougars, and furtive enemies. Turning out the lantern, I went happily to work, diverting my mind with imaginary wilderness adventures.

About a half hour into the work, I heard a noise upstairs in the church. I swore angrily to myself. It is probably Dennis, I thought. He is returning to get his tools.

As usual when interruptions occur, I was at a particularly sensitive stage of the developing process. I had to keep the chemical bath in continual agitation over the film and couldn't leave the side of the tub. Stuck there, I hoped I could stop him before he lit a lantern and ruined everything. As I heard the heavy stone scraping away from the floor overhead I shouted, "Dennis!"

No answer. I heard the ladder creak.

"Hello? Dennis?"

I heard the stone being slowly pushed back into place.

"I say," I shouted. "This is Charles Castle. I'm developing pictures down here. So for God's sake, don't light any lights for a moment, will you?"

I heard whoever it was leap down from the ladder onto the bare earth.

At first, I was frightened that whoever it was would bring a light and ruin my pictures. Now I feared for my own safety.

"Who is it?" I cried, seized by a paroxysm of terror.

After all, I was naked, defenseless, and alone in the darkness. I could not light a light or stop agitating the chemicals without ruining my work. And for all I knew that work was the priceless fairy photographs I had been seeking.

My mind filled with pictures of Paolo and Shorty. It was they! Come to get me!

"That's enough now," I cried. "Who are you? What do you want?"

"Oh dear," came a voice from the darkness. "Have I frightened you?"

"Linda?" I said. "Linda Drain? Is it you?"

"Yes. Yes, I'm afraid it is. I'm so sorry. I'd really rather creep back up the ladder now. I'm so ashamed of myself."

"Ashamed? What for?"

"For frightening—I mean—startling you."

"I wasn't frightened. I was just thinking of those two—Paolo and Shorty—who attacked us on the train. And then you came down."

"Oh, I'm so sorry. I really just came down to see if I could help."

"Help?"

"I'd told you I'd been reading up on photography."

"I'm afraid there's not much—you aren't planning to light a light, are you?"

"No. I didn't bring one."

"That's good."

"Would it ruin the pictures?"

"Yes. That. And, you see, I—well—remember that precaution I told you about? The thing I needed the mineral oil for? To protect against dust? Well, I'm taking that precaution right now."

"Are you afraid that I've brought dust into the room?"

"It's not your fault. But you probably have. Unless—"

"Yes?"

"Unless you've taken off your clothes and covered yourself with mineral oil. Ha ha."

"But I have."

"You have?"

"Yes. I did it upstairs. Before I came down."

My head swam in the darkness. Massive quantities of blood were either rushing to my brain or departing from it.

"You know, Linda, I appreciate that you . . . What I mean to say is . . . this might not look good if anyone should—"

"No one will know. And anyway, it's all scientific, or artistic, what have you. I mean, it's like a doctor and patient, artist and model. And we don't even have to see each other if we don't turn on a light."

"That's true."

"Now—is there anything I can help you with?"

"Yes . . . yes, I suppose there is."

I decided to let her agitate the chemical bath while I prepared a water bath in another tub. Handing the tray to her proved difficult. It is hard to judge distances in complete darkness without touching the thing you are trying to reach. And I was sedulously trying to avoid touching flesh.

As the minutes passed, however, I found I could sense where she was by the smell of the oil on her body, the warmth of her breath, and the sound of her voice. Handing things back and forth got easier. But having Linda "help" me was making the work far more difficult than it might have otherwise been. Still, I enjoyed her conversation, and it was not long before we were preparing the final bath.

"Almost finished," I said.

"And then?"

"We'll be able to turn the lights on."

"Oh dear."

"So maybe you ought to go up and get dressed."

"I can't say I'm looking forward to it."

"Why not?"

"I'm covered with this oil. Can you imagine putting a dress on over that?"

"Well, here. Here's a towel. Towel yourself off."

"That's very kind."

"Think nothing—Now where is that? I think I've dropped it."

"Let me help you."

"No, I—"

As we groped on the floor in the darkness, my hand brushed against some part of her body. It was smooth, warm, and oily.

"Oh," I said. "Sorry."

"No, I'm sorry."

"No, I'm—"

From the sound of her voice, I could tell her back was now turned toward me. The next thing my hand brushed against was smooth and giving.

"Dear me," she said.

"Yes," I agreed.

My heart was pounding. A delightful tension filled every part of my body. I knew quite well just where my blood was going at that moment. As one part of my mind told me the hundred and one correct, respectable, and decent things I should say and do next, another part of my mind said "Oh hell—" and I reached my hand out in the darkness.

The first thing I grabbed was Linda's elbow. She reacted instantly, coiling her arm up around mine. Then the rest of her body followed. In a second we were belly to belly, slap close in the darkness.

The floor was hard and gritty; but Linda had the towel in hand and we parted long enough to allow her to spread it on the floor before slithering back around one another. I recall great waves of perfect sensation (working in the dark wonderfully sharpens the senses); kisses were more profound than any I had ever felt; the essence of kisses. We lost ourselves in each other. Such sliding, rolling, perfect disembodied pleasure I have never known. For life is hard. It is cruel and there is no justice. We are born, we suffer, and we die. But it may all be worthwhile, if only for moments such as those I enjoyed with Linda Drain in the basement of that church.

For Linda's part, she expressed her enjoyment loudly. This is a type of vocalization I ordinarily relish, and this occasion was no exception—but, unfortunately, it covered the sound of someone walking around upstairs. We did not hear the stone being pulled away from the floor. Nor did we hear the footsteps on the ladder. In fact, we didn't know we had company at all until the intruder was already in the room and blinding us with a lantern.

"Dennis!" I shouted, as my eyes adjusted to the light.

The handyman stood before us, toolbox in hand. His face was a picture of wonder and confusion. He watched with frank curiosity as Linda scrambled up the ladder, trying to cover herself with the towel. Then he stared at me as I clumsily got into my pants.

"Looking for something?" I asked bitterly.

He held up the box of tools.

"Found them." A great idiot grin spread over his face.

CHAPTER TWENTY-SEVEN

How I Concocted a Useful Experiment

PUTTING ON CLOTHES over oily skin is a distinctly unpleasant experience. I no sooner had begun to do so when I thought better of it. That is how I came to be removing my pants and toweling myself down as I gave Dennis a short course on how pictures are developed.

"And so," I concluded, "the photographer has one great enemy which must be suppressed at all costs. Do you remember what that enemy is?"

"Uh—" Dennis worked at bringing the idea forward.

"Dust!" I said. "Don't you remember? Dust. That's why we develop pictures without clothes on. All photographers do that."

"You and Mrs. Drain," Dennis giggled in his deep, incongruous baritone. "You were naked."

"Well, of course. But it's nothing to laugh about. It's a serious, scientific matter. Only a child would laugh about something like that. And you're a grown-up, aren't you?"

"I'm a grown-up," Dennis said seriously. "I'm twenty." (Actually, he was forty.)

"Twenty? Well, well, well. You know better, then,

right? I hope you won't make a joke about what you've seen here this evening. I hope you won't do anything childish."

"Huh?"

"You don't want people to laugh at you, do you?"

"No!"

"Then be sure not to tell anybody about what you saw down here this evening. If you do, people will laugh at you. They'll say you're childish. Because what we were doing down here was a perfectly ordinary thing. It's like when you take your clothes off for the doctor. Do you understand what I'm saying?"

Dennis nodded.

"Good. So, since we're both adults, we'll never mention the whole thing again. To anybody. Especially to Rev. Drain. I mean, he already knows about it anyway. So he would think you were very childish for bringing it up."

"Oh."

"So you understand?" I said, toweling off my feet and putting my trousers back on.

Dennis nodded.

"You're a good helper, Dennis."

"I know. I'm a good one."

"Good-bye, now."

"Good-bye."

"I'm staying."

"Hm?"

"I'm staying down here in the darkroom. You're going."

"I'm going? Yes. Oh, yes. I'm going."

Was Dennis—as simpleminded as he was—convinced of what I was telling him? I thought so. It was not as if I was talking to an ordinary person, who had the ordinary person's arsenal of conversational dissimulations—poker faces, nods of agreement, sympathetic smiles, frowns, sad eyes, and furrowed brows—to deflect attention from what they were really thinking, hearing, or understanding. Dennis never learned any of these subtle tricks. Everything he thought showed up on his face. So I knew that what I had said had struck home. Especially the part about being laughed at. I saw his face register a distinct bull's eye at that one.

I waited until he had climbed the ladder. Then I collapsed onto my trunk, the only place to sit down there.

It had been the most unusual carnal situation I had ever found myself in. But what did it mean for my future relations with Linda? Our affair was not proceeding in an orderly way. We had not advanced by small steps but had plunged straightaway into hot, slippery passion. I had no desire to carry on behind Rev. Drain's back. There would be much to talk about when Linda and I next saw each other. Perhaps, I thought, it was time to tell Linda about the fairies. Explaining the whole thing would be much easier if I had some fairy photographs to show her.

Hoping that that was what I had, I got up and rushed over to the developing table. I lifted the negatives from the bath and held them up to the light. I held my breath. I saw spots.

Success! The spots were on the negatives, of course. They were the same kind of spots that were on the photos Walsmear had brought me in London. Admittedly, I had hoped that with a better camera, I might have gotten something clearer. But here, at last, was something to work with. And what might I find when I enlarged these spots? There would certainly be something to show Linda.

Slipping the negatives under the enlarger, I saw that they were not really any different from the Walsmear photos. The spots were still only a blur. And it was only by enlarging and studying each and every one that I might be able to find one that showed the shadow of a fairy figure. If only I could get a clear image. If only they weren't so washed out by the light.

Of course. It suddenly occurred to me. When had I myself seen the fairies? At night, of course. So why was I shooting pictures during the day? Who needed daylight? The fairies generated their own light. The thing to do was to get out there in the dark. That would do it.

Or would it? There were some technical problems. Yes, the fairies provided their own source of illumination; but their very brightness combined with their quickness of movement meant that I would have to use a very short exposure. The result, I feared, would be like a photograph of a candle taken in a dark room. The flame would show up, but the rest of the room would not. And so, if I took a picture of a fairy in the dark garden, the fairy herself might show up, but the figure would stand against a black background. There would be nothing to measure the figure against. It could be a naked figure of any size standing anyplace. All the indicators of her "fairyness" would be invisible.

Rather than do any further work on the negatives I had on hand, I rushed back to the Starry Night to conduct some experiments. It was late. I had to tiptoe past the remnants of Esmirelda's engagement party snoring in the barroom. I stopped Cole, ready for bed in an old-fashioned nightshirt, on his way back from the privy. He grumblingly lent me what I needed: a candle, a lantern, an electric torch, and a lightbulb. I took them all back to my room. There, I set up my field camera and photographed these various light sources at every imaginable camera setting. I buried them in sheets, blankets, and Esmirelda's cast-off apron to simulate possible intensities of brightness, and noted everything I did in a notebook whose pages were soon black with markings. My goal was to find the settings that would give me a clear picture of both the light source and the flowered wallpaper behind. Those would be the settings I could use to shoot the elves and fairies at night and show not only their bare little behinds, but the garden as well.

By the time I had exhausted all the possible combinations of light and setting, it was almost dawn. Nonetheless, I slept only a few hours. I was up early, and full of plans. My first task of the day would be to develop my test pictures. In between the stages of development, and after I was finished, I planned to hunt for wildflowers—in particular the little flower that allowed one to see the fairies. I would divide the neighborhood of Burkinwell up into sectors and scour each one until I'd found another patch of the magic blossoms. If necessary, I would do the same for the whole island of Britain.

Toting a sackful of film, I hurried to the church. Inside, however, I found Rev. Drain pacing the ground between the door and the altar. He was dressed in black and wearing his clerical collar, and had his hands folded tightly at chest level. He did not see me come through the door.

I knew I would have to face Drain at some point after having committed adultery with his wife.

I can't say that my conscience bothered me. At one time, it might have tortured me. But not now. For one thing, I was aware of Rev. Drain's own specialized brand of sexual activity outside the marriage bed. And more importantly, I was very much aware of being The Man Who Had Seen the Fairies. To me, the world had suddenly burst open with potential. Anything was possible. Maybe anything was permitted. One thing I knew for certain was that everything we knew about science, religion, and philosophy would have to be thrown out once the world had acknowledged the existence of the fairies. Of what importance was an ethical bagatelle like adultery in a situation like that? How could anyone expect me to respect the bonds of matrimony at a time when I was coming to question the very bonds of the material world? Were not all things suddenly permeable?

On the other hand, here was this husband I had wronged. I would soon stand face to face with him in his church. And as I approached him, I could tell by his expression that he was agitated about something. Had Linda been seized with remorse? Had she leaned across the tousled morning sheets and told him? Or was he still ignorant, and could I get by with just a short exchange of pleasantries?

I coughed as I came toward him. He looked up.

"Castle," he said, taking his chin thoughtfully between thumb and forefinger. "You're a civilized man."

"I beg your pardon?"

"I mean, we're both civilized men, are we not?"

"I would like to think so."

Was he about to demand satisfaction? Would his seconds be calling on me in the morning?

"Would you," he asked, "get rid of the church?"

"The church?"

"Yes."

"Well—I suppose—no. No, I don't think so. I mean, it serves a purpose, doesn't it? Gives people hope. Ordinary people need something, I suppose—King James . . . language . . . very beautiful . . . morals and civilized values . . . Ten Commandments . . ."

"No, no, no," Drain waved his hand. "Not the Church. The church—small c. This building. The one we're standing in. There's not really much to it, is there? It's not one of the architectural gems of England. In fact, it's really kind of pathetic, isn't it?"

"It's not Chartres," I agreed. "But there's something comforting about these old places."

"That's right. You're American. You wouldn't understand. That's the whole value of England to you. It doesn't matter to you how nasty and inefficient we are over here. All you want us to do is preserve something old out of our shared culture. But you can't stop progress, Castle. I'd like to tear this place down. Put up a modern church."

"I don't think your parishioners would agree."

"Probably not," he sighed. "Sometimes I wonder where the Church—capital c now—would be if it weren't for the appeal of these ancient buildings."

Trying to lighten things up, I gave a little laugh. "For my part," I said, "I quite approve of them. That is, I don't know how they are for praying. But they're fine for developing pictures. You know, the darkroom?"

"Oh yes, the pictures." Drain nodded absently. "How is all that going? Getting some nice views then?"

"Some beautiful landscapes and gardens."

"That's all very nice, Castle. But you know, I'm coming more and more to think that there's not much out there. In the world I mean. I think it's all right here.

In the body. Those Eastern chaps may have a better grasp of things than we do in that respect. Your Hindus. They emphasize discipline of the flesh. Exercise. Concentration. I'm the same way."

He looked up at me.

"You wouldn't believe some of the things I've felt, Castle. Some of the sensations." His eyes focused on some distant point. "The sensations," he whispered, and walked past me. I heard him exit the side door.

I went down to the cellar, more than imagining what he was talking about. If it was his nights in the garden, there was indeed food for spiritual thought there.

Fully clothed, I developed the test prints. By checking them against my notes, I got a pretty good idea of which settings would get me the best pictures of the fairies. When I climbed back up into the church, Rev. Drain was gone. There were voices coming from the choir. I looked up and saw Dennis's golden head poking above the shadows. Next to him stood Linda. She was pointing at the wood paneling and gesturing authoritatively. A moment later Dennis stuck a couple of nails between his lips and climbed the ladder. While he pounded away, Linda turned around. She waved. I waved back. She pointed surreptitiously at Dennis and winked.

"Okay?" I mouthed.

She nodded and disappeared.

I met her in the vestibule. We kissed.

"I'm sorry for running off like that yesterday," she said. "But can you imagine—?" She burst out laughing at the recollection.

"I don't have to," I said, rolling my eyes toward the choir. Dennis was still pounding away.

"I wouldn't worry about him," she said. "He's so

innocent. Nothing makes an impression. But tell me, how are your pictures?"

"Oh, they're fine. Fine. I'm very pleased."

"So where are you off to now?"

"Now?"

I stared into her clear, relaxed face. There was not a trace of powder or makeup on her strong brow and shapely nose. And it was not missed. I wondered how much I could tell her. How much I should involve her in the fairy situation. Should I let it all out now, or should I wait?

I decided to wait. I had a fantasy. I would hand her a crisp, exquisitely detailed photograph of a fairy. She would gasp. There would be no doubt. She would love me and fall into my arms. To show her anything less than the perfect photograph of a fairy would be to see her turn her eyes to me doubtfully. To tell her the whole messy story of Doyle, Walsmear, and the other photographs would be to court her scorn, or worse, pity.

"I'm going botanizing," I said, unfolding my sketch of the magic wildflower. "I'd like to photograph one of these. They're very rare. A decent photograph could be quite valuable."

"Really?"

"Yes. Have you ever seen a flower like this? It's very small. Not much bigger than your little finger."

She thought she may have, but couldn't really remember where. I told her I was determined to search Burkinwell until I found one. She asked if she could come along. But before I could answer, her husband came bounding up the steps of the church and into the vestibule. As I was standing rather close to Linda, I jumped back. This might have aroused another man's suspicions, but Drain hardly noticed. In fact, he barely acknowledged us in passing.

"Oh, darling," Linda called after him. "Do you mind if I go out with Charles here? We're going to look for a certain wildflower. Botanizing, he calls it, don't you, Charles?"

"Do as you like, dear," said Drain, striding down the aisle. "I have a great deal of work to do."

Linda smiled at me and shrugged. "There we go then."

We walked out into the afternoon sunshine.

With all that has followed, the sweetness of that afternoon has stayed in my memory. I think back in wonder on the simple hope that filled me then. How I held in my bosom the greatest secret of the age: My awareness that I had the power, with a single revelation, to change the course of historical, artistic, scientific, and religious thought. I believed then that I was enjoying my last moments of privacy, that soon I would be engulfed by worldwide fame. It was delicious to know all this imminent grandeur, and yet to be able to enjoy these simple pleasures; to walk on a pleasant summer afternoon through a small English town at the side of a delightful woman, visiting small gardens, chatting with householders, marching through open fields, and resting at the bottom of shade trees. The sky was gloriously clear. And when no one could see us, Linda took my arm and we walked side by side like a proper couple walking through a park in London, a thing I hoped we two would do together someday soon.

We talked about all sorts of things, among them Templeton and his daughters.

"He is not fit to care for them," Linda said angrily.

"It is a disgrace. You saw how it was when you were there. They are completely unsupervised. I've already contacted the child welfare authorities. I'm going to see if I can get Anna and Clara remanded to us as guardians."

"Us?"

"Since my husband is a clergyman, I don't expect there will be much trouble. And you know they're such lovely girls. They deserve so much better. And I—I can't have children of my own. . . ."

It was a disappointment to hear her talk about a future "us" with the Rev. Drain. I had some hopes—but then, what did I expect?

"Have you ever taken it up with Templeton?" I asked.

"Yes. In an indirect way. But if you come even close to the subject with him, he goes all hysterical. He's really rather like an old woman sometimes."

A degenerate, syphilitic old woman, I thought. By coincidence, we just then emerged from the copse at the far end of the field directly across the road from Templeton's cottage. I could see its roof, chimney, and pointed flanking trees in the distance. The ground over which we now walked was the very place where I had spotted the fairy fog as I sat against the garden wall two nights previous.

I wondered again how widely the fairies were scattered across Burkinwell, England, the world? However much that might be, the magic flowers that enabled one to see them were not so easy to come by. There were none to be found alongside the farmer's ditch, around the trees, or in any of the other spots nearby, otherwise rich with wildflowers purple, gold, and orange.

Despite my disappointment, I was not at all unhappy. Being with Linda filled me with hope of a thousand kinds. One of the flowers would turn up, I knew. Perhaps their season was over. So what? They'd come back next year. In the meantime—I walked Linda back to the rectory.

There I asked the inevitable question: "When will I see you again?"

"Soon," she whispered.

CHAPTER TWENTY-EIGHT

How I Saved the Templetons from Burglars

THE NIGHT WAS DAMP. Ragged clouds sailed before a quarter moon. They took the shape of rearing horses, baroque mermen, and glowering prophets. With my camera equipment slung over my shoulder, I kicked a stone before me down the dirt road. Dim light came from nearby houses. I took the opportunity to scan the verges for the "magic" wildflowers. Alas, there were none. I was disappointed to be going out to photograph the fairies at night without even the means of seeing them, but I had a pretty good idea of where the fairies tended to gather; if, indeed, they were out this night. All I really had to do would be to point my camera at the great tree in the garden. If the camera followed its propensity of capturing on film that which is invisible to the naked eye, I should have my fairies.

There were no lights on in Templeton's cottage. I

could have simply entered the garden through the front gate, but I was, after all, trespassing, and that policeman had been alerted to me. So I took the long way around, crossing to the field on the other side of the road and going down a bit before crossing back into the woods behind the factory, which was dark and eerie in the uncertain moonlight. Glass crunched underfoot as I walked alongside it, pushing away charred beams and climbing over ruined walls. Before I had left the Starry Night, I'd had a few glasses of beer. Not unnaturally, I now felt the need to relieve myself.

Even though I could look around and see that I was alone, modesty would not let me relieve myself out in the "open," as it were. So I found a hollow doorframe and went into what was once the building's interior to do my business. I was in the midst of doing so when I was startled by the sound of footsteps. It was most awkward. For I could not stop the stream without soiling myself, yet I was afraid the steady trickle would give me away. And as the steps came closer, and the stream seemed as if it would never end, I cursed all beer, brewers, and bartenders of the world. I promised, if the Lord would save me, never to touch another glass.

It finally stopped. As the last drop fell, I looked up and saw two men passing the empty doorframe, not seeing me where I stood. I could not identify them from a quick glance in the dark; but they were headed toward the garden, as I was.

Buttoning up, I took slow steps on in the same direction. With the factory wall between us, the two did not suspect that they were being shadowed. While they rustled through the weeds and kicked aside branches and timbers as they walked, I tiptoed and leaped like Nijinsky through the iron bars, fallen timbers, and broken machinery inside the factory. At one point, however, my foot struck what must have been a nut or a screw, sending it pinging off a section of metal shelving. The rustling progress outside came to a halt. All I could hear was my own thin emission of breath.

"You hear something?" asked one of the men.

There was a moment of silence.

"There's rats in there," answered the other.

My shirt was instantly drenched in sweat. I shivered. The voices: I recognized them. Even from those few syllables. The two men outside were none other than Paolo and Shorty. I dropped against the wall so that I might hear what else they had to say.

"You got the floor plan?" Shorty was speaking.

"Got it," said Paolo.

"Let's have a look."

"What's to look at? The stuff is in the library."

"So where's the library?"

"In the house."

"Where in the house? What room is it?"

"It's the room with all the books. Don't worry, we'll find it."

"What if we wake somebody?"

"We get rid of them."

"Oh yeah?"

"What of it?"

"If we wake anyone, we don't get paid."

"Says who?"

"Pocus."

"Pocus? They're going to pin it on him anyway. He doesn't have a chance."

"You want to double-cross him?"

Paolo laughed. "Of course. Whatever the hell these pictures are he wants they're worth a lot of money to that Arthur Conan Doyle in London. You read the papers in that bastard's bag. The one from the train."

"So what are you saying? I don't get it."

"I'm saying I don't care if we have to get rid of the whole family in there. You understand? They'll pin it on Walsmear, I'll see to that."

Shorty inhaled sharply. "I don't—"

"Oh, shut up."

I heard them start moving again. They were taking care to creep more quietly now. Only this time, I wasn't following. I was standing stock-still, stunned and terrified. How could Walsmear have been so stupid? He'd hired Paolo and Shorty—of all people—to break into Templeton's house and steal the photographs.

Those two insane, violent men in the same house with Anna and Clara! It could not happen. I wouldn't let it. I had to raise the alarm. Help! Help! But how could I shout? It would do no good. The nearest neighbor was too far to hear. And I would only reveal myself to Paolo and Shorty. They, in turn, would surely kill me.

Was there any way to stop them?

The only thing for me to do would be to get away at that very moment without being seen. I could get out onto the road, run to the cottage, and rouse Templeton and the girls before Paolo and Shorty got there. The villains would be too cowardly to attack a house that was fully lit and where they were expected. But even if they were mad enough to do that, we still had the chance of escape through the doors and windows. That, at least, was a hope.

I rehearsed this plan mentally as I made my way back through the factory to the road. Unfortunately, being so preoccupied, I accidently stepped on a board hidden under a pile of soot. This board balanced a panel of a dozen or so glass squares and an empty bucket. These shot up in the air and came crashing down, giving the night the percussive color of a Stravinsky ballet.

Hurriedly disentangling myself from the camera strap that had fallen down around my legs, I took off at a run through a hole in the wall. Flying through the woods, I made for the road. But I could hear footfalls behind. I turned to see Paolo and Shorty in pursuit.

Trying to evade them, I zigged and zagged, feinted, and spun. But this cleverness—as the cleverness we fancy in ourselves always does—slowed me down. And I was soon tackled from behind.

After the jarring crash into the dirt and leaves, there was a brief tussle. I grabbed at cloth and hair, rolling about in a miasma of Paolo and Shorty's horrible breath. Then I did something unaccountable.

Paolo's long arm was around the lower part of my face, squeezing and choking. Managing to free my jaw for a moment, I gasped for breath. Then I earnestly whispered, "Quiet, you idiots, quiet! Do you want us to get caught?"

This comment made no impression. For the moment. Paolo's arm closed once more around my throat. But I managed to free my jaw once more.

"You'll ruin everything," I hissed. "Quiet."

"Paolo," Shorty made a motion to stay his partner's murderous grip. "What's he saying."

"I dunno."

"Find out who he is."

"Who are you?" Paolo snorted foully in my ear.

"Do you want to get us arrested?" I answered, roughly. "Can't you keep quiet?"

I felt my arm twisted behind my back. Paolo almost pulled it off as he stood me up.

"Who are you?" he asked, bending over to look at my face.

I was bent almost double and gasping with pain. "It's me? Don't you remember?"

"No."

"The train. From London. The compartment. You carried my bags. Ouch—stop, stop, stop."

Shorty now bent to look in my face. "It's him," he said. "It really is him."

"Goddamn." Paolo let go of my arm and pushed me to the ground. "It's him, is it? Let's get rid of him."

"No, no, no, you idiots," I said. "I can help you."

Making up facts as I went along, I tried to convince them that I was there that night for the same reason that they were. That Walsmear had also asked me to break into the cottage and steal the photographs.

"I wish he'd told me he'd hired professionals," I said, with feigned bitterness. "Then I wouldn't have to be out here tonight. That bastard. I'll get him for this."

Paolo and Shorty consulted with brief looks. I could tell they almost believed me.

"We can't trust anyone," Paolo finally said.

"You can trust me," I said. "And I can prove it. I've been in that cottage. I stayed there. I know exactly where the photographs are. I can lead you there."

"What's in it for you?"

"Oh, nothing. I mean, no money. I'm in it for the same reason as Walsmear. We're on the same side. Ask him, he'll tell you."

That must have been the wrong thing to say. Paolo moved quickly. He flipped me over in the dirt and began tying my wrists together with his belt. Shorty leaned over and held a gleaming blade to my throat.

I protested. But Paolo sat roughly on my back and lit a cigarette.

"What's wrong?" I asked. "Don't you believe I can help you?"

Paolo ignored my question. "How do you know what we're doing here?" he asked.

"Well, I—I overheard—"

"If you were listening to us, you heard everything."

"Everything?"

"Yeah," Shorty chimed in. "You heard him say we were going to double-cross Pocus."

"That's right," from Paolo. "And if you're on his side—"

"Oh, I won't tell," I said beggingly. "I promise. I'll help you get the pictures. But I won't tell."

"Shut up," said Paolo. He brought the lit point of his cigarette right up to my eye. Then he slowly crushed it out in the dirt an inch or so in front of my face. "You'll help us, all right. You'll show us where the pictures are. Or we'll kill you."

He and Shorty dragged me to my feet. I still saw the cigarette ash. It lingered like an orange sunset in my aftervision.

"C'mon," Paolo said. "Let's get into that house."

I was led through the woods with my wrists tied and Paolo gripping the back of my shirt. He did not, however, grip tightly. I thought about breaking free. I could make a desperate dash for the road, screaming my lungs out all the way. It seemed like my only hope. But the moment I considered doing it, my muscles uncontrollably tensed in preparation. Paolo sensed this and tightened his grip. With his other hand, he pulled out a knife and pressed it into my back.

"Don't be clever," he warned. "Clever means I cut your kidney out."

"I'm not clever," I said. "I'm trying to help you. Don't you understand that? Can't you untie my hands?"

"In time, in time," was his reply.

We came to the ferny glade. We swished through, three abreast. At every step, I measured my chances of writhing free. They did not seem good. If I attempted to escape, all I could look forward to was quick recapture. After that, a knifing. I could have shouted and screamed before I died, but I had no guarantee that anyone would hear me.

As I saw it, my only hope was to accompany Paolo and Shorty into the house. Once we were there, I would lead them straight to the photographs and get them out. We could do the job quietly and directly without waking anyone. Of course, they'd probably kill me afterward. But at least Anna and Clara would be spared.

Beyond the ferny glade, we came up behind Old Splendor. Here we stopped and I was pushed down to my knees. Paolo and Shorty crouched to either side of me. The garden stretched before us. At the end of the flagstoned path, I saw the sleeping face of the cottage, wrapped in peace.

Paolo shook my shoulder. "Which door?"

I looked up at him.

"Which door is easiest?" he asked.

"This one right in front of us," I said, truthfully. "You just have to give it a little push. It'll open right up. They never lock it. So for God's sake, don't go kicking it in or anything."

"Don't tell me what to do." Paolo kneed me in the back. "So once we're inside, where is the library?"

"Turn right when you get inside the front door. Go through the sitting room. The library's right after that. The pictures are in the desk. In the upper right hand drawer. It's unlocked."

"Anything else?"

"What?"

"Anything you forgot? A dog, maybe?"

"Well, no, I—"

I glanced at Shorty. He appeared to be hiding something behind his back. He twitched a little. I saw that it was a length of pipe as long as a man's forearm. That pipe was meant for my head, I knew. I'd be coshed the moment the two were sure they'd extracted all the helpful information I knew. Could I stall them?

"Let me think now . . ." I said, trying to move out of Shorty's range.

"No, you don't." Paolo thought I was making my move, and grabbed for the nearest part of my body. It happened to be my face. He took it into his whole palm and squeezed it like a grapefruit. I kicked at his stomach but he jumped around and locked my head in his arm. I could not move and expected at any moment to feel the knife plunge into my body.

But something had happened. I could feel Paolo's body tense and go still. Though I was still crushed under his stinking armpit, I could hear him whispering to Shorty. I looked up, but all I could see was the side of Paolo's shirt. Suddenly, I was released. A split second later, a foot slammed into my face. I could feel the grit and almost taste the shoe leather. The shock passed like an ugly black wave through my brain. When it had passed, I was lying on my stomach. Paolo had his knee in my back and his forearm around my mouth. Opening my eyes, all I could see was a bit of his shirt and a nobbly mound that could only have been one of the tree's huge roots. Paolo was hardly breathing and Shorty was silent.

Since I didn't know what was going on, I tried not to worry about it. Instead, I lay there feeling terrifically sorry for myself. I almost sobbed recalling the last night I had been in the garden. How ironic, I thought. As I was being brutally held prisoner by two vicious thugs, the air around us was probably filled with invisible fairies. Perhaps they were mating. I imaged the elves' pursuit, the capture, and the swirl of spinning bodies. I thought about the lovely fairies with whom I had disported, and how they were now dancing with equal indifference down Shorty's back and over Paolo's head into the garden.

If only the two criminals knew. If they held perfectly still, they could actually have felt the fairies. If they held perfectly still and concentrated all their attention on the most delicate nuances of sensation in their skin.

The silence was finally broken by Paolo. "Who is it?" he whispered.

"Dunno," said Shorty.

"What's he doing?"

"Can't tell."

I felt Paolo's fingers creep across my scalp. He grabbed a handful of my hair and roughly jerked my head upward.

"Keep quiet," he said. "And look straight ahead. See that? Who is that?"

I painfully raised my eyes.

"Oh God," I prayed. "Not tonight. Please, not tonight."

It was Rev. Drain. He was stark naked and tripping gingerly down the flagstoned path.

"You know him?"

"Yes," I said, trying to control my fear and despair.

"Who is he?"

"The minister."

"The fucking minister? Naked in the garden? What's he doing?"

"He comes here at night."

"What for?"

I should have told them he came there to pray; but I was addled with horror and half-suspected that the idea of prayer would enrage the evil men beyond control.

"He does a funny thing here. It's a funny—sexual—thing. He does it all alone. Don't bother him, I beg you."

"Alone? Or with you?"

"What?"

"That's it," Paolo whispered inches from my face. "I thought there was something funny about you being out here. You're a fucking sod, you are. That's what you're up to. You and him. You're disgusting. You make me sick."

"No, no—"

"Oh fuck," Shorty exclaimed. "He's coming this way."

I could see what Drain was doing. He had been testing various areas of the garden. I guessed that he was searching for the one that would produce the effect he was looking for. His search was taking him closer to the mighty tree, and I guessed that he would be coming even closer. As I had observed, the tree seemed to be a kind of Charing Cross for the local fairydom.

How often did Drain come to that spot, I wondered. And how—how in the name of heaven had he discovered the indescribably subtle sensation of fairies dancing on his skin in this of all places? I myself, of course, had felt the fairies. But I had been looking for them. And I could see them. Drain, however, couldn't see the fairies. I could tell by looking at him. He was easing his way across the garden guided solely by his sense of touch. He could not know the exact nature of what he was feeling. He probably only knew that it was real and that it felt good.

A remarkable man.

Now that I've had time to think about it, I can imagine his chance discovery of the *thing* on one of his long midnight runs—his first encounter with the otherworldly sensation. It's a bright moonlit night, a week, a month, a year earlier? He is probably improvising a route, trotting through fields, past the factory, and then through the ferny glade. It has been a fierce, energetic run. But now he is on the point of collapse. He is at the end of his physical energy. Hot, sweaty, and breathing hard, he staggers past the great tree and into the Templetons' garden. There, feeling the soft grass under his feet, he drops onto his back. In an ecstasy of exhaustion, he lies there, staring into the starry sky. Perhaps a daffodil hangs over his face, or a lacy cloud of baby's breath. Maybe a branch, heavy with pink blossoms, hides the moon. So pleasant! The air is scented with intoxicating spring perfumes. He closes his eyes. He can feel the sweat evaporating off his skin. His pores contract in waves of delicious coolness.

Suddenly, he feels something on—or in—his arm, leg, or belly.

What is it? Does he try to brush it away? Pesky insect! Or does he sense that it is something else? The fairy touch is like nothing else in nature. And not by any definition disagreeable.

So Drain lies there, keyed to a high pitch of sensitivity, feeling this unaccountable sensation pattering over, around, and through him and what must he think? He thinks, "I must go along with this feeling. I must lie here and follow it wherever it takes me." And where it took him was—

Well, just then, it was bringing him closer to Paolo, Shorty, and myself, where we hid behind the great tree. He was surely closing in on a strong concentration of the sensation he sought. Fairies must have been cascading down the roots of the tree like Hindus down the banks of the Ganges. Drain was pursuing the best spot with the fetishist's hair-splitting niceness. He wouldn't stop, I knew, until he'd found just the right place.

As I prayed that he would give up and turn back, I felt the knife blade pressing into my back.

Paolo's mouth pressed damply into my ear. "Say something to him," he said.

"What?"

"Think of something."

I couldn't bring myself to do it. Whatever I said would have brought Drain's solitary pleasure to an end. My words would tear him from his beautifully private world of self-delighting idiosyncrasy and drag him into the world I currently occupied: a world of pain, confusion, horror, and evil.

Paolo pressed the knife more deeply into my back.

It tore through my coat and broke the skin of my back.

I cried out.

Drain heard. He jumped up into a crouch. Every muscle in his body popped alert. He was motionless, but for a slight twitch under his eye.

"What—who—" he stammered. "Who is that?"

Still in a crouch, he moved a little forward until he spotted me.

"Castle? Is that you? Who is that with you? Oh, my goodness. Well, well, well." A desperate smile spread over his features. "I suppose," he said, "you must be wondering. I know this looks—I mean, it's quite simple, really—"

He stood up in a matter-of-fact way, silent for a moment. He was frantically, no doubt, trying out explanations and excuses in his mind.

I didn't want him to get any closer.

"Drain," I said, feeling the knife just inside my skin. "Run."

The syllable "run" was no sooner out of my mouth than my arm was violently twisted. It felt like my shoulder blade was being torn out like a turkey wing. And it was all for nothing. Drain didn't understand. He was preoccupied with his own shame.

The poor man. I imagine what must have been going through his mind. Whoever I was with, he probably guessed he was destroyed. He had been found out. How could he explain? The effort of lying and of keeping up a lie would have been too much for him. What was in store for him? Disgrace, ridicule. He came toward us now with his eyes cast down and his powerful chest heaving.

To me, it is unspeakably tragic that Drain's spirit

was crushed the moment before Shorty came up behind him with the lead pipe and did the same to his skull.

"Run!" I screamed.

But Drain, mortally struck, pitched forward. He landed against me, the shoulder of his carcass taking another blow from the pipe—a blow that was meant for my head.

I made a grab for the weapon. It was on the downswing and I thought I had a chance. But in a moment, I found myself in a welter of arms and legs. With Drain sagging amid us, I felt myself being grabbed, struck, poked, and pulled. The moment I was able to struggle free, the knife blade swung at my head. I ducked, and was half-blinded as it ripped across the boney ridge over my eye.

Nonetheless, I was free. I ran in the direction where there was no one to obstruct me. I screamed loudly. I screamed for help, mother, the police, and Jesus Christ. I ran across the garden, vaulted the wall, crossed the road, and ran through the field across the road. I thought I heard footsteps behind me. I was actually happy when I thought this. If the villains are chasing me, I thought, they are not in the cottage harming the Templetons. And if I make enough ruckus, and draw them far enough away, there is little likelihood that they will return.

At the same time, I was sure that I was only moments from death. I was sorry to go this way. I was also sorry that no one would ever know how I sacrificed myself to save the Templetons. I would never enjoy their gratitude—or Linda's admiration—for my deed.

How long did I have? As I made it across the field

and into the little woods, I looked behind me. I slowed down. There was no one there. Whoever was following me had dropped away. Or they were hiding.

I dived onto my belly and crawled into a shallow ditch. Peering over the edge, I scanned the fields and woods. But all was dark and peaceful. The chimney of the cottage merged with the silhouettes of the treetops on the horizon. Overhead, clouds were rolling over the stars.

I slid farther down into the ditch. Fear, horror, and tension raced through me like Alpine cataracts. My head throbbed. Sweat poured down my face. But it was not sweat: It was blood from the gash over my eye. Faint and frightened, I looked down into the ditch. There was a kind of tunnel there. A man-sized pipe made of brick. It was dark. I crept into it and lost consciousness. From thence I was pulled the next morning and placed under arrest for the murder of Rev. Drain.

CHAPTER TWENTY-NINE

How I Am Spending the Last Night of My Life

Actually, I am not writing this at all. Who would be foolish enough to think that a condemned man, on the night before his execution, would have the stamina or patience to commit such a mass of words to paper? Where would he get the paper? Does anyone think that jailers are eager to supply condemned prisoners with reams of paper, unlimited ink, not to mention coffee and other stimulants necessary to keep the mind fresh while in the act of composition?

Writing this? Not at all. I am thinking it. And I am thinking it all while in the act of sketching a fairy with a piece of charcoal on the single sheet of paper I have been allowed on my final evening. Of course, I am drawing from memory, and not from life; and as I try to capture the look of a fairy exactly as I remember it, I've had to do a lot of smudging and crude erasures, leaving the paper as gray and shadowy as that first photographic enlargement that so electrified Walsmear and I back on my London rooftop that delightful spring morning. So it is that the more accurate my picture becomes, the more difficult it is to see; and when it is complete, I imagine that the figure may very well be rendered invisible to all but those who are looking for it among the clouds and rubbings—if at all even to them.

My little fairy is a female one; for female is the shape of my desire. But how much more interesting—in retrospect—were the males, with their disproportionate heads and chaplets of thick hair. Where are they now, my elvish mates? They who, after all, wanted nothing more than what Rev. Drain got from his fairy mistresses; or what I and the minister's wife longed for from one another. So many of the elves dead, necks broken by Anna and Clara—their elvish souls filled with concupiscence, they were crushed by the terrible power of innocence. But what I am asking is: Did the elves have souls?

I have no doubt that at this time tomorrow, I will

be seated opposite Rev. Drain in some celestial chair, discussing the incredible chain of events that brought both our lives to a fatal cross. I have no doubt that I will be doing that—or I will not be doing that. One or the other.

If I am, my hope is that we will be surrounded by jolly elves, sporting down sunbeams and spinning through the clouds with spry, fairy mates. Perhaps, however, the elves and fairies have no souls. Perhaps they are more like cats: seeming to share some of our feelings and sensibilities, but dying a final sort of death, from which no spirit emerges, and which marks the completion of a life, as our human deaths never seem satisfactorily to do.

The moon has passed down behind one of the guard towers. It has become very dark in here. I can hardly see my drawing anymore. How annoying. This will be the only record of what a fairy looks like for a long time to come. Brian Templeton destroyed the fairy photographs in his possession. And my copies and enlargements disappeared among the possessions auctioned off to pay my debts and legal fees.

It is unfortunate that my counsel advised against mentioning the fairies at the trial. Toward the end of the proceedings, when I could see the trend of things going heavily against me, I ignored this advice and demanded a hearing. Standing before the courtroom and the world—such as it was represented by the newspapers—I told the whole story, in rough, spontaneous outline. There was an impressive silence in the courtroom as I did so. I interpreted it as the bated breath of awe. Later, I was told that the courtroom was shocked by the desperate audacity of what they thought was a last-minute attempt to portray myself as insane. The move also brought chaos to my counselors, as my representatives climbed over each other like toads in a shoebox in their attempts to dissociate themselves from my defense.

Not that I had ever had a chance of escaping the charges. After poor, simple Dennis, the church handyman, spoke as a witness for the state, the rest of the trial was a mere formality. Sitting there in his—or somebody's—best clothes, he told in crude, innocent terms what he saw that day in the church cellar; how he came upon Linda Drain and myself "naked and uh—slippery" in the dark—thus providing a surprisingly many-faceted motive for my supposed commission of the crime of murder against Rev. Drain. It was a beautiful move for the prosecution. Linda Drain and I were not simple adulterers, taking a room at a strange hotel. We were jaded voluptuaries, far beyond the pleasures of mere coupling; to achieve satisfaction in lust, we had to oil our bodies and commit our naked outrages beneath the very altar of the town church. It was a scene Aleister Crowley might have relished; and which the London press certainly did.

So were my bona fides as a pervert firmly established. And so it became possible to believe that I was capable of anything—including a midnight tryst with Linda's husband in a secluded garden.

Oh, the world knows me and my story well by now: How I, a financially dissolute foreigner, met Mrs. Drain on the way to Burkinwell, where we were attacked by two low-life criminals, probably former confederates of mine getting revenge for a crooked deal gone bad. Why was I going to Burkinwell? Well, the disgraced policeman Walsmear and I had been known to have met in London, and we were concocting a scheme to get hold of Templeton's property and sell it to the London consortium which was eager to get hold of it for reasons of their own—mainly the seam of coal that was believed to run beneath it. Our plan was to confound and frighten the high-strung Templeton with a preposterous story that his garden was somehow enchanted. But our little scheme floundered on my omnivorous appetite for sexual love. Of Rev. Drain and his wife, I had been having relations with both. It was one of the most appalling examples of vice ever encountered in that part of England. But why kill Rev. Drain? Why not? I had already demonstrated that I was capable of any monstrosity. But a little mysterious midnight murder in the "enchanted" garden would possibly be the last straw for Templeton, and encourage him to sell out more quickly to us. Or perhaps Drain had finally refused my proposals, hoping to swear off sodomy, and I killed him in a rage.

It is not necessary to prove motive.

Of my confederate Walsmear, he had disappeared. To America, it is believed. With Esmirelda, the loose-moraled girl who worked at the inn. The girl's absence had been a great loss to her father, Cole, proprietor of the Starry Night.

I could not convince the court that any of this was untrue. And the final proof of my monstrosity was that I wanted to call the two little Templeton girls into court to support my outlandish story of traveling to Burkinwell to photograph fairies in their garden.

Of course, there were some witnesses who could have saved me. One was Brian Templeton. Oh yes, he informed the court, I was a perfectly respectable and docile guest while invalid in his home; but as I grew more healthy, and was discharged from his home,

I became more strangely and violently attached to the girls and the garden, until such time as he had to report me to the authorities (as the policeman who'd bicycled by was called upon to affirm). Yes, I'd babbled some nonsense about fairies, Templeton attested. And as for the girls, they would naturally be drawn to that sort of talk and made to believe all sorts of things.

"There are, however," he said, "no such things as fairies. No fairies in my garden. No fairies anywhere."

As far as believers in fairies were concerned, Sir Arthur Conan Doyle found himself on a tour of the Far East soon after the crime—and therefore was unavailable to appear in court. While he was in Australia, his fairy photographs were published to a gratifying burst of incredulity from the press; but, surprisingly, the absurd forgeries found many believers among the public, leading the newspapers to courteously retreat from mockery to a position of charmed skepticism.

I have lived now through my last sunset. That was several hours ago. It glowed through the bars of my high window, a pink fan across the ceiling.

Far to the west, I imagine, Michael Walsmear and his bride Esmirelda are growing roseate in this same sunset. I wish them happiness in my vast homeland. In my fancy, I see them sitting on a bench among the lengthening shadows of Boston Common, the colorful leaves of the New England autumn underfoot, Esmirelda growing big with child—a child I dare to dream carries part of myself back to the land of my birth. Walsmear, I suspect, will make a good Boston cop. And for Gypsy thrills, I'd suggest he haunt the rooming houses and alleyways behind the theaters of the

McLarty district. He may learn some new magic tricks there. And may he never recall the night he sent two ruffians to rifle his friend's home; two monsters to perform a task no man would accept. Two monsters, whom, as far as the trial was concerned, may not have existed at all.

Giving Paolo and Shorty more solidity than the fairies I claimed were the doctor who treated Mrs. Frosse, the older woman who had been attacked with us in the compartment on the train, as well as the conductor. Mrs. Frosse herself was besmirched by a campaign in the press, which dug up some information about her brother, who'd apparently once forged some signatures and got himself sacked by the Admiralty. Detective Cubb came forward and testified that Linda Drain, Mrs. Frosse, and myself did indeed appear before him claiming to have been attacked by two men on the train; although beyond that fact none of us could agree, he said, our descriptions of the attackers being contradictory, and when they were not contradictory, vague.

As to what happened to me that night at the Gypsy camp—well, everybody knows what goes on in the Gypsy camp.

It was a trial that might have occurred in Alice's Wonderland. And in the topsy-turvyland witness box, only Linda Drain confessed to anything.

I will never forget, as long as I live (and beyond, I hope), the sight of her in the courtroom, the shaft of light falling upon her chair, as she sat so bravely erect, in her dark suit and dark, round hat with two stiff wings coming down along either side of her cheeks, hiding the upper part of her face in a horseshoe of shadow, within which her eyes caught the light: two fierce and determined little sparks, glittering with truth.

Before the world, she told how, indeed, there had been a young man in London, whom she had been going to see when I stepped into her life. And that the idea of a darkroom under the altar had been entirely her own, as had been the instigation of what had occurred there before the eyes of the startled handyman.

The truth did not save me. Especially when she truthfully told that I had never mentioned to her anything about fairies, or my desire to photograph them.

Good-bye, dear Linda. I am crushed by what I have caused you. But now you know all, as I should have told you from the beginning. I should have enlisted both you and your husband as my partners in a merry quest for the fairies; a search that may not have produced fays, but which may have brought us a friendship we could still be enjoying. Now, however, my shame forces me to avert my eyes, to avoid speech, to avoid thinking of you and what your life might become after this. I cannot see you. I could not see you this afternoon, when my jailers told me I had a visitor—yourself—waiting outside to come in.

No, no, no, it was impossible to let you see me here in this dark cell, to let you take away the image of me sitting slope-shouldered on an iron bedstead. I told them to send you away, without a word, without a sign, without a notion—which might comfort me—that we will ever meet again even in that next world. (I vow, by the way, to keep my silence there. I will not communicate with anyone by Ouija board, table rapping, or mediumistic trance.)

With the greatest agony—for you alone were one

who might understand and comfort me—I banished you from my final day, and now the pain and horror of having severed my last human contact has struck me full force.

You left. You left the prison, left London, and will leave this England that knows your secrets, I hope. Before you left, you gave the jailer this envelope for me. This envelope I have not yet opened. I finger it now, wondering at the note inside. Why read it? Why not tear it up now and cast it down into the hole in the corner? What can you possibly say to me that will not make my going harder—or easier, and yet more difficult in the way that I desire not comfort. Yes. I will destroy this envelope. But I won't tear it up. For then I might catch a glimpse of your handwriting. I will crumple it up and bowl it down the hole. I feel the paper now beneath my fingers. I tap the point of my index finger against the hard corner of the envelope. I will cast it away. Now. Now. Cast it away. Now.

No. I will save the blank envelope. Of what comfort to me is a blank envelope? It is no comfort, but a reminder. That I will save. I will keep it on my person, and be hung with it in my pocket tomorrow. I will open the envelope, throw the note unread into the hole, and save the envelope. I could not read the note anyway. It is too dark in here. I would have to squint, and put my eyes very close to the paper. I cannot accidentally read it. So I will take the note out *now.* I tear open the envelope. I reach inside.

There is no note inside the envelope. There is something else. I pull it out, and hold it up toward the high window.

It is a tiny wildflower. The very flower I had told

Linda to search for. The very flower which Anna and Clara . . . Linda remembered. And during the trial, she heard. She heard me say that the flower enabled one to see the fairies. She was listening even as the others turned their heads away in embarrassment at the outrageousness of my claims—my attempts, they thought, to feign insanity.

But of what use is it to me now? How much better to return it to Linda, to have her eat it, to see what I saw, to enjoy the world of fairies, the unspeakable delight of their presence and touch. Better still, she could bring it to scientists, an eminent scientist, and have him eat it and see the fairies for himself. Thus would begin the new age of fairy study, fairy natural history, fairy religion and humanities. I must get this back to her somehow. Put it in an envelope. Write her a note. I need paper. Paper and an envelope. I pound on the door to my cell. Who is on duty now? Walter, I think.

"Walter, Walter," I call. "Come here. I need something."

Walter's brisk steps slap down the stone corridor. The sliver opens in the door, and I see Walter's sympathetic, but dutiful, gray eyes.

"What is it?" he asks.

Something suddenly occurs to me. "Nothing," I say.

"Are you sure?" he asks.

"Positive," I say.

"Got the jitters, then?" he asks.

"No, nothing like that."

"You can see the minister if you like. He's sleeping in the warden's house. At your call."

"No. I don't want to see him."

"It might help."

"No, no, no," I trail off, and wander back to my cot.

Walter takes a last look and slides the slot closed.

What has occurred to me is this: If Linda found one of these flowers, she must have found more. From what I saw of Templeton's garden, they grow in clusters. That means Linda may have picked some for herself—for the scientific authorities—but mostly for herself, I hope. Even now, she might be standing in a garden somewhere, enjoying the fairy touch, their merry race to nowhere, the sight of their dance and whirling, midair coupling.

Linda! Have you seen them? Have you seen the fairies? The thought thrills me, it excites me. I imagine her recalling what I said in court, and very hesitatingly taking the flower between her thumb and index finger—as I am doing now. I imagine her closing her eyes, and gently placing it on her tongue—as I am also doing now. And, just like this, chewing and swallowing the slightly bitter blossom. So tomorrow I shall die with the rough parts of this flower still in my stomach.

I lie down on my cot and stare up at the ceiling, where the dim aureole of starlight shines through the high, barred window. Thank you, Linda. My cell remains dark. There are no fairies in prison. But if I were somewhere else—

Wait. What is this? Up in the window. A hazy light. It grows more solid. It is like the end of a tapering ribbon, curling through the bars of the window. It is a tendril of the fairy mist—reaching, just barely, into my cell.

Where does it come from? The garden! The prisoners' garden in the courtyard down below! My heart beats faster. There are no fairies, just the fairy mist;

but if I could look out of the cell window, perhaps I could see them.

The cell window, however, is so high. So far away. At least fifteen feet up. If only I could climb up there. I go to the corner of my cell. The walls are stone, closely set, almost smooth. I run my hands over the walls. There are cracks here, but they are so small. Perhaps if I can fit my fingers in there. No. I cannot. But my nails. My fingernails. There. Ouch. Can I raise myself up on them? Yes. The pain is—ah, but I can do it. But not from the floor. From the bed. I'll get a running jump from the bed, hit the wall, cling to one of the interstices with my fingernails. Here we go now. Jump.

I scrabble for only a moment before finding purchase. My nails dig into the cracks. They begin to separate from the flesh beneath them. Quickly, I pull myself up to the next interstice. Beneath me, my bare feet hold to the wall with friction, barely supporting my weight, sliding slowly downward as the stone rips the skin. I pull myself up. The fingernails separate further. I must move quickly before they pull off. The feet are a bloody mess now. But the raw flesh provides greater purchase. Up now, boy. What is pain to you who are about to see the fairies for the last time? I hoist myself again. How am I holding on? How am I wedged here? If I breathe I shall fall. If only I can grab one of the bars on the window. So close, so tantalizingly close. The fairy mist shines above me. I will go for it. I have the edge of the window. My fingers are slipping. Hold on, Charles, hold on. By the fingertips of one hand. Swing yourself by those fingertips. That's it. Now, bring the other hand up. There you are. You are clinging to the edge of the window. Don't look down. Reach up. Grab a bar. There. You've got it.

Pull yourself up. Grab another bar with the other hand. Up, up, up. Pull your head up and look out there.

Stars. The sky is full of stars. There is a guard tower. And a wall. That's where the stars stop. The fairy mist cascades down from where I hold myself with the most painful effort. I look down toward the prison garden. I see figures. Tiny figures. And beyond them, the mist grows red . . . there is something there. . . .

Good God. The gallows. Something red there, a purplish red; I sense conflict, great conflict there; limbs clambering over limbs; something horrid, red, purple, and wet. I will not look, there. I will not look. I will look down at the fairies. Yes. I reach one hand through the bars. Do they see me? Will they trip upward these thirty feet into the air? I see tiny faces looking my way. They are beginning to move, to clamber, to dance their funny slow-motion climb up the fairy mist to where I am reaching out to them, the muscles in the arm that holds me up beginning to snap and tear from the strain, even as my chest seems to rip in half over my ribs, and warm saliva gushes from my mouth. No, not saliva. Blood.

But I see the lead fairy. See her face, the curious happy eyes as she rises toward my fingers. The fairy mist seems to push forward ahead of them. It pours through the bars; down over my shoulders. It must be filling the cell. I turn my trembling palm upward. The fairy laughingly places a toe there. A thrill passes up my arm. I look into her eyes, bright, tiny, delighted. I cannot hold on any longer.

I am falling. For a moment, I savor the weightlessness. Then my back strikes the edge of the bed. I feel a sharp snap, such as I have never felt before. Something has been severed, something profound.

The fairy mist has seeped into every corner of the cell, curling in vegetable profusion. The fairies are dancing down upon me in troupes, falling over me like a rain of petals. Their hair, their feet, their tiny faces. They clamber over me. I long to embrace them, but I cannot move. They are on my chest, my arms, my face . . .

I am ravished.

O.

About the Author

Ohio-born **Steve Szilagyi** (pronounced Sil-ah-jee) graduated with honors from Columbia University, winning the Columbia Bennett Cerf Award for Fiction for his unpublished story collection *The Night Sophia Loren's Dress Caught Fire in a Restaurant.* A painter and illustrator, Szilagyi has published drawings in *New York* magazine and other national publications. *Photographing Fairies* is his first novel.